UNLUCKY MEL

UNLUCKY MEL

A Novel

AGGELIKI PELEKIDIS

AN IMPRINT OF CORNELL UNIVERSITY PRESS
ITHACA AND LONDON

Copyright © 2024 by Aggeliki Pelekidis

All rights reserved. Except for brief quotations in a review, this book, or parts thereof, must not be reproduced in any form without permission in writing from the publisher. For information, address Cornell University Press, Sage House, 512 East State Street, Ithaca, New York 14850. Visit our website at cornellpress.cornell.edu.

First published 2024 by Cornell University Press

Printed in the United States of America

Library of Congress Cataloging-in-Publication Data

Names: Pelekidis, Aggeliki, author.
Title: Unlucky Mel : a novel / Aggeliki Pelekidis.
Description: Ithaca : Three Hills, an imprint of Cornell University
   Press, 2024.
Identifiers: LCCN 2024003238 (print) | LCCN 2024003239 (ebook) |
   ISBN 9781501776304 (hardcover) | ISBN 9781501776724 (pdf) |
   ISBN 9781501776731 (epub)
Subjects: LCSH: Doctoral students—Fiction. | LCGFT: Novels.
Classification: LCC PS3616.E35846 U55 2024 (print) | LCC
   PS3616.E35846 (ebook) | DDC 813/.6—dc23/eng/20240209
LC record available at https://lccn.loc.gov/2024003238
LC ebook record available at https://lccn.loc.gov/2024003239

This is a work of fiction. Names, characters, places, and incidents are either the product of the author's imagination or are used fictitiously, and any resemblance to any persons, living or dead, business establishments, events, or locales is entirely coincidental. In certain instances in which the author makes references to historical events and real persons, those references are made solely in a fictional context.

For Voula and Dinos,
how I wish you were both here to see this

UNLUCKY MEL

1

Despite its being well before 8:00 a.m. on a Monday morning, Parking Lot M at Vestal University is full. Melody Hollings drives up and down the rows, unwilling to venture into Lot N, which is farther away from the classrooms she teaches in three days a week. Finally, she wedges her old brown Sentra in next to a new silver BMW that straddles the yellow line between spaces. Resisting an urge to smash her door into the nicer car, which has a VU student parking tag on its back window, Mel opens it the width of a cantaloupe and slides out sideways, dragging her messenger bag behind her. She looks around to see if she's alone, then reaches into her bag for a Post-it note pad and pen. She scribbles, "Park within the lines!" and walks around to the driver's side to stick the tiny sheet onto the rearview mirror of the BMW before glancing around again to check if anyone has seen her.

Approaching from the direction of Lot N is Cicely Hernandez. They've been cordial acquaintances for several years, since Mel started working on her PhD in creative writing and Cicely on her doctorate in English lit. Yet Mel has never moved the relationship beyond that, despite Cicely's friendly overtures, because she's afraid something stupid will emerge from her mouth, revealing how out of place she is in a PhD program.

Without thinking, she drops down between the BMW and the car next to it, like an eel slithering back into its lair to avoid a shark. While she waits for Cicely to pass, she rubs her index finger across the rust forming at the base of the not-BMW. Mel reaches into her bag to retrieve a letter she received from the graduate office at VU:

September 1, 2006

    Dear Ms. Hollings:

    Please be advised that you will no longer be funded by the end of this academic year and working as a graduate instructor in the

English department will no longer be possible. We can offer these limited assignments only to funded, incoming graduate students. I hope you will take this notice as a strong recommendation that you graduate at the end of this year. We wish you the best of luck in all your endeavors and look forward to adding you to the ranks of our successful alumni!

>Sincerely,
>Amber Lester
>Director of the Graduate Program

Above her, the cloudless sky is a cheerful blue that reminds her of a crayon. Mel's shoulders slump. What if she doesn't land a job after graduation? She waits for several more moments to allow Cicely to move out of sight. A young man carrying a North Face backpack stops short at the sight of her hunkered down between the two cars like a medieval crone tending a cauldron. He starts toward her, a concerned look on his face, but Mel shoos him away. Confused, the student shrugs and moves on.

Mel rises, only to find Cicely directly across from her in the parking lot. She waves as though she's just seen her.

As they meet up, Cicely looks puzzled. "I thought I saw you but then you just disappeared. What were you doing?"

"Who, me?" Mel says, buying time. She feigns dawning comprehension. "Oh, you mean over there?" She points back at the spot where she'd hidden. "Dropped my pen and, wouldn't you know it, it rolled under the next car."

Cicely looks skeptical, an expression Mel has seen on her so often during their literature classes that she wonders if this is how she appears in her sleep.

"You're here early," Cicely says. "Do you teach now?"

Mel nods. "Yeah, in a little bit. Hey . . . did you get one of these too?" She hands Cicely the letter she received, which Cicely skims before handing it back.

"Oh, yeah. A bunch of us got it. VU wants everyone about to graduate to know they need to leave the nest at the end of the year." Cicely flutters her hands like a bird taking wing.

In her best James-Cagney-thirties-gangster voice Melody says, "That's why I'm here early, you see. I gotta see a man, you see, 'bout a job, you see." Cicely looks confused, so in a normal tone Mel adds, "Professor Pollon. I'm hoping he'll hire me for one of those lecturer gigs they bestow on a fortunate few. In case I don't land a job for next year."

Cicely snorts. "Good luck with that. I know of at least four people trying to nail him down for one of those."

"Great," Mel says, wondering what chance she stands when the only time she had Pollon as a professor was during her first semester, in his *Hamlet* class. Although she's been at VU for six straight years between her master's and PhD, he probably doesn't know who she is.

Mel and Cicely fall into step, crossing the parking lot toward West Drive, which circles VU's perimeter and makes the central campus footprint resemble a brain in profile. The university stretches across several acres of hills, making walking across campus a test of endurance and fitness Mel barely passes. The central buildings were built in the fifties and sixties, with a fallout shelter rectangularity, while the ones around the perimeter look more modern. North of the campus runs the Susquehanna River, a muddy, sediment-filled waterway prone to flooding. In the six years since Mel returned to her alma mater as a graduate student, the university, like the river, has overflowed beyond its original boundaries with new dorms, classrooms, recreation and health centers, and a sports stadium. Its status as a "public Ivy" ensures a healthy inflow of middle- to upper-middle-class students, mostly from Long Island, with a corresponding decrease of students like herself, from lower-middle-class local families.

For Mel, the start of the fall semester means the end of a summer spent being a writer, not just a graduate composition instructor and PhD candidate. Despite teaching two online writing classes to make some extra money, she floated through June, July, and

August, catching up on reading and working on a blog she was temporarily calling *Portrait of a Hypercritical Dame: Musings from a PhD Student*. She'd finished a full revision of her novel by the end of the spring semester and given the manuscript to her best friend in the program, Ben Howe, to edit over the summer. Soon, he'll return it to her filled with suggestions for how to improve it, like he'd done so expertly with the short stories she workshopped in their creative writing classes. The thought of this sends a thrill of anticipation through her. Her mentor, Professor Abe Pater, had recommended she put the book aside for the summer so that when she revisited it with Ben's comments in hand, it would feel unfamiliar. The novel's flaws would be more visible, like seeing a former lover after a long separation and noticing his protruding nostril hairs and tendency to pick at scabs.

A car driven by a young woman barely stops to let them through the crosswalk. As they pass in front of it, Mel turns away from Cicely and shoots the driver her best Edward G. Robinson scowl.

"How are the jobs in creative writing this year?" Cicely asks.

"Meh," Mel says. "I've been applying to anything that remotely matches my background, but so many want a published book. And I don't think I can live in Idaho or Georgia." Two nights earlier, her father called her at midnight to tell her about a dream he'd had that his neighbor and former close friend Haruto Tanaka, or Oji, as Mel has called him her entire life, was running a drug ring out of his house with the Japanese yakuza. "It felt so real," he told her. "Do you think it could be true?" Leaving him to work in another state was becoming less and less likely as an option.

A flock of male students dressed in running gear jogs past them as effortlessly as a herd of gazelles. Mel watches them with envy.

"Well, hang in there. There'll be more openings in October," Cicely says. Melody imagines that poster of a kitten hanging from a branch, but with her own terrified face superimposed over the animal's head. The camera pulls back and the branch she's clinging to stretches out over a mile-deep gorge in the Grand Canyon.

"I was thinking of submitting some of my papers from English classes I've taken over the years. Make myself more hirable."

"You could try, but literary criticism journals are hard to get into." Cicely shrugs. "Your blog posts are funny and smart. Maybe write more of those and build that up to make yourself more marketable?"

Mel discards her notion of achieving literary greatness. At least her blog has an audience of one.

Ahead of them a double staircase leads up to the first floor of the Science II building, where one of Mel's first-year writing classes meets. Her yearly stipend is $14K plus free tuition with the two online classes she taught earning her only an additional $6K thanks to low enrollment, because what student wants to take Advanced Argumentation during the summer? She made more than double this managing the office at Kiddie Kare, where she worked for many years after receiving her BA from VU. Her class load consists of forty students. Sometimes, when she's in the midst of providing constructive feedback on all of their personal essays covering such momentous occasions as receiving one's driver's license or overcoming a sprained ankle to play the best soccer game of one's life, or argument papers advocating the legalization of marijuana or lowering the drinking age to eighteen, she considers that unless she gets a book published, she'll have to teach comp for the rest of her academic career. Then she imagines selling off all her belongings and flying to Tibet to become a monk.

"How's your diss going?" Mel asks Cicely, the standard question to ask PhDs, similar to the way adults ask preschoolers how old they are.

"I've got the first five chapters done. I'll defend it in the spring."

"Cool!" Mel says, thinking, must be nice. "What's it called?"

"The Aporetic Coeval Origins of Latina/Latino Transnationality; an Ethico-Ontological Approach."

Mel goads her brain into deciphering this jibber-jabber. Is there an academic's version of Boggle with words instead of letters that graduate students use to concoct titles for their dissertations? She arranges her face into the required expression of admiration. "Great."

Cicely stops short midway up the staircase and grabs Mel's forearm. "Guess who I heard was wandering around the library last Thursday night?"

"Who?"

"Professor Pater."

"Really?" Mel continues walking. "That's weird."

"I guess he looked bad, like a ghost of himself."

"Are you sure it was Abe Pater? I don't see him coming back here after what happened last semester."

Cicely shrugs. "That's what I heard."

"Hmm," Mel says. It was Abe who started the creative writing program decades earlier. His abrupt and unexpected departure from VU's English faculty had been a shock to the department. Had he been fired? Forced into early retirement? Left in disgust? No one knew, but his absence put Melody in a tough spot because he'd been the chair of her dissertation committee.

"I'm dead to the department," Abe had told Melody the last time she saw him. It was a week before the spring semester ended. He'd looked tight around the mouth. Abe was tall with a second-trimester belly. His long gray hair was gathered in a ponytail at the nape of his neck. He wore his normal uniform: ill-fitting pleated pants, a wrinkled short-sleeved button-down shirt with palm trees scattered across it, a tie as a belt. He'd been packing books into a box, one of several that surrounded his feet like wood piled around a witch tied to a stake. "Going off to finish up a book. And get away from these lunatics."

Mel's stomach had shrunk at his words. "Will you be able to edit my novel before I give it to my dissertation committee? I'll have a second draft ready after Ben reads it this summer."

Abe had looked uncomfortable. "I'm sorry, Mel. I should have told you sooner: I can't be the chair of your committee."

Mel had sat down in the chair beside his desk. "Well, that sucks."

Abe had smiled at her. "I wish you had the faith in your writing that it deserves. You should apply for the Emerging Writer postdoc fellowship. It's for a fiction writer the year after you graduate. It'll buy you time to write and publish more, in case you don't find a job right after graduation. And you know academia is all about publications."

"Are you sticking around long enough to be on the selection committee?"

Abe shook his head. "It'll be the Tina show."

"Great," Mel said, considering the last time she'd passed the director of the creative writing program in the hall near her office, Dr. Tina Petrakis had looked at her with zero recognition. "She doesn't even know who I am."

Abe shrugged. "I still think you stand a good chance of winning. Between you and me, Ben's your only real competition, and he won't apply since he doesn't want to hang around after he graduates."

"He does hate it here."

"There you have it." Abe had said this as though it absolved him for abandoning her.

Thinking about Abe reminds Mel she'd better put together a committee, starting with a new chair. But who to ask when there are so few creative writing professors at VU? The English department is filled with older literature faculty, and the university has refused to hire writing professors to balance things out. With Abe gone, the only creative faculty left are poets and nonfiction writers.

Mel and Cicely take the stairs up to Science II, and Melody shifts the weight of her heavy messenger bag onto her back. She'd like to pause and catch her breath but refuses to show Cicely how out of shape she is.

"Do anything fun this weekend?" Cicely asks.

"Hung out with my dad, graded papers as usual. Watched some movies with the boyfriend."

"You mean your partner?" Cicely says.

"Is that what I'm supposed to call Drake?"

"I mean, you're not a teenager, right?"

"Not quite," Melody says, breathing heavily. She plasters an exaggerated coy expression on her face, an out-of-breath Mae West fishing for a compliment, but Cicely stays as earnest as an evangelical pastor. Or is the problem that, thanks to Mel's seventy-three-year-old movie buff father, many of her cultural references are anachronistic? Because she worked at Kiddie Kare for years after graduating from VU, Mel is older than most of the other master's and PhD students, who entered grad school straight from completing their BAs. Take Cicely and Drake, who are both in their mid-twenties. There are times when Mel feels ancient compared to the rest of her cohort, aside from Ben, who's also in his early thirties.

"How long have you two been together?" Cicely asks.

"Almost two years," Melody says, noting Cicely's calm breathing. She recalls from casual conversations before classes they've taken together that Cicely does yoga and often rides her bike to and from VU.

"Exactly. Doesn't it feel weird referring to him as your boyfriend?"

"I suppose. But if we get married, not that that's on the table, is it okay if I refer to him as my husband?"

Cicely shakes her head. "Definitely not. Too patriarchal. He'll still be your partner. 'Husband,'" she says, caging that dangerous word in air quotes, "has too many hegemonic connotations."

Mel ponders this for a moment while studying Cicely's long dark-gray cardigan and its yarn cysts. She imagines the two of them as companionable chimpanzees sitting on a large sun-warmed rock, Mel picking the fuzz balls off Cicely's sweater. She snorts at the thought, but instantly alters her face into a studiously attentive expression. Mel also knows Cicely has a long-distance "partner" who teaches at a school somewhere in the Midwest. But how much of a partnership can they have with that many miles between them?

Then she thinks of the word "pardner" and pictures Drake, with his round belly and Wayne Newton black hair, wearing a cowboy outfit complete with ten-gallon hat, chaps, and spurs. The chaps are ass-less and he's riding a horse to a fossil dig in Colorado. Better not think of that, she warns herself, but the image of Drake's ass, its mottled white and pink skin, forces itself on her like a drunken frat boy.

They cut through the Science II building and back outdoors, taking the wide concrete path leading to the Library Tower, where the English department is located. Ahead of them, Melody spots an unmistakable pairing: the Moe-from-the-Three-Stooges haircut of Professor Sig Pollon, the chair of the English department, and the curly blond hair of his Labradoodle, Gertie. Kelly, the department's secretary, has informed Mel that Pollon usually arrives in the office at 8:00 a.m.

"Professor Pollon!" she screams. Two groundskeepers turn to look, as does Pollon, who stares at her blankly. It's at that moment that Gertie decides to squat on the lawn. Pollon continues walking, forcing the hunched-over dog to trudge behind him. As soon as she's finished, he picks up speed.

"Go," Cicely says, giving her blessing as if Melody is a Crusader departing for the Holy Land.

2

Melody builds up to an awkward trot, her messenger bag bouncing off her lower back, causing something sharp (a pen or the corner of her laptop) to jab her. What is it about running in public that makes her feel like everyone around her is a figure-skating judge, analyzing her ungainly form, scoring it according to some criterion based on gait and elegance that she lacks? She's never been athletic. When she runs, she has to remind herself to keep her arms tucked close to her body and not held outward like a baby bird attempting flight. Other people have muscle memory; Mel has muscle amnesia.

Ahead of her, Pollon and his toothpick legs speed up. Gertie, whom he often brings to work, runs alongside him. "Spindleshanks," a word she learned and grew fond of thanks to Pollon's *Hamlet* course, occurs to Melody, and she pictures a dictionary entry for the term accompanied by a black-and-white illustration of his long, gangling form running in cargo shorts. During the warmer months of the academic year, Pollon either wears the same pair of olive cargo shorts every day or has several identical ones. Mel has considered buying a pair in a different color and leaving them anonymously in his mailbox. Except she doesn't know his size and he'd probably find out it was her. What if he thought she was hitting on him? Mel imagines stroking Pollon's thin, freckled forearm and batting her eyelashes, à la Claudette Colbert flirting with Clark Gable. Or he could view it as a bribe. Not that this would be unheard of, given the tight competition among grad students to teach anything other than first-year writing or to be granted one of the research and writing fellowships the department confers via a mysterious selection process.

Pollon is in his early sixties and yet he easily outpaces her. On her left, Melody passes a fenced-in construction site that will eventually become the new home of VU's expanding management school.

Jackhammers and the beeping of construction vehicles make her feel as though she's walking through Fred Flintstone's Slate Rock and Gravel Company. Prior to the groundbreaking, she could cut diagonally across a large grassy quad to get to the Library Tower. There are construction sites across the campus for new dorms, a nearly complete engineering building, and a larger health center to accommodate more students, but there's never any money to hire new faculty in the humanities.

Once upon a time, VU's English department and creative writing program were prestigious with a well-known reputation that guaranteed their graduates employment. Now it's an aging actor, heavily reliant on Photoshop to make it look younger and more attractive. Vestal University had shifted its focus away from the humanities toward a business model bent on producing graduating classes of readers of spreadsheets and Excel documents. Funds for humanities programs dried up. Professors who retired or left were replaced with cheaper adjuncts and even cheaper graduate students. English courses were supplanted by composition classes to teach students from all disciplines how to write, because why would a management student ever want to take a class on eighteenth-century literature? English and creative writing graduate students were lucky if they had the opportunity to teach in their fields.

No wonder whenever Mel sees Professor Pollon on campus he's running—not toward somewhere, but away from the aggressive pursuit of desperate grad students. He's VU's version of the Fugitive.

Past the quad, Pollon opens one of the doors leading into the Library Tower to allow Gertie to proceed ahead of him. A few moments later Mel follows him inside and immediately slips on the wet floor. She lands backward on her well-padded ass to the sound of a loud gasp she can't place, then springs up, embarrassment acting like nitromethane to her atrophied muscles. An instantaneous cramp causes her to look behind her for the sniper who shot her right buttock, but she sees only the faces of the coffee kiosk's entire staff of students staring at her.

"Mrs. Hollings! I was hoping to run into you. Are you okay?"

Melody shakes her head disgustedly at the yellow "Caution—Wet Floor" sign. She turns to find Joshua "Joshie" Grubber, a sophomore in her first-year writing course who spends most of their afternoon class on his phone, texting. He'd emailed her before the beginning of the semester to let her know that while he'd failed the first-year writing class he'd taken the previous spring with another professor due to an unforeseen fraternity-pledging-related illness, he'd heard great things about her and looked forward to her class. She'd asked him not to call her "Mrs. Hollings" during their first email exchange but gave up in the face of Joshie's persistence in using a title that conveys a married state when the male equivalent "Mr." doesn't.

"I'm fine. Just on my way to a meeting," she says. Dragging her cramped-up right leg behind her, Mel unsuccessfully tries to breathe away the pain.

"Mind if I walk with you? I want to ask you about my research paper topic."

"Sure," Mel says, gesturing in the direction Pollon went.

Beyond the kiosk, a hallway with pale-gray walls and dim lighting leads to the English department, with offices on both sides inhabited by literature faculty. Creative writing professors, with the exception of the director and co-director, are relegated to the basement below. The doors on either side of the hall have long vertical windows often covered over on the inside to prevent anyone from witnessing professors in captivity engaging in their natural behaviors, which include plotting coups against their enemies and writing articles in fluent academese, a language that's incomprehensible to the layperson, undergraduate, or creative writing major.

"Cool," Joshie says. "So I want to write about poverty. I think poor people should take financial literacy classes so they learn how to manage their money better and not need as much help from the government."

"Hmm," Mel says thoughtfully, hoping to convey both encouragement and healthy skepticism. "You want to be careful about going into this with an argument already in mind, because you may find that scholarly research contradicts the opinions you've formed over time based on your environment. They could lead you to look for sources that confirm your bias, which we've talked about in class. Poverty is a huge and complicated topic, so the first thing you'll need to do is figure out what scholars have to say about the causes of poverty, like wage stagnation, inflation, child care costs, generational poverty, among other things."

"That's true. I hadn't thought of that." Joshie seems crushed, as though she's told him his puppy has cancer. "So I shouldn't write about this?"

"No, you should, but without having your argument already figured out when you haven't dug into the research yet. Remember how we talked in class about starting with a good research question instead?" At Joshie's confused nod, Mel adds, "How about we meet during office hours to talk about it more so I'm not late to my meeting? You can email me to set up a time."

At the end of the hall, Pollon pauses in front of the English department bulletin board to rip down a piece of purple paper and crumple it into a ball before disappearing inside the office. The heavy door closes behind him and Gertie with a slam as loud as a gunshot.

"Okay, I'll do that," Joshie says, looking more hopeful. Mel mentally places low odds on his ever coming to her office hours.

She waves goodbye and speeds up to catch Pollon before he can hide behind his locked office door. If she doesn't land an academic job for next year, she could be in limbo for god knows how long. Could she work at Kiddie Kare again? The thought fills her with dread, especially as she remembers how the owner, Trisha Monroe, often tried to involve Mel in her church. New Wave religious music would play from Trisha's office all day, the singers swearing their undying passion for Jesus like obsessed former flames that Jesus should take out a restraining order against. Or will Mel need to tag along with Drake wherever he's hired, like a remora, unable to make it on her own? They haven't spoken about this yet, and Mel has been reluctant to broach the subject in case Drake isn't ready to take that step with her. He is, after all, a lot younger than her.

After carefully closing the English department door to avoid alerting anyone to her presence, she stops in front of the department secretary's office right next to Pollon's. His door is shut. This semester, Kelly's hair is the bright burgundy of a McMansion dining room. Her eyes are darkly lined with black. The faint smell of patchouli oil hovers around her.

"I just saw Professor Pollon. Is he in there?" Mel asks breathlessly.

Kelly's look is one a mother of ten might give her youngest and most annoying child. "He's not here."

"Where'd he go?"

While staring at her monitor, Kelly points down the hall to a door that exits out onto the wide hallway connecting the library to the coffee kiosk. There are far too many exits out of the English department.

"Man, he's fast! When does he have office hours this semester?"

"Hell if I know. It's not like he keeps them." Several colorful fairy statuettes stand in battle formation around Kelly's computer. She continues typing without looking at Mel.

"Can I make an appointment with him?"

"Sure. Send him an email."

"He doesn't respond to them."

"I know."

"Thanks," Mel tells Kelly with a smile, thinking, you've been very unhelpful.

Kelly relents and looks up at Mel. "I know. He's a pain. I'll text you the next time he ends up in his office for any length of time."

"I really appreciate it!" Mel says. "I'm kinda freaking out over what's going to happen to me after I graduate. My dad has been acting a little off since I moved out. I don't know what's going on with him."

Kelly nods. "Same thing happened to my mom a couple of years after my dad died. Turned out she had a massive glioblastoma in her brain and died within two weeks of us finding out."

"Jesus," Mel says. Could that be what's wrong with her father? Is his odd behavior an early sign?

"Life is tough," Kelly says, continuing with her typing.

Mel nods at this profound statement. "You're not lying," she says.

She considers leaving a Post-it note on Professor Pollon's door, but what would be the point? On her way out of the English department, she stops by the large wall cabinet that holds all the departmental mailboxes. She can never remember whether her box is above or below her name. Today, Ben's slot, which is below hers, is empty, but Melody finds a letter from New York University addressed to Ben in hers. She imagines it's a request to give a reading, since Ben graduated from the MFA program and taught there, and she shoves it into his mailbox. She shouldn't compare herself to him. He's been writing for a lot longer, starting with the creative writing instructors at his private Manhattan high school. But one day she'll catch up, if she keeps working hard at it, and especially if he helps her with her novel the way she's always helped him with all his writing. This is one thing she can pride herself on: her ability to spot what other people's work needs and help them improve it. There's no point in wishing she had the years of experience Ben had. Instead, she can focus on the positive: that his proficiency will help make her own book better.

3

Two days later, Mel arrives outside the room where her first class takes place. She takes a seat behind her classroom's bulky instructor's desk, so big it reminds her of a gladiator's chariot, and tries to ignore the distinctive perfume of eau d'engineer that hovers in the air. Her first class in the morning takes place in Room 59 of the Science II building, and the students who occupy this space prior to Mel's composition class are predominately male. She imagines tiny aggressive male sweat particles floating in the clammy atmosphere, clinging to her skin and embedding themselves in her lungs.

She would open the windows to let in the dulcet strains of construction projects happening across campus, but they're welded shut from decades of paint. Her classroom is unrenovated, unlike the five-star suite in another building that Ben was assigned for his two back-to-back creative writing classes, with its new flat-screen TV, SMART Board, DVD player, and desk with inputs for all kinds of devices. The walls in Ben's classroom are a pale green reminiscent of budding pea shoots; his windows open wide to invite in fresh air. Mel's morning classroom is a repository for broken desks with a chalkboard that's usually covered by the previous professor's lecture notes of hieroglyphic mathematical formulas. Her second class takes place later in the day in an equally unrenovated room.

Mel smiles at her twenty students, whose names she's still memorizing a few weeks into the fall semester, as they arrive and take their habitual seats. The periphery pupils sit with a cadaver's stillness that renders them invisible to predatory professors. Front sitters dominate classroom discussions. Actor/students wear expressions of mild interest they enhance with occasional nods. Melody smiles and hopes she looks welcoming yet professorly, all while feeling like an impostor though she's taught composition for more than four years and nearly has her doctorate. Next year, she'll hopefully be standing in front of a fiction class teaching at a university away from her hometown as a tenure-track assistant professor. She imagines a dozen students gathered around her in a book-filled classroom at Harvard, their chins held in the palms of their hands as they absorb every wise word about writing she bequeaths upon them. She exhales a mouthful of fragrant pipe smoke that forms itself into a perfect miniature nimbus cloud. There are probably rules about smoking in Ivy League classrooms, but once she has a few best-selling literary novels under her belt, the school will let her get away with almost anything.

But in reality, whatever job she lands will involve exactly what she's doing now: teaching first-year writing. Most creative writing positions expect entry-level assistant professors to have a published book. So not only does she have to revise her dissertation to graduate, but she has to land a publication deal as well, and maybe even an agent, before any of this becomes a possibility.

"You know what, let's do a circle so I don't feel like a weirdo up here," she tells her students. They look for confirmation from their peers before getting up to comply. "C'mon now. Hop to it." Mel looks at an imaginary watch on her wrist. "I don't have all day, folks. We need to get our learning on."

The single buzz of her phone sounds like a cicada trapped in her messenger bag. Melody pulls it out and reads the text from Oji, her almost-uncle. A few months earlier, when she moved in with Drake, she'd asked Oji to call her if anything weird happened at her father's house. "Call me," the text says.

Except this was the third such text in a month.

As her students continue to file in and arrange their seats into a mango shape, she walks out into the hallway to make the call. Two young women stand in the corridor. A young man with forward-sweeping black hair—a twenty-first-century emo Heathcliff—stops in front of them. Melody pictures herself wearing a pith helmet and khaki vest, holding a pair of binoculars and a pad on which she jots her field notes. She's a zoologist observing the mating rituals of bonobos in a jungle located within the Democratic Republic of the Congo.

The young man hugs the smaller woman, who accepts the contact with the resignation of an annoyed cat. "Later," he says, giving them an admiral's salute before walking off down the hall. They watch him briefly before turning back to each other.

"What's up with him?" the taller student asks.

The smaller woman shrugs. "We hooked up at the Alpha Omega party."

Undergraduates seem so young now that Mel's in her thirties. She's heard rumors of male graduate instructors dating some of their own students. Disgusting. Mel thinks about talking to the young women about consent and boundaries while realizing how much her own perspective has evolved over the past few years, but she has a phone call to make.

"Hi, Oji. What's going on?"

"It's your father," he says, his voice worried. "I haven't seen him in two days."

4

Thirty minutes later, Mel arrives in Chenango Forks, a residential area north of Vestal University. She turns onto Winston Drive, which takes her to her father's house on Maplewood. There are still plenty of maples in the neighborhood, but they're mostly in back and side yards. The small subdivision is close to Chenango Forks' elementary, middle, and high schools, all of which Melody attended.

She pulls into her father's narrow driveway and feels some relief. His red Ford Taurus is there, though it's parked at a diagonal, its front left tire planted in the weed-filled flowerbed in the corner between the driveway and the concrete path leading to his front door. His right front fender is only inches away from the rust-pocked black post light in the center of the flowerbed, while his back bumper looks like someone sanded it. Though it's past 10:00 a.m., the frosted light fixture on the iron post glows, as do the multicolored Christmas lights swooping irregularly from a gutter that's pulling away from the house.

The first time Oji called to report that her father wasn't answering the door even though his car was in the driveway, Mel had raced over, filled with dread at the thought of finding him unconscious at the bottom of the basement stairs, his legs at angles only cartoon characters could achieve. From glimpses down the stairwell, however, she knew how much stuff was crammed down there from floor to ceiling, so the reality was that even if he fell down those stairs, his landing would be cushioned by a variety of useless items. Then there were the spiders the size of golf balls—one of which once ended up in Mel's hair. She'd fled back up the stairs screaming for her father to get it out. So she'd been as terrified at the thought of having to set foot down there again as she was at what condition she might find her father in. But when she'd arrived at his house, she found him taking a bubble bath with several large porcelain figurines he said needed cleaning. "Didn't want to waste all the warm sudsy water."

There have been other false alarms over the summer, and she's not sure if Oji is taking her casual request to keep an eye on her father too seriously or if her father's behavior has become something to worry about. He is seventy-three, after all, but he also has an agenda: to make her resume the role of his full-time companion. On top of ignoring Oji's knocks on the door, he's made occasional late-night calls to ask Mel if she knows where something is. In a recent one, he whispered that someone was breaking into the house, as if the best course of action was to call his bookish and unathletic only child rather than the police. He tried to convince her that his neighborhood was the primary target of a nefarious ring of thieves bent on stealing men's underwear, the occasional shoe, and beloved knickknacks.

Now, as she exits her car, Mel considers the fact that her father's home resembles a run-down antique store. The porch posts and railings with their chipping paint remind her of a barnacle-encrusted whale. A giant slug that looks like a puppy fetus rests on the walkway to the house. Mel grimaces as she takes an exaggerated step over it. Stacked on the porch are several empty flowerpots near two battered rocking chairs. She trips over a bucket filled with car wash items. An old nonworking barbecue that her father insists he will one day fix squats at one end of the porch.

She hears Oji's front door open. His gait as he crosses his yard to her father's is that of a race walker: arms pumping, fists gently clenched, back as straight as celery. Mel kisses his cheek. He's only an inch or two taller than her, but thin and fit. His yard and house are the Felix to her dad's Oscar. It's hard to believe that Oji is five years older than him. The deep grooves that arc down from his eyes to the sides of his chin tighten as he smiles at her consolingly. When he squeezes her forearm, Melody pats his hand in a "there, there" gesture. Oji is the only neighbor or friend her dad hasn't alienated over the years. Once they had been much closer, and Oji's house had been a second home to Mel whenever her father needed someone to look after her. They'd had barbeques in each other's backyards, dinners, and movie nights. But as Mel grew older and needed both men less, their relationship faded like that of a long-married couple suffering from empty nest syndrome.

"I'm sorry I have to text you when you're teaching," Oji says.

Kelly had sounded understanding in the reply email she sent to Mel, but what if Mel's having to cancel her morning class makes her look bad to the department? She shrugs. "So what's going on this time?" she asks him.

"Yesterday when I went for a run, his car was in the driveway. I knocked on the door when I came back to say good morning, but no answer. I looked outside every hour and saw nothing. No Collin all day." Oji shakes his head. "Last night I knocked on the door many times, but nobody was home."

Melody nods and fans out her keys. She had hoped moving into Drake's apartment would accustom her father to her not being around because the plan was that post-graduation, she'd be working in another state. There'd even been a transition period of a few months when Mel slept over at Drake's several nights a week before moving in. Yet here she is, still at her father's beck and call, having to cancel class, though it pleased Mel's students almost as much as if she'd told them they'd each won a monetary prize.

When she opens the front door, the smell that greets her is that of a 1930s men's club. She imagines W. C. Fields ensconced in a wing chair, sucking on a cigar, while Fatty Arbuckle holds court beside him. Dad's smoking again, she thinks, but there's a tang beneath the odor, perhaps of cat urine—poor Swift probably needs his litter cleaned—and unwashed male body. The scent is diabolical in its ability to cause an instantaneous mood-lowering reaction; it could be used in prisons to subdue rioting inmates.

"Dad. Are you home?" she calls out, but there's no response.

"You want me to wait here?" Oji asks from the porch. How depressing it is that she's now embarrassed to let him see the inside of her father's house when he used to be a regular visitor.

"No, that's okay. Let me see what's going on and then I'll come over." Melody remains standing in the doorway to block Oji's view. Her father has always enjoyed acquiring new possessions, but never to this degree. Loneliness and too much time on his hands must be driving this transition to hoarding. He needs a hobby, one that gets him out of the house to socialize with people his own age and doesn't involve buying things. But where to find something like that? Especially for someone like her father, who'd see right through an adult day care situation and rebel against it.

"I'll make tea." Oji jumps down from the porch, his arms adding to his momentum, a Japanese Jack LaLanne.

Melody closes the door behind her. A large white-and-gray tabby cat emerges from beneath a chair in the dining room and runs to twirl around her calves.

"Hey, buddy," she says, leaning down to pet him. "How's my boy?" Jonathan Swift, Swift for short, meows in response. "Dad, where are you?" Melody calls out again. She hears a sound down the hall.

Her father's house has an open floor plan with the living room, dining room, and kitchen forming a right angle on one side and three bedrooms and a bathroom at the other end. The drawn shades and closed curtains and stacks of boxes and bins block sunlight from penetrating into the room. Mel flicks on the overhead light in the living room. The switch plate of pocked metal is in the form of an eagle with outspread wings clutching three arrows in one claw and a sheaf of wheat in the other. The living room, like the porch, the garage, and the rest of the house, is now almost filled with boxes, bags, and bins. Resting on these are stacks upon stacks: the huge collection of Motown records her father doesn't listen to anymore because he keeps losing the hearing aids he swears he doesn't need, magazines of DIY projects for homemade furniture, and several wicker baskets compressed together to form a skyscraper bird's nest. A pair of balled-up socks sits on the dusty coffee table next to a mug half-filled with what might once have been coffee but now resembles tan pudding. Next to the socks, an ashtray overflows with butts and ash. The dust covering any visible surface is thick enough to cause an asthma attack.

An old brown sofa dominates the room. A fraying recliner, whose sides double as Swift's scratching posts, crouches beside it. A worn stuffed bear sitting in the middle of the couch faces the TV as if waiting for it to be turned on. Melody recognizes the stuffed animal as one she'd had as a child. She hasn't seen it in years.

Mel heads toward the bedrooms, towers of boxes and other items narrowing the hall. The smell of cat litter wafts from the bathroom. She hears movement from behind the door to the spare bedroom. Inside, the full-sized bed is covered with piles of clothes and picture frames. Her father kneels on the other side of the bed, reaching underneath it. The walls in this room, at least what can be seen of them between hangings of hunting scenes or wildlife, are tongue-and-groove pine, her father's attempt to turn this room into a mini-hunting lodge. The head of a deer with only half its antlers hangs above the bed, its expression one of blank resignation. Mel glances at it, thinks about how her mother died on Highway 88. Whether or not her father shot this animal during his brief period of interest in hunting after his wife died is an unknown, but Mel vaguely recalls him owning a rifle.

"Dad. What's going on? Why didn't you answer the door when Oji stopped by?"

Her father straightens up and turns toward her. Even on his knees, his height is obvious. He's wearing a dark-green-plaid flannel shirt. His eyebrows need a trim, as does his white hair, which is still thick and sticks out from his head like a pulled-apart cotton ball. He looks at Melody with a confused expression in his muddy-green eyes. Mel wonders if this is what she'll look like one day, though hopefully in a more feminine version. "Hi, kiddo. What are you doing here?"

"Seeing what's up with you. Where have you been?"

"Home."

"Okay. So why did you ignore Oji stopping by?"

"When did he do that?'

"Yesterday. And last night."

He looks thoughtful. "Today's Friday, right?"

Mel frowns. "It's Wednesday."

Her father cocks his head. "Where are all my Halloween decorations?"

"In the hall closet. On the top shelf to the right. Where I put them last time I tried to clean the house." This had happened at the end of the summer, when it became clear that her absence was allowing her father to indulge in his collecting predilection. It had started off well, with her dad eager to have her help and keen to purge. They began in the kitchen, where they'd filled three large boxes. Then progress stalled in the living room when her father refused to donate or throw anything out. "I need that," "I can sell this," "That's a collector's item," "This reminds me of your mother." When Melody pressed him, his annoyance grew. "You can go now," he said, sitting down on the couch and turning on the TV. Melody left to seek refuge at Drake's clean and uncluttered apartment, where the only knickknacks he owned were his childhood collection of plastic dinosaurs neatly arranged in a wall-mounted display cabinet. She sat on the sofa her boyfriend had inherited from his parents, took several deep breaths of odor-free and dustless air, and realized her father's house was no longer her home. Not that Drake's was either, with all the cast-off furniture he'd gotten from his parents and only her books and clothing establishing her presence.

"Phew," her father says. He looks around the room as though seeing it for the first time. "This room is a mess."

"So clean it. Aren't you embarrassed by how the house looks?" Pushing against the bed with his hand, her father rises from the floor. Melody can almost hear the clank of his old joints. His shirt is partially tucked into the front of his wrinkled pants. "Why do you want those decorations anyway? Halloween's over a month away and they're all falling apart."

"I like to make it festive around here. God knows this neighborhood could use a little cheering up. Have you seen how depressing it looks nowadays?"

Melody thinks of all the neat yards of the well-maintained houses surrounding her father's. His neighbors now give her tentative smiles when they see her, as if she might be a carrier of her father's hoarding virus. "You still have the Christmas lights up."

"People need the holiday spirit year-round."

Mel wonders where her father's newfound desire to draw attention to his house comes from. Like an aging Joan Crawford, is he slathering on cosmetics to conceal the effects of time?

He stares down at her for a long moment, his blank expression turning to one of cunning as quickly as that of F. Murray Abraham as Antonio Salieri in *Amadeus*, one of his favorite movies. Mel widens her eyes at his performance. Once upon a time, her father played small supporting roles in productions at the Chenango River Playhouse. Mel has watched many old VHS tapes of her father acting, his expressive face and willingness to appear absurd leading to several small comedic parts. He'd also served as a grip and procurer of furniture and household decor for sets, the perfect outlet for his collecting hobby. Her mother, who'd been an art teacher in the Chenango Forks schools, created the backdrops for a number of their productions. When Mel watched those videos, she felt a swell of pride at seeing how her mother managed to create such beautiful settings on the smallest budget.

"Oji came in last night and stole a bunch of stuff," he tells her. "Did you know that?"

"Stop. You know he didn't do that. You probably dreamt it. He doesn't have keys to the house anymore. You made him give them back last spring."

"Maybe he jimmied the lock."

"That's ridiculous. Besides, there's nothing in here anybody would want. And how would you know if anything's missing? There's so much of it." She gestures around the crowded room.

"What're you kidding me? There's tons of valuable stuff in here if you know what you're looking for. You need to start selling some of it for me. I'll give you a cut. It'll be your inheritance."

Mel groans. "I don't have time for that. You're perfectly capable of selling this stuff yourself. Why don't you rent a booth at Charlie Brown Antiques again?"

"They charge too much and it's not the same anymore," he says with exaggerated sadness. "Nothing's the same now that I live all alone."

"Oh my god. C'mon, Dad. I can't live with my father for the rest of my life. I'm graduating in the spring, and who knows where I'll be working next September."

"Do you think it's right for you to live with a man before marriage? Is this how I raised you?"

"It's the twenty-first century. This is how people do things now."

"Well, I don't like it, and neither will your mother when I tell her."

Mel stiffens. Does her father really believe that his wife and her mother, who has been dead for over twenty-five years, is alive? She scrutinizes his face to see if this is another one of his performances, but it's hard to tell. Great, she thinks, something else she can add to her list of things to worry about.

5

Mel's memories of her mother involve paper, crayons, scissors, and glue. Her mother had attended Vestal University herself as an art major. After graduating in the 1970s, she participated in the local performing arts community, which at the time boasted several theaters and a vibrant Tri-Cities Opera, while also being the art teacher for all three of the Chenango Forks schools.

One day, near the end of second grade, Mel's father picked her up from school several hours before her mother would usually get her so they could walk home together. Instead of driving back to the house, he took her to get ice cream at Humdinger's on Front Street.

Once they sat down at a table, he said, "Your mother isn't with us anymore."

Melody thought her father was joking. "Why?" she said, digging her spoon into the cup of soft vanilla ice cream with caramel. Her father had given her permission to order a sundae, and not only a scoop. She'd asked if they could stay to eat their ice cream and he glanced at the empty picnic tables in front of the ice cream stand before he agreed. Four lanes of traffic provided a backdrop of automotive rumbling to their conversation. In the parking lot next door, people entered and exited the local veterinarian's office with their pets.

"Something bad happened."

Mel stopped eating to stare at her father, noting how serious his expression was.

"Your mother was on her way to a meeting in Albany this morning for her teachers' union. And she was in a car accident, Mel. She didn't make it." He looked away from her to work his mouth in a strange way, like Mel did when she choked down medicine.

"When will she be home?"

"She won't be, kiddo. That's what I'm trying to tell you. She's never coming home . . . because she passed away." Her father looked away from her to face the cars driving on Front Street, unabashedly crying and forcing the drivers to bear witness. His shoulders shook. "I can't believe it, I just can't believe it," he muttered.

Mel instantly joined her father in crying. One of her friends from school had "lost" her father several months earlier from a heart attack, something Mel assumed meant he could be found. She remembered how dazed and quiet Natalie had been for weeks afterward, how their teacher, Miss Morton, had spoken to the class before Natalie came back to school to explain that hearts can stop working properly in grownups and to ask them to be extra nice to Natalie.

Mel wiped away her tears. "Did she have a heart attack?"

"Heart attack? No, that's not what happened. She was in a car accident on 88." A few years later, he would explain that her mother had swerved to avoid hitting a deer, which caused the car to spin out of control before slamming into the guardrail on the driver's side.

Mel dug into her ice cream, bite after bite of sweetness melting in her mouth, swirling around her tongue. She concentrated on the delicious taste. In the parking lot next door, a young man was coaxing a fluffy golden puppy on a leash to follow him from his car to the vet's entrance. "I want to go home," she said, pushing her empty dish of ice cream away.

"Okay, let's go. It's going to be you and me now, kiddo. I'm gonna need your help." Her father took her hand as they walked back to their car. He stopped by a garbage can to dump the Styrofoam ice cream dish.

"With what?" Melody said.

"Well, taking care of you. I gotta work and we need to make sure you get your homework done and don't go to school looking like a Chenango County scumbag."

"What's that?"

His eyebrows lifted. "Something pool cleaners use to get all the crap out of the water."

Melody stored this word for later use. Which ended up getting her into trouble with Miss Morton when she used it in a story she made up for "Tale Time" about a family whose pool and house were cleaned each night "by fairies with scumbags."

The funeral and wake were a blur. Many of Mel's parents' friends and co-workers came to pay their respects. They'd had a thriving social life because of her mother. Mel's maternal grandparents drove up from Tennessee but stayed for only two days at a hotel. They'd never liked her father and had been estranged from their only daughter for years for a variety of reasons Mel didn't learn about until much later, her mother's lack of religious belief being one of them. Mel watched her grandparents' fervent praying, how they held their hands up above their heads with their eyes closed and rocked, making them the center of attention at the service. She'd lifted her own hands up, but her father had patted her leg and smiled gently at her. "You don't want to look like those yahoos, do you, Mel?"

After the service, Mel never saw her maternal grandparents again, though she did receive the occasional Christmas present and birthday card from them, so thick with religious messages and trite phrases about the Lord and all his mysterious reasons for manipulating people's lives. Eventually the cards and gifts slowed and then stopped coming until one day her dad told her that her grandfather had died, and then a few years later her grandmother, neither of which conjured up any emotion in Mel. Her paternal grandparents had been long gone, having passed before Mel was born.

In the years after her mother's death, Melody's life settled into a routine. During the school year, she walked home, let herself inside, did her homework, and read until her father came home for dinner. Their neighborhood had already been well established when Mel's parents bought the house in 1976. As the first generation of residents aged and moved out or died, younger couples moved in. But by the time their children were born, Mel was already a teenager, who'd missed out on riding bikes in the street or playing tag and hide-and-seek with neighborhood children her own age. Her father's work schedule as head of maintenance at Chenango Community College made play dates with school friends rare. Besides, few parents felt comfortable allowing their daughters to stay overnight at a single man's house.

Initially, all their meals could be opened, microwaved, and eaten. When she and her dad went to the supermarket to buy groceries, they filled their cart with boxes, plastic containers, and jars. After dinner, Melody cleaned or did laundry with her father, until she was old enough to do this by herself, then they would watch TV. Often she read in her room until she fell asleep. During the summers, she was home alone, though Oji was available if she needed anything. Sometimes she'd stay with school friends on the weekends. Occasionally she wandered over to Oji's house, when she was lonely and tired of reading. Melody gained weight during these years because with no one around to supervise her eating, she ate what she wanted when she wanted.

"You're alone too much, Melody," Oji would tell her. "Why don't you come here more? We can go for walks. Or we can garden. I can take you to the zoo. Or maybe I can take you to a friend's house? Too much time alone is not good."

"I like being alone. It's hard to read when people are around." Melody had been looking forward to the summer when she could stay in her room and read all day. She already had a stack of books from her last visit to the library in downtown Binghamton waiting for her on the first shelf of her bookcase, where she kept unread paperbacks. A newer librarian had given her a skeptical look when she'd checked out so many, until the one who knew Melody chimed in, "Don't worry, she'll read them all."

"Books are good. But there is more to life than words on paper. There is nature. There are friends."

But Mel had already learned the adult habit of ignoring conversations she didn't want to hear.

Now, standing in her father's den, Mel wonders how to take his comment about her dead mother. "How are you going to tell Mom anything when she's dead? Besides, didn't you two live together before you were married?"

He nods but wrinkles his face with disgust. "Not for long because it wasn't the right thing to do. And I never brought a strange woman here to live with us, did I?"

"No, you didn't, but that's because none of them could put up with you for long."

Melody had enjoyed some of her father's long-term girlfriends after her mother's death. There was Claudia, who had red hair and wore green eyeliner and mascara. She helped Melody organize her closet and put together outfits, and bought Mel her first pair of high heels. Fortunately, she'd also been around when Mel experienced her first period. But Claudia's relationship with her father ended after several years, though Melody never knew why. After her, he didn't see anyone for longer than a few months at a time.

"That's not a nice thing to say."

"You're right. I'm sorry. Did you take your medicine this morning?"

"'Course I did. All three pills."

"Are you sure?"

Now he looks annoyed. "I'm not a child."

"Yeah, you only pretend you are, when it suits you, so I can take care of you. Which is why I bought you that pill dispenser. Is it still by the kitchen sink?"

Mel heads to the kitchen with her father following her. What looks like a lawnmower engine rests on newspapers on the counter. Beside the fridge are at least thirty salt and pepper shakers neatly arranged in rows. Mel wonders what her father plans to do with these—are they a donation to a church, nursing home, or hospital? The sink itself is filled with food-encrusted pots and dishes, the same plates they've had since she was a child: thick beige porcelain with small blue flowers around the edges. The smell of acrid pasta sauce and the swampy odor of a dirty drain assaults her nostrils when she leans over the sink to reach for her father's pill case. She'd filled it the previous Saturday and it's thankfully up to date. At least he's taking his meds as prescribed. On the black fridge are three neon-yellow Post-it notes Melody left for her father. One tells him to take his medicine, another to feed Swift and clean his litter, and a third to "Eat Something! And not fast food!"

She gestures at the pill organizer. "Good work taking your meds, Dad."

"Those aren't mine."

"Whose are they?"

"Your mother's."

"Stop it."

Her father shakes his head. "She comes to visit me. More often than you do."

"Then maybe she's the one who stole your stuff."

Her father looks pinned down by this. He glances around the kitchen as though searching for a way out. The table in the center has a stack of mail on it. A dusty fake ficus tree in the corner is festooned with plastic supermarket bags that hang like overripe fruit. Every expression on her father's face seems rehearsed to Melody, as though he's performing before a packed house. But is there something more to his behavior that her departure triggered? He wasn't this much of a slob or hoarder when she lived with him. That could be because she was constantly picking up after him and secretly throwing out things that she knew he wouldn't miss. It had taken near constant vigilance and work to live with him. No wonder she jumped at the chance to move in with Drake when he asked her. This thought gives Mel a twinge of guilt. But that isn't the only reason she left her father's home; she left because she loves her boyfriend.

"Your mother's not a thief."

Melody closes her eyes and wishes her mother were alive so she could occupy her father's time. Had her mother been the type of wife who monitored her husband's health, setting up doctors' appointments and making sure he ate well? Or did she expect him to handle his own well-being? Mel doesn't know, but it would be nice to have him not be so dependent on her. If all goes as planned with Ben critiquing her novel, she'll graduate at the end of the year and land a job elsewhere—with Drake—which means she'll finally be able to leave her hometown. That gives her a year to help her father learn to live without her.

"Did you feed Swift yet?"

"'Course. But I haven't eaten in days."

"All right, King Collin. I'll make you breakfast." She puts a hand on his forearm. "And I promise to come over more. Okay?"

"You don't have to do that. I know how busy you are with school. And the boyfriend. What's his name again? Something strange. Crick. Crack. Cake. Besides, I got a new friend."

He ambles into the living room and picks the stuffed bear up off the couch. Long black eyelashes surround its large blue eyes. A red ribbon with frayed edges circles its throat. Her father shakes the bear in her direction, like a tambourine.

"Funny stuff, Dad."

"She keeps me company when I watch TV." Her father sits on the couch with the bear next to him and grabs the remote. Melody looks at him with concern before opening the fridge.

6

A few days later, on her way to her afternoon composition class in the Library Tower, Melody hears Ben's voice coming from Professor Pater's former office. The door is open, allowing light to flood the dim hallway leading to the English department. Mel pauses by a box of books placed against the wall not far from Ben's office, with "FREE" written on the side. Unable to stop herself from obtaining more books at no cost, she crouches down to look at the titles. *Surrounded by Idiots*, *How to Win Friends and Influence People*, *How to Lead When You're Not in Charge*, and *Think Big, Act Small*. What an odd assortment of self-help books. She takes *Surrounded by Idiots* out of the box and glances through it. The margins are marked in a script she recognizes. Are these Ben's? Feeling embarrassed, as though she'd caught him doing something shameful, she puts the book back and moves on. Who would have thought someone as outwardly confident as Ben would read stuff like this? But maybe he had to work at cultivating that persona, a thought that makes Mel appreciate him more.

She pauses in front of his door and Ben gives her a friendly smile and wave. He sits behind Abe's old desk, in her mentor's ergonomic black leather chair, dressed in a perfectly ironed blue shirt and jeans. A young woman with long blond hair, wearing a black sweater and pants, sits in the chair across from him. He leans back, one leg crossed over the other, posed for an author photo. The bookcase behind him and his thick black glasses make him look even more the professor. One deserving of the chili peppers on fire that grace so many of his positive reviews on GradeYourProfessor.com—something she knows he takes pride in despite his insistence on the meaninglessness of the site.

She wonders how he managed to get Professor Pater's upstairs office. Had Abe passed him the keys like an academic torch? Was he elevating Ben above the rest of the rabble to be their king? Abe could have offered it to them to share. Had he thought she was unworthy, a petty vassal who should pay homage to the more published King Ben? She imagines offering Ben a roasted suckling pig on a platter as he lounges behind a long food-laden table, discussing important fiefdom matters with his honored retainers. The crown perched on his head glimmers gold in the torchlight, as does his blond hair. He sips from a chalice, nods dismissively to Mel as she places the pig on the table. She bows obsequiously and scuttles backward over a rush-strewn floor.

Outside his new office door, she tips an imaginary top hat and launches into a shuffle off to Buffalo tap step down the hall—and practically runs into Sherry Turner, a former student from the spring semester. Mel stops mid-shuffle, embarrassed, before continuing on to her class. Sherry waves as they pass each other, pauses momentarily in front of Ben's office, then hurries on.

Mel and Ben met four years earlier when they both started the PhD program and took one of Abe's creative writing workshops. The reading list featured Updike, Fitzgerald, Hemingway, Carver, Cheever, and Chekhov, all the forefathers of short story writing, plus Ann Beattie. Abe's criticism pushed Melody to improve her work, with some of the most helpful feedback coming from Ben.

Mel had been surprised by their instantaneous connection. But they share a similar sense of humor, plus an admiration for many of the same writers. Not long into their friendship, they became each other's beta readers, meeting for meals and coffee to hash out ideas and offer suggestions to each other about their stories in a mutually beneficial exchange. Ben often needed extra help with his literary criticism classes too, his theoretical background somehow being weaker than Mel's, despite his private high school and undergraduate education.

The rest of their classmates often offered comments that were too vague to be helpful or too complimentary to be taken seriously. Like Jeannie Tremin, a non-matriculated student whose stories took place in sweat lodges and cabins and included hikes in the woods where characters encountered a beneficent nature and symbolic animals. Crows had wise eyes, trees stretched thoughtful arms to the sky, and the earth forgave in Jeannie's stories. She was a writer of modern folktales, she informed everyone.

"Your story," she told Melody one day, ". . . is wonderful." Her expression of earnest intensity pinned Mel to her seat. Jeannie stood and reached across the table to clasp Melody's hand in a way that almost brought tears to her eyes.

Then there were the students who were less complimentary, like Ashwini Patel. Not that Mel could blame her. A chapter of a novel Ashwini submitted to be workshopped took place in a romanticized version of colonial India, with lordships and ladies, upper-caste Indians, Madeira wine, and parasols.

"This is a wonderful parody of British colonial literature," an impressed-looking Abe told Ashwini.

"It's not a parody."

Mel caught the evil glint in Ben's eyes.

"It's not?" An awkward pause followed as Abe recovered. Although Professor Pater was rigorous and helpful with his feedback, he was also ill-equipped to teach genre fiction, and it was clear to Mel from his reading list for the class that he valued a certain kind of "serious literature" of the male-dominant variety. She would have liked to have seen a much more diverse group of writers on his syllabus instead of only ones that made her question whether she belonged among them. "Well, that may be a mistake of a novice writer."

Ashwini's face stiffened. "I was accepted into the program because of my writing."

"I'm sure you were. But that doesn't mean there isn't room for improvement."

"Professor Petrakis told me to take this class because I have experience writing historical fiction. For my master's thesis I wrote a historical novella."

"Where did you do that?"

"St. John Fisher."
"Which is where?"
"Rochester."
"Oh."

The class had gone on, but after that, Ashwini's comments on both Mel's and Ben's stories were more biting than they'd been. She and Ben created work in line with Abe's tastes and literary preferences, earning his praise when they workshopped their stories. To broker a truce, Mel found a craft book on writing historical fiction and sent Ashwini a link to it. "I don't know if you already have this book, but you should write what you want," she wrote. Ashwini emailed back a thank-you and softened toward Mel after that. Though her comments on Ben's work remained critical. Unlike Mel, he was able to shrug it off, easily ignoring what he called "amateurish" commentary.

Even though he had far more published stories under his belt, Ben treated Mel like an equal. He had been writing for at least a decade and had received his MFA before deciding to pursue a PhD at VU to better his chances of finding a tenure-track job. Melody had read and commented on Ben's dissertation, a novel called *The Stinkfist Chronicle*, over the previous winter break. They'd brainstormed and discussed the book on the phone, working out plot problems, adding layers of detail, and fleshing out characters. Melody had been fired up by the exchange of ideas and the cooperative effort, and the fact that someone with Ben's level of talent appreciated her feedback and often implemented it. This continued throughout spring semester, with Ben giving her chapters he'd revised, until he finished it in April.

"I owe you big-time," he'd said, handing her a coffee he'd bought her. They sat at a table at the coffee kiosk in the Library Tower. In another three weeks, summer break would begin, creating a tangible feeling of joy exuded by the kiosk workers, faculty, and students. "I cannot wait to dive into your novel after the semester's over. Once I finish my last field exam and input final grades, I'm all yours."

"Awesome! I'll give it to you after classes are done."

"Did that plot book Abe recommended help?"

"So much. You should check it out, not that your book needs help like that."

"Yeah, characterization is more my thing," he said absently, watching several undergraduates sitting at a nearby table. One young woman stuck her straw into the whipped cream at the top of her drink and licked it off in a suggestive manner, as her friends laughed at her. Mel lightly kicked him in the shin and shook her head at him. Ben smiled guiltily.

"I can't tell you how much I appreciate your editing it." To have Ben read and enjoy her book would help eradicate some of the impostor syndrome Mel carried despite having arrived at her final year of graduate school. Hopefully that feeling of inferiority would go away once she became an assistant professor and climbed up the ranks of academia. Or, even better, if her novel was published.

"After all the help you gave me on my book, it's the least I can do. And you know how much I love reading your stuff."

"Did you hear what happened at some of the PhD defenses?" At Ben's curious look, Mel continued. "A few poets turned in manuscripts that were barely finished, and Abe wouldn't let them pass until they submitted complete revisions. He and Tina got into an argument after one defense. I bet she didn't appreciate his interfering with her favored few poets. You think she'll be extra tough on fiction dissertations in the spring?"

"I'm not worried." He sat back and folded his hands across his torso.

"Of course not. Your book is awesome. Are you applying for the postdoc fellowship? Abe told me I should, to give me another year to write before going on the job market."

"Hell no. I have no desire to stay up here after graduating." He looked around the kiosk, which had recently been remodeled to resemble a three-star hotel lobby, with faint contempt twisting one side of his mouth. "But you should go for it."

Mel nodded, feeling relieved. "You probably won't have a hard time being hired as an assistant professor anyway. Not with all your publications. And if you can land an agent with your book . . ."

"That's the plan." He sipped his coffee, a confident look on his face. If he had any anxiety over his future, he hid it well. Ben gestured toward a short middle-aged woman waiting in the line. "Do you know Professor Ivanov in comp lit?" Mel shook her head.

"I met her at the English department–comp lit mixer."

"You went to that?"

He shrugged. "You gotta make those connections, Mel! When I told her I was a creative writing major she said, 'I'm not sure I understand creative writing degrees. Shouldn't you just write?'" he said, in a falsetto Russian voice that sounded more like an old Italian man.

"Nice accent. What'd you say to that?"

"I told her creative writing programs make it possible for writers to learn their craft over the years without starving to death. It's not like back in the day, when a writer could earn a living publishing stories. Not to mention they all had mentors, editors, and fellow writers who helped them develop their work."

Mel was impressed. She'd never have the courage to challenge a professor that way. "Well, we've certainly helped each other," she said.

"Exactly. Anyway, she didn't seem convinced."

At the end of that spring semester, Melody had practically run to the basement office Ben shared with three other PhD candidates to give him her finished manuscript. The space was crowded with two desks and four uncomfortable-looking old chairs upholstered in an apricot color popular during the seventies.

"Here you go," she said, handing him the box that held her baby. It was two years of hard work with Abe's most recent feedback incorporated into the latest version. She was proud of the writing she'd produced. More than this, she was looking forward to taking Ben's criticism and pushing the book to evolve. She imagined him laughing at the funny parts and nodding reflectively at the profound ones. He would read her book and know, without a doubt, that she was his equal. But he would also point out all the flaws and opportunities she'd missed.

When he took the box from her, Ben's hands sank. "Well, I guess I know what I'll be up to this summer," he said with an exaggerated look of alarm.

They hadn't seen each other over the summer since Ben spent his in Manhattan in an apartment that his parents owned on the Upper East Side, patronizing the literary scene. He took any opportunity to do readings, which Mel dreaded. To her disappointment, he'd already texted her to say he hadn't been able to work on her book much during the summer because of his father demanding that Ben pay rent on the parental apartment, which required him to bartend. But he had to have made some helpful suggestions she could use. In the meantime, Mel only allowed herself to write brief notes for the book when ideas for revisions occurred to her.

Now, he calls out to Melody, who turns back around to see him standing in the hall.

"Hey, want to get dinner tonight? We need to catch up," he says.

"Sure, but let's eat at my place." If she left it to Ben, they'd eat out every time they met, which she can't afford. She hadn't planned on having anyone over, but this would give her the opportunity to ask him for her manuscript. "I need to pick you up, right? Or did you finally buy a car?" she asks him jokingly, because for the past several years, she's been Ben's personal chauffeur when he didn't use a local taxi service.

"Funny stuff. What would I do with it in Manhattan? What time?" Ben asks.

"Six-ish?"

"Great. See you later."

That afternoon, when Melody arrives home after classes, she finds Drake standing at the kitchen sink, rinsing dishes, holding them to the light to make sure not a speck of grime is left on them, and placing them in the drying rack. His jeans sag in the ass; his T-shirt from his summer trip doing fieldwork at Dinosaur National Monument in Utah is a faded rust color. Their kitchenette, which was an afterthought when the apartment was created out of the second floor of a single-family home, is tucked into the back of the house. It has a tiny fridge and an equally small stove, with little storage space. But the entire apartment is always immaculate thanks to Drake. Mel had bought only a few items to decorate to reflect her developing style. Too many years of living with her father and with home decor he scavenged had turned Mel into a minimalist. Less stuff meant less cleaning. Though book hoarding is always permitted.

"Howdy, pardner," she says, hugging him from behind. She burrows her nose into his neck to inhale the smell of his clean skin.

He twists around to give her a peck on her cheek. "Okay? Hello."

"I saw Ben today, in Abe's office, which is now his."

Drake shakes his head. "That guy. How'd he manage that?"

"No idea. He was meeting with a student so I didn't ask." Melody retrieves a glass from the cabinet to the left of the sink and turns the tap to cold. She bumps Drake out of the way with her hip. The profile of the attractive woman in Ben's office comes back to her. Her own silhouette springs to mind, but in caricature form: an oversized nose, small eyes, high cheekbones. "I think she might be a new master's student because she looks older than an undergraduate. I've never seen her before, but she's pretty."

"Sure she is."

Mel shrugs with what she imagines to be French insouciance. "I don't buy the rumors. Is it important to him that his students love him and think he's 'the coolest professor ever'?" She says this last bit in what she hopes is an adoring undergraduate's voice. "Yes, but you know how competitive and gossipy graduate students are. Plus, he is kinda good-looking in an academic sort of way, if you like that sort of thing. It's a cutthroat gig," she says, trying to sound worldly. "He's coming over for dinner tonight. I'm picking him up in a bit."

"I swear we feed him more than we feed your dad. What is he, our kid?"

After the last time she visited her father, she'd come home and asked Drake to make larger portions of food whenever he cooked so she could bring meals to her father regularly, and he'd happily acquiesced. "Yeah, yeah, I know. But don't forget how often Ted's over here."

Drake concedes this with a tilt of his head.

Melody leans against the opposite counter. "So, you're not my boyfriend anymore. We're partners now."

"Okay," he says, with a quizzical look. "But we're still dating, right?"

"C'mon. We've moved on from there." Her tone is one of exaggerated scoffing.

"Shouldn't I have been consulted? I don't know how comfortable I am being someone's partner. Sounds businesslike." Is Drake trying to be funny, or is there annoyance in his tone? That's one thing she doesn't like about him: his dead-man-talking voice that makes it hard to tell whether he's being sarcastic or serious.

"What's wrong with being my partner?" Mel asks, keeping her intonation light. She notes the fat peeking out from beneath Drake's too short T-shirt, which is wet in front from his leaning against the sink. Then she thinks about how, when he goes down on her, it's like he's on a beach in the Caribbean that he never wants to leave. Her previous partners treated oral sex like a trip to the DMV. Mel would never have thought when she first met him at the Belmar that he would be such a good lover. They'd both been drunk that night and ended up sloppy making out in the parking lot of the bar before Cicely came out and offered to be Mel's designated driver.

"Nothing at all," Drake says, grabbing her hand and pulling her close to him. "I was thinking about what happens after we graduate. Why don't we stick together and take the better job offer either one of us gets? We could be each other's partner hire."

A surge of relief fills Mel. Drake's most promising lead is right at VU, where his adviser in the paleontology department is starting a new program she wants him to work for in an administrative position. It won't involve fieldwork, which Drake enjoys as much as teaching, but it's practically a sure thing, which means Mel will be able to stay local and watch over her father. If she tags along with Drake to a different job, she would need to figure out what to do about her dad. Yes, she'd have to teach whatever classes Drake's university employer would give her, but at least she'd be working. Who knows, maybe he'll be hired someplace she'd want to live—or she could be the one to land the better job.

"That sounds like a plan, pardner!" Mel says, hugging him tightly.

7

When Swift, who still lives with Mel's father, vomits several times and refuses to eat for a day, Mel decides to bring him to the vet. She spends several minutes searching her father's garage, digging through his hoard there where cobwebs hang from the rafters like dirty lace, before finding Swift's cat carrier, which is filled with mildew-splotched magazines. A pervasive chemically sweet smell fills the space, emanating from a back corner she has no desire to investigate. Mel covers her nose and mouth with her sweater and tries not to breathe deeply before fleeing the garage to find the garbage cans stationed in the side yard. She empties the carrier, then brings it into the bathroom to rinse it out in the tub. But the ring around the tub's perimeter and the scummy film coating the porcelain are impossible to ignore. There are crumbs of litter scattered in front of Swift's cat box that crunch beneath her feet. She'd have to kneel in them to clean out the carrier.

Mel finds her father's broom and dustpan in the hall closet and sweeps up the litter. She takes two supermarket plastic bags off the ficus tree in the kitchen and doubles them. Bathtub cleaner and a scrub brush are in the cabinet below the kitchen sink, which, as always, is filled with dirty dishes. On the way back to the bathroom, Mel shoots a vicious scowl at her father's profile, but he's too immersed in his TV show to notice.

"Dad, the litter box needs to be cleaned and your tub is a disgrace."

He waves her off. "Who cares? Not like anyone comes over to see it."

"That's because it's such a mess here you can't invite anyone over."

He ignores her and Mel shakes her head at him. She cleans the litter box, ties the bags together by their handles, and takes them to the garbage can outside.

Back in the bathroom, she runs hot water in the tub and squirts cleaner in a zigzag on the sides. Fifteen minutes of scrubbing later, a layer of grit and slime drains away, and the tub walls are glossy white. The word "grit" reminds her of Stephen King's book *On Writing*. For King, domestic distractions from writing were "the grit that formed the pearl." That's easy for him to say, Melody thinks, as she cups water into her hands and throws it at the particles. Actual grit, as in dirt and grime, are probably not a part of his daily existence. His wife, Tabitha, most likely hires someone to do all the cleaning, cooking, shopping, and laundry. Melody imagines King—isn't he eight feet tall?—scrubbing a tub. What she needed when she lived with her father was a "wife," or what that used to mean. More like a housekeeper or a cleaning service, but her father would never allow a stranger into his home, out of fear that some treasured item would be thrown away. Only Mel is allowed to clean his house. How many hours over the years has she spent doing housework that could have been spent writing? She can still recall her amazed relief when she and Drake first started spending time together and she saw how clean he was and that he knew how to cook.

Melody rises from the tub with the front of her white shirt stained by the bright-green cleaner. She gives her reflection in the vanity mirror a disapproving look. With wet hands, she tries to smooth back the frizzy tufts of hair emerging from her ballerina bun before tightening it higher up on her head. How is it that her undergraduate students can do this to their hair and look so stylish, while she looks like a kindergartener at the end of the school day? The tighter bun only hurts her scalp, so she loosens it and makes a gorilla face at herself: tongue tucked beneath her pulled-down top lip. What she wouldn't give for straight hair, the kind so many of her students have that looks so sleek and polished.

A glance at the sink, mirror, and countertop results in phase two of the bathroom cleanup, which leads to phase three: the toilet bowl and floors. An hour and a half later, Mel stands in the bathroom doorway surveying her work with both pleasure and resentment. She could do this forever, move from room to room in her father's house before going on to the yard—forget about the garage and basement, a space that causes an involuntary shiver of horror in Mel on the rare occasions when she thinks of the giant spider getting stuck in her hair—and spend the rest of her life cleaning up after him.

"Just stop!" she says to herself. But it comes out loud enough for her father to hear her in the living room.

"Who're you talking to?"

"Myself."

"But I'm the crazy one."

Mel returns the cleaning supplies beneath the kitchen sink. She left the door to the garage open, letting in the unheated air along with the potent odor of something sugary but noxious. She shuts the door. "What's that stench in the garage, Dad?"

"What stench?" He glances away from the set, an old block of a TV as wide as a monster truck tire. He's watching a Cary Grant movie on TCM. *Bringing Up Baby*. How appropriate, Mel thinks.

"You don't smell it? It reminds me of cotton candy but with a nuclear waste undertone. Is there something in the garage you need to throw out or take to the dump?" Dumb question, Mel thinks. There are many somethings in the garage that should be discarded.

"How do I know? Don't go in there much. Too crowded."

"So maybe you should start whittling the mess down, so you can get in there?"

He nods. "I'll put that on my to-do list," he says, licking the nib of a pretend pen before acting out the motions of scribbling a note on an imaginary pad of paper.

"You're hilarious."

"Thank you." He nods at her, fake serious.

"Well, you need to check it out. It's not going to get better if you ignore it." Mel inwardly groans over her own words. Isn't this what she's doing about her father? Her dissertation committee? She needs to take him to his doctor for a checkup. God knows the last time he had one. And figure out who's going to be the chair of her committee.

"That's how it's always smelled in there. You don't remember because you don't live here anymore."

"Right, which is why you need to clean up after yourself since you're the only one making the messes. You're retired so you have plenty of time to do that."

"Good point," he says, his eyes never leaving the TV.

Mel glares at him. She looks for Swift, who only emerges from the self-imposed exile instigated by the sight of the cat carrier when she shakes his bag of treats. She manages to grab him before he disappears, but the process of getting him in the carrier is as easy as putting a star-shaped plastic piece in the square hole of a game of Perfection.

In the driveway, Mel watches her father buckling the teddy bear into the back seat of her car. She studies him carefully, looking for signs of she doesn't know what. That he's acting this way just to worry her?

"Maybe a car seat would be safer," her father says. "Your old one is in the garage somewhere. I could find it in no time."

"Are you being serious right now? It's a stuffed animal, Dad." Swift's low yowls of fear emerge from the carrier on the seat beside the teddy bear. Mel gets into her car. "Besides, the less time Swift has to be cooped up in here, the better. It's okay, buddy," she says, looking into her rearview mirror at Swift, then at the bear, which is slumped over as if in a drunken stupor.

"He was fine the other day," her father says, getting into Melody's car.

She glances at her father. "This is another reason you need to keep the house clean. You can't leave garbage out that he'll eat."

"I thought it might be a candy wrapper, but what kind of dumb creature eats something like that? It doesn't taste good. I know because I tried it."

Mel gives her father the side-eye but says nothing. She backs out of the driveway and heads to their vet, recalling the time her father faked breaking his elbow at work to take two weeks off during August so they could visit the world's largest yard sale, the 127 Corridor Sale. She would have been around fourteen. Mel can still remember her father's glee as he told her how he'd pretended to trip on a broken paver outside Chenango Community College's administration building right in front of his boss, then clutched his supposedly injured elbow and moaned. "You should have seen Ned's face!" he'd said as he was driving. "He thought he'd have a lawsuit on his hands. Giving me a couple weeks off to recover is a bargain compared to that."

They'd driven down to Jamestown, Tennessee, in her dad's old green minivan, heading toward Michigan. They traveled the sale for almost four days, stopping at any stand that caught his eye, and staying in cheap motels each night. They ate at local diners in the mornings and grabbed whatever fast food was nearby for lunch and dinner. Only when the minivan was full did they head back home.

It takes just a few minutes to arrive at the vet, where Mel finds a parking spot. Though it's only a little after 6:00 in the evening, the sky is starting to darken. A tree whose leaves have all turned a reddish brown stands forlornly in the berm separating the road from the parking lot. Her father starts to retrieve the bear out of the car, but Melody stops him. "You don't want to wake her up, right?" she says, feeling ridiculous. This is what it has come to, playing along with her father's performance.

Her father nods. "You're probably right. But won't she be cold out here?"

"C'mon, Dad," she says, pretending disbelief over his ignorance. "She's a bear. They're covered in thick fur."

He concedes and follows Mel inside, where she checks in with the receptionist. She and her father sit in hard plastic chairs with curved backs designed for someone of a particular height that's not Mel's. To her right hangs a poster depicting an assortment of animal skin diseases caused by biting insects, such as ticks, fleas, and mosquitoes. Graphic photos of bloated ticks, pus-filled skin eruptions, and infected bites dominate the top two thirds of the poster. At the bottom, a posed dog and cat pointedly stare at Melody. The tagline beside them reads, "IF You Love Your Pets . . . PROTEKTRIX." Melody looks away, but the image of the tick, sucking the blood of its host while passing on a life-threatening disease, stays embedded in her mind.

The elderly woman sitting across from them rises and drags her small fluffy dog on a bejeweled leash to the front desk. Her purple puffy coat comes down to her knees and is covered in white dog hairs. At the hem in the back, the coat looks as though it's been chewed. "Lucy has more personality than most people I know," the woman tells the receptionist, who wears the patiently bored expression of a teenage lifeguard. She hands a clipboard to the receptionist. The dog, who lies prostrate and listless on the floor, stares off at nothing, a heroin addict chasing the dragon. Melody wonders what kind of people this woman knows. But then, pet owners see more in their beloved companions than what's there because they want to see these same qualities in themselves. She considers Swift, who is slow. He's named after Jonathan Swift, Mel's favorite satirist, but is of average intelligence and not particularly attractive, with blotches of tabby gray on his otherwise white body. Swift does sit in strange positions like a feline bodhisattva, however. And he's extremely friendly, dog-like even. Compared to several of the graduate students and faculty in the English department, maybe Swift does have more personality than some people Mel knows.

Her father elbows her. "Personality, my ass," he says, loud enough for the woman to turn around and shoot him a questioning look. It's then that Melody realizes her father has two different boots on—both have laces, but one is black while the other is dark brown. She points down to his feet and gives him a wide-eyed look that he shrugs off.

Lucy's owner turns back around without saying anything to her father, and Melody is grateful.

"You can come right in here," the receptionist tells the woman, walking to the examination room on the left.

"C'mon Lucy, honey," the woman says, trying to coax the dog to stand up. Lucy ignores her and keeps her head on her front paws. "We're only getting your annual exam," the woman says, looking at Melody and shaking her head in proud disbelief. "It's like she knows she's getting an S-H-O-T," the woman spells out, a hand cupped around her mouth in case Lucy is also a lip-reader. She tugs on the leash, which elicits no response. Then pulls harder. Until she's dragging Lucy across the slick tile floor. "We do this at home all the time," she tells the receptionist as she heads toward the exam room, pulling her dog behind her like a mop. "Lucy loves it."

"I've seen dirty socks with more life in them than that thing," her father says before the door closes behind the woman. "Never liked those yip-yip dogs."

"Dad, stop."

"What? She didn't hear me. The old bat."

"You're an old bat. You can't even match your shoes."

"Is this how you talk to your father? The one who raised you all by himself, with no help from anyone?"

"Don't start."

"What? You don't want to hear the truth? How a single man sacrificed his entire life to give his only child everything she could ever desire? They could make a movie out of my life. It's got everything. Tragedy. Sacrifice. Paternal love."

"You're practically Jesus, Dad."

"You should write the story of our lives. Forget that book about those women. Who wants to read about three women fighting with each other all the time? And cheating on their husbands."

"Husband, Dad. Just one of the women cheats. The others do all sorts of things with their lives, like travel, have careers, move away. Besides, how would you know what the book's about when you haven't read it?" What if this is what Ben thinks of her novel? That it's trite and badly written? Could this be why he hasn't critiqued it yet and is afraid to tell her? But he's loved her other work. He's consistently complimented her writing over the years.

Her father waves her off. "I know what you've told me about it. And that's old hat."

"So books about women's lives are 'old hat' and what we really need are more stories about men and fathers because that hasn't been done before. Right. Maybe I should quit writing and move back in with you. I can go back to work at Kiddie Kare and be an office manager with a PhD for the rest of my life."

"Now look who's exaggerating."

"Dr. Fossweller is ready for Swift," the receptionist says, walking over to the other exam room.

"Fossweller's still here?" Mel's father asks. "Man reminds me of a damn reptile the way he stares at you without blinking. Don't his eyes dry out?" he asks the receptionist.

"Dad, be quiet." Mel smiles awkwardly at the receptionist, who maintains a blank face. Her hairstyle reminds Melody of the kind young boys wore in the fifties: short at the sides with a greased-back wave on top. "You stay out here. I'll go in." She presses on her father's arm to keep him in his seat and grabs Swift's carrier. A forlorn meow comes from her cat, followed by the coughing bark of another round of vomiting she'll have to clean up. She can only imagine the hidden locations where Swift has done this throughout her father's house, the piles that will have hardened to concrete by the time she finds them, if she ever does. Not waiting to give her father a chance to protest, she rushes into the room and closes the door behind her. Her last glimpse of him is of his look of surprise. While Fossweller examines Swift, he'll probably tell the receptionist that Melody beats him.

"A hundred seventy-five dollars just for fluids and anti-nausea meds? What kind of horseshit is that?" her father says before they've fully exited the vet's reception area.

"We're lucky it wasn't worse than that."

Melody holds the carrier, which she was able to wipe down in the exam room while waiting for Dr. Fossweller. Swift's feet, however, are stained yellow from standing in his vomit. The poor baby. She'll clean him when she brings him back to the apartment. She'd called Drake while in the room with Swift to make sure this was okay. "Of course you can bring him here," he said. As much as she hates to leave her father without company, she can't take the chance of Swift eating a wrapper, or worse, a string. Dr. Fossweller had warned her of what this could lead to: surgery or death. Swift can no longer live with her father. Hell, her father should no longer live with her father.

Melody starts her car and backs out of the parking spot. "We're going to Target."

"No, I want to go to Walmart," her father says. "Let's go there."

"I hate Walmart. It's the devil."

"They're cheap, and with what you're making, that's where you should be shopping. Don't be a snob."

The parking lot of the Walmart on the Vestal Parkway is filled. Inside the pet section of the glaringly lit store, Melody grabs a plastic litter box and a container of clumping litter from the shelf below it.

"Why are you buying this stuff? I have it all at home," her father says.

"Swift's staying with me now." She avoids looking at him.

"You can't take him. Isn't your boyfriend allergic to cats?"

"Where'd you get that from?"

"You said so."

"No I didn't."

"Well, I remember you telling me that. Or maybe he did when we went for breakfast."

"I never once said Drake's allergic to cats. And I'm sure he didn't either. You must be thinking of someone else."

"Fine. Now I'm the one making up stories." Her father's mouth sets in a pout. "First you leave, now you take my only companion."

"Clean the house and you can have him back. Besides, don't you have a new friend now?" She gestures at the teddy bear sticking out from under his coat while scrutinizing her father's expression. How far is he willing to go with this new behavior?

He scowls. "Yeah, but she can't talk back."

"Thank god for that," Mel mutters to herself.

They arrive at the express checkout lane to stand in line behind a woman whose son sits in the cart while her daughter stands beside it. The woman has a full cart of groceries she stacks on the conveyor belt.

Her father points to the sign that says "15 Items or Less." The other checkout aisles around them are also filled. In the one to their right is a family consisting of a father speaking on his cellphone in what sounds to Mel like Russian; his wife, a short woman who gently touches his sleeve on occasion to get his attention; and his teenage daughter and son, who have opened a container of crackers and eat from it until their father violently wrenches the box from his son's hands, while still on the phone, and puts it on the conveyor belt. Like diplomats aghast at the rude manners of a foreign ambassador, the teens share a look but say nothing.

"Mama, can I get one of these?" the little girl ahead of them asks. She emerges from between the cart and the shelf of candy holding a giant ring pop for her mother to inspect. She's tiny, about five years old. Her pink jacket is darkly stained from the wrists to the elbows as if she's a squid fisherman.

"No, Sissy, that's not good for you," the woman says in a sweetly patient voice. The woman wears a man's-sized parka. She reaches over her son to take items out of the cart as the cashier scans and bags her groceries in a random fashion: a whole chicken with laundry bleach, milk with shampoo, lettuce with crayons.

The little girl's shoulders slump and she puts the candy back in a box of chocolate bars.

"What about this one, Mama?" she says, holding up a plastic container filled with sparkly gum.

"I have to pee," the little boy says, clutching his crotch.

The woman lets out a low growl of frustration that Mel can empathize with. "Sissy, put that back right now. We're not buying garbage. Brother, you don't have to pee. You went before we left the house."

Melody's father looks at her and makes a face, but she turns away from him so as not to invite other comments. Is it possible the woman named her daughter Sissy and her son Brother? No, probably not. Mel's glance falls on the racks of tabloid newspapers across from the candy shelves. One cover features a photo of a haggard-looking actress. Smaller photos of other makeup-less actresses surround the larger one. The bold headline advertises a ten-page exposé of "Celebrities Revealed!" as though a massive conspiracy is about to be unveiled in the tabloid's pages. This would make for a good blog post, Mel thinks, about the pressure put on female actors to look inhumanly perfect in their daily lives.

"Can I have a strawberry, Mama?" the little boy asks, reaching for the translucent plastic container of berries his mother has placed on the belt.

"No. We have to pay for them first," she says, with a brittle smile at the cashier, whose raised eyebrows convey several emotions: indifference, exhaustion, existential angst. "It's stealing if we eat them before doing that."

"For chrissakes, let him have a strawberry," Mel's father volunteers. "It's not like you're buying them by the pound."

Mel cringes. Why is he telling this woman how to raise her children? Thankfully, both the woman and the cashier ignore him, though the little boy gives Collin a comradely nod. They're men in the trenches and need to stick together if they're going to win the war against oppressive women. Melody attempts to do her usual thing when she's out with her father, which is to disassociate from the scene to observe the performances around her. She wonders if the development of this writerly trait has been inspired by her father's ability to embarrass her in public. Mel would often drift away from him in stores, leaving him to have awkward encounters with strangers on his own. During a late teenage phase when she was reading superhero comic books, she nicknamed her father The Rebuker. His mission: to reprimand anyone he encountered who did something he viewed as wrong. From not saying thank you to neglecting to hold a door open to cutting in front of you in line, The Rebuker was there with a gesture of disgust or a cutting comment.

The little boy continues staring at The Rebuker as his mother pushes her cart out of the aisle. Mel's father gives him a salute the boy clumsily returns.

Finally, it's Melody and her father's turn to have their few items rung up. He opens his coat to retrieve his wallet, insisting he'll pay, and the stuffed bear falls onto the conveyor belt.

"Why did you bring that in here?" Mel asks before turning to the cashier. "It's his. Or was mine. We didn't take it. Look at it. It's old and crappy."

The cashier, a large white woman with dark blond cornrows, wears long nails with zebra stripes painted on them. She gives the bear and Collin a skeptical look. "Ain't you a little old for that?"

"Your nails could be as big as shovels and they still won't hide the size of your ass," her father says.

Melody inhales sharply, her body tensing. This is much worse than her father's normal brusqueness. She reaches over and clasps his bicep. The cashier, who had turned to face her co-worker in the next aisle to exchange pantomimes of fainting from exhaustion, now turns back to them. "What you say to me, old man?"

"Nothing, nothing," Melody says. "Don't listen to him. He's old and senile." She guides her father out of the lane. "Go sit there," she tells him, ignoring his injured expression and pointing toward a bench outside the in-house optometrist across from the checkout aisles.

Back at the register, the cashier lets out a doubtful "humph" sound. "You lucky I'm tired," she says over her shoulder as she scans Melody's items.

"I'm so sorry," Melody says.

"Girl, I'm sorry for you, too, with a daddy like that."

"You have no idea," she tells the woman.

8

A few days later, Swift is still exploring the uncluttered apartment like a pleasantly surprised prospective buyer.

As Melody grades papers at the dining room table, Drake relaxes on the couch to watch ESPN or, as Mel likes to call some of the programs on this channel, his man gossip shows. Now and then she looks up at the TV, where a very attractive blond woman attempts to be heard among several male cohosts.

"Jeez, you think her skirt is short enough? Or her heels high enough? Why do all the male commentators on ESPN look like they're heading into a business meeting, while the women dress like they're going clubbing?"

Drake nods. "Yeah, it's messed up. And they're all attractive, like that's a requirement of the job. But look at the male analysts. They get to be overweight, old, and ugly."

He rises from the couch without disturbing Swift, who is in loaf form at his feet, and comes to hug her from behind. "Anything new going on with your dad?"

Mel leans back and puts her arms over Drake's. "Just the usual weirdness. I have to take him for a checkup, but I'm terrified of what Dr. Loomba will find. What if it's brain cancer?"

Drake sits down next to her. "But what if it's not? Maybe his meds are doing something to him. Maybe it's just loneliness. It sucks, but you're the only one who can figure this out."

"Like I always have. A part of me just wants a break. Do you have any idea how much work is involved in being Collin's daughter? How am I supposed to leave for a job if something's seriously wrong with him?"

"Because my job here will make it so you won't have to."

"You accepted the VU job?"

"Yep. And I've already talked to my adviser about a partner hire and she said it should be no problem."

"That's amazing!" She gives Drake a tight hug, then sits back to contemplate the news. She is guaranteed a job after graduating. Maybe not a great one, and one that means she's not leaving her hometown, but still, it's work that will allow her to earn a living and continue to keep an eye on her father.

"See? You keep thinking of the worst-case scenario, like it's a given. Sometimes it's not and things work out for the best."

Mel sighs but doesn't agree with Drake. He's never had the worst happen, like his mother suddenly dying, to shape his way of thinking. "I still think I should apply for other jobs, in case something turns up that lets me teach creative writing. As if I don't have enough to do right now. I filled out one application the other day that wanted sixty pages of materials. It's insane."

"Oh, I know. I was right there with you." Drake looks thoughtful. "But you know, I should probably keep applying too, in case a job that includes fieldwork happens."

After he goes to bed, Melody stays up, sitting on the couch and reading emails with the TV on for background noise. With her laptop resting on a pillow in front of her, she occasionally looks up at the cooking show she's watching, then types responses to students, deletes junk emails, and processes rejections from magazines she's submitted to, or for grants and fellowships she won't be receiving. The world likes to tell her "No!" So many noes and so few yeses. But then she remembers how much she loves the process of writing when she's doing it. That will have to be enough. She opens the folder on her desktop that contains notes full of ideas for her novel manuscript and reads one, then revises a small section of the book. But the open loop of such a huge incomplete project nags at her.

A GEICO commercial comes on and Mel watches it absently. It cuts between two scenes, one of a pig who quickly and easily settles an accident because GEICO is so efficient, and the second of a man who is not a GEICO customer and is therefore on hold with his insurance company while his beautiful girlfriend waits impatiently in the background. The last scene is of the woman driving off with the pig. She has, apparently, grown tired of waiting and, like most beautiful women, is shallow and fickle enough to bail on her boyfriend to have a good time with a pig.

Melody saves her novel and closes it, then deletes the note that inspired the revision. A small feeling of accomplishment fills her, something she hasn't felt in a while because her blog posts don't provide it. But she will finish her novel *and* have a job—an actual job— after she graduates.

She scrolls through Facebook, landing on a post covering the latest VIDA Count. The organization was created, it says, to "tally the gender disparity in major literary publications and book reviews." Unsurprisingly, the post points out that books written by men get reviewed more often than ones by women, and that magazine and journal writing is dominated by male writers too. It isn't only Melody receiving noes; it's women in general. She considers the personal consequences of this. If a woman writer like herself has a harder time getting her book reviewed, she sells fewer copies, which means she's less likely to get published again. And if her writing is less frequently accepted by magazines and journals, that means fewer publications to put on her curriculum vitae, which reduces her chances of being hired for an assistant professor job or receiving tenure, because both depend on publications.

Mel shares the VIDA article with her Facebook friends, of which she has a few hundred—from her undergraduate days and high school, her years working at Kiddie Kare, and her grad student years at VU. Mel visits Ben's Facebook to see what's been taking up his extra time, scrolling through his posts and ignoring the feeling she's stalking him. There aren't many entries because he isn't a big social media guy, but one fills her with joy: "Working on a friend's MS right now and let me tell you, the writing is spectacular!" She's buoyed up by restored confidence. Her talented friend whose opinion she values the most believes in her.

Below this post is one sharing an article from a popular men's magazine of "The 50 Books Every Man Should Read." The list includes obvious choices, like Hemingway, Faulkner, DeLillo, and Twain. Many of the books Melody has read and enjoyed, like *A Confederacy of Dunces*. She also sees Flannery O'Connor's name and scans the rest of the list, expecting to find more women writers. Except there aren't any. Not a single other female writer besides O'Connor. Melody considers her publications in literary journals; the first prize she recently won, judged by a well-known writer, a female one; and the Distinguished Thesis Award she won at VU for her MA thesis, which was a short story collection. She wonders what she might accomplish if she only had a penis.

Across from her is a huge filled bookcase. At least half the books were written by women and people of color, along with a selection of LGBT books. But that's not enough. From now on, she decides, she'll do her best to buy more books written by marginalized writers, talk about them on social media, leave reviews on Amazon, and make sure they dominate her syllabi when she gets the chance to teach creative writing. If that ever happens.

Melody scrolls past several more posts from friends and acquaintances, stopping at one written by a graduate of VU, Frederick Schultz, now an associate professor at a university in Illinois and the editor of the school's literary magazine. "I know I probably shouldn't admit this," Frederick writes, "but I find I don't often read books written by women. Probably because I have a hard time relating to a female protagonist."

Melody exhales hard and reads the comments, hoping someone has criticized Frederick for his admission and what it reveals. She's read thousands of books over the decades that featured male protagonists, and she's had no problem relating to them. Does this mean that women have better imaginations? Or are they simply used to reading male perspectives because writing is dominated by men? But instead of anyone calling Frederick out, they've left only kindly recommendations of women writers he should read. Melody considers several reactions: unfriending Frederick, adding some suggestions of her own, or telling him off.

Instead she writes: "Your reading habits have serious consequences for female writers. That you're in a position of power as an editor and professor makes this even more problematic." She adds a link to the VIDA article.

Over the following day, several people like Mel's comment, mostly women. Many add their own remarks that echo hers. And she realizes she's taken up the Rebuker mantle from her father, which isn't a bad thing when it's used for a good purpose.

9

Mel's afternoon class has just ended when Drake calls to remind her to pick up a quarter-scale replica of a T. rex head from outside the paleontology department's office before it's thrown out. She'd completely forgotten about it, a case of selective amnesia.

"Not sure I understand why you would want something as big as that in our apartment," Mel says. She has a vision of their home evolving into a space her father would feel comfortable in, filled with models of dinosaurs.

"It'll look cool. Besides, what about all your books?"

"They're alphabetically organized and neat," she says, omitting the stacks of books on the dining table, beside their bed, and next to the couch.

Was it her purposefully forgetting or something more worrying? As she drives across campus through a cold drizzle to the paleontology department, Melody considers what she can do to improve her memory so that years from now, she can avoid some of the issues plaguing her father. There are ginkgo biloba tablets, except she'd forget to take them. She's heard that some cognitive exercises can pump up the brain's centers of recall, and there's a plethora of books and articles that give examples of cerebral calisthenics, but when would she have the time? Her father could probably use these exercises more than her, but he would never do them.

The T. rex head is made of papier-mâché over Styrofoam designed to resemble pocked and mottled lizard skin, with fake scar tracks around the neck meant to signify battles the T. rex fought. Its palm-sized yellow eyes stare off at nothing, reminding Melody of some of her students. The head was a cross-disciplinary project between the paleontology and art departments, encouraged by the school's administration to diminish departmental "silos" and create a more unified institution. Ted, Drake's friend and a fellow PhD candidate in his discipline, helps her carry it to her car.

"This thing is ridiculous. Can you explain to me why Drake wants it so bad?"

"It's free?" Ted shrugs and turns his palms outward. His work boots, jeans, and denim shirt are all dusty, as if he's stepped away from a fossil dig on campus. On special occasions, Ted wears a brown leather hat to "keep out the sun," though that glowing orb is as rare as a brontosaurus bone in Binghamton. "They were going to throw it out. At least now T. has a home."

"All I know is he'd better never say another word if I bring home more books."

"You could put it in your living room. It'd make a great conversation piece."

Melody looks at Ted doubtfully. "Won't work. I think he's going to hang it from the ceiling somewhere."

"How 'bout your bedroom?" Ted gives her a double eyebrow raise behind his large square glasses.

"You're a funny guy, Ted. Don't give him any ideas."

Melody drives to the parking lot nearest the Chenango Room, a dining hall on campus where she's meeting Ben to "talk." He'd texted her the day before to set it up, which has to mean he's finished her manuscript. Finally she can close this loop. Mel's fear that she won't complete the book on time to defend it in the spring—or find a new chair for her dissertation committee—looms large. She really needs to get moving on that. And what if Tina is as hard on the fiction dissertations this year as Abe was on the poetry ones the prior spring?

On the radio, a promo ad for 92.5 KGB plays. The voice of a stereotypical young dude says, "We got stuck behind a girl texting while she drove. Hey slut, stop texting! When we drove past her, we threw a beer at her car!"

Melody makes a disgusted sound. Why does the area's sole alternative rock station assume its listeners are fourteen-year-old misogynists? She switches to the local NPR station and classical music broadcasts from the Sentra's speakers. Maybe only classical music should be allowed to influence her brain, because she read somewhere that people who listen to it have higher IQs. More likely it's that smart people listen to classical music, not that classical music makes them more intelligent. The song that's playing is one she recalls from her childhood years watching Looney Toons, and she imagines Elmer Fudd dressed in Viking regalia singing, "Kill da wabbit, kill da wabbit!" She cringes at the realization that her knowledge of several centuries of important music rests precariously on a stack of animation reels.

As Mel walks to the Chenango Room, she spots Ben outside the entrance talking to a young woman with brown hair, whose back is to her. She studies Ben's neutral expression, the one she's seen him wear in literature classes when a graduate student interprets a text in a wildly inaccurate way. Does Ben ever doubt if he's intelligent enough? Probably not. How nice it would be to feel that certain. The woman turns to leave, and Mel sees it's Sherry Turner, her former student. This is at least the second time she's seen Sherry seek Ben out. Not good, she thinks.

Then Ben spots Mel. "Hey, how's it going?" There's relief in his eyes, though Mel isn't sure why.

"Busy and stressed. I have forty annotated bibliographies to grade over the next week."

"Christ, that sounds awful." He gestures for her to head away from the Chenango Room toward the road that circles the inner campus and she falls in step with him.

"Oh yeah, it is. How about you?"

"No complaints."

An older woman with her hair piled into a large bouffant updo passes by them on her way to the Chenango Room and Mel recognizes her as one of the waitstaff. Her pink-frosted lips make her look like she just rehearsed for a gig on *Laugh-In*. If she told Ben that, he'd know what she's talking about. Still, she needs to find more current cultural references instead of the old ones she's adopted thanks to her father's TV-watching habits. How many of these have ended up in her book to make it outdated—and possibly offensive?

"I had a story accepted the other day," she tells him.

"Awesome. Please tell me the mail guy story got picked up. I love that one."

"That's the one."

"Who took it?"

"The online version of *Red Wheelbarrow*."

"Ah, that's great. Too bad it's not print though." Ben looks contemplative.

"At my stage of the writing game, I'll take either," Mel says. But his comment deflates her.

As they approach the entrance to the engineering building, with its large expanse of windows, they find a group of prospective students and their parents on a tour of the campus led by a VU student guide. Mel pastes a serious expression on her face, hoping that she and Ben look like colleagues deep in conversation about important contemporary issues in literature. She catches a glimpse of their reflections in the windows as they pass the building and wonders if onlookers are more likely to see Ben as her mentor and her as the mentee. How easily he fits the part of a professor. She gives her fleeting reflection a disgruntled look and hurries to catch up with Ben, who has forged ahead.

"How's your dad?" he asks.

"Well, he might be acting senile to get me to move back in or he might be legit senile. Hard to tell." Mel tells him about the state of the house and how he's been talking to her old teddy bear.

Ben's eyes widen. "No way. That's not good." Then he adds, "But it does give you material to write about."

"Someday, but right now, it's too depressing. I'm taking him to his doctor to figure out what's going on. He could use a cleaning lady or home care attendant so I don't have to be his maid and companion. Though he probably won't go for that." Mel stares blankly at the surrounding hills, barely noting the orange and yellow leaves of the trees.

She considers her father's likely reaction to her proposing they hire someone to help take care of him. "I don't need no nursemaid," he'd say.

Ben nods. "That's a good idea. Don't get caught up in being his housekeeper. It'll suck the life out of your writing time. How's the job search going?"

Mel takes a deep breath before responding, wondering why Ben is setting such a grueling pace walking around the campus loop. "You know I was hoping to leave the area for a tenure-track job. But Drake took a job here, and I'll be his partner hire. Given everything that's going on with my dad, it's my best option, though I'd prefer the fellowship if I'm going to stay local. If I win it, it'll look good on my CV, plus it'll give me time to publish more and teach creative writing. But . . . so much for leaving," Mel says, her shoulders slumping.

Ben looks sympathetic. "You don't have to stay a partner hire. Use it for the experience while you look for something else."

Mel shrugs. "And go through the whole application process all over again? It's like having another job that doesn't pay. What's with these schools that want a cover letter, your CV, a statement of teaching philosophy, your student evaluations for the past year, recommendation letters from three faculty members, a sample syllabus and assignments, plus a writing sample?"

"That's ridiculous. I don't bother applying to those. The only thing they should be asking for in round one is a cover letter and CV."

Mel sighs in near breathless agreement. Why are they walking so fast? She takes a quick look behind them, but no one is in hot pursuit. They've reached the eastern part of the campus and he presses on. She stops and stares at him with dawning realization. "Are you trying to get me to exercise? Is that why we went on this walk?" Ben is an avid gym-goer who has tried on numerous occasions to talk her into a membership at Planet Fitness so he'll have company when he works out. But Mel has steadfastly refused to join him, blaming it on her lack of fitness and not her lack of funds.

He grins at her. "See? You're a lot fitter than you think."

"You're hilarious," Mel says. "How about you? How are your applications going?"

"I've applied mostly in New York City and some other bigger cities. I'd live in Boston, I suppose, or Philadelphia. Maybe Chicago."

"Everyone says you need to graduate before hiring committees will look at you. Or get a book published." She hopes this last bit will lead to Ben's telling her he has her book ready.

"You worry too much over stuff you can't control," he says. "Stop doing that to yourself. It'll all work out."

She gives Ben a withering side-eye but his focus remains straight ahead. Where does he get this certainty and optimism? His family, what little he reveals of it to Mel, is well off, so that probably helps. His mother worked in real estate in New Jersey and is supportive of his writing. His father is somewhat doubtful, being a retired CEO for a large investment firm in Manhattan, though he apparently likes the idea of having a "doctor" in the family. The worst Ben has complained about when it comes to his father are his half-joking comments about Ben being a bum for having summers off and about writing being a "hobby." The only major difficulty he's ever revealed to Mel was that he went through a period of heavy drinking as an undergraduate when he was trying to emulate Hemingway and Faulkner. It occurs to her that he's always been interested in hearing about her family history but rarely reciprocates with details regarding his own. Is that because there are none, which seems impossible to believe, or because they might tarnish the curated persona he's created?

"Easier said than done," she says. Mel slows her pace, hoping Ben will follow suit. He does not, but instead turns and beckons her to catch up to him. Groaning inwardly, she scurries forward and steels herself. "About my novel. Please tell me it's done so I can get that off my back."

"Well, there's good news and bad news," he says, looking ahead at the newly built recreation center to their right. "The good news is that I just signed with an agent and she's trying to sell my book."

"Holy shit, Ben! That's fantastic! I'm so happy for you." Melody grabs his forearm, shaking it like an elderly pit bull with a favorite toy.

Ben smiles. "I can't believe it myself."

"How many agents did you have to pitch?"

"Actually, she contacted me because she read one of my stories. Asked me if I had anything bigger finished. I showed her *The Stinkfist Chronicle* and she loved it."

"Look at you, not even having to query to land an agent." Mel shakes her head in wonderment.

Ben lets out a hard, sad breath. "That part felt great, and she loved the book. But she wanted me to make it more marketable before taking me on, and that plus bartending took up my summer. I haven't had a chance to jump into your novel, though believe me, that's what I really want to do."

"Oh." Mel imagines a giant "Acme" anvil landing on her. She thinks about his recent Facebook post. Whose manuscript was he talking about if he hadn't touched hers? Doesn't he realize when he posts things like that, she can see them and know that he has time for someone else's work but not hers? "Does that mean you won't be able to read it?"

"No, definitely not. I totally owe you and I'm dying to start because I know it's going to be great. I just need more time."

Mel's gloomy outlook breaks to allow rays of relief to peek through. "Could you have it done before Thanksgiving so I can work on it during the break? That gives you over a month to read it."

He nods gratefully. "That sounds totally doable."

"Great," Mel says in a neutral voice while sending him a strongly intoned subliminal suggestion willing him to follow through.

10

After they finish their circuit of the campus, Melody and Ben head to his office so he can drop off his messenger bag. Once again, Mel can't help but think that this is the type of campus office she dreams of having one day: plenty of shelves for books, walls to hang art on, a space both inviting and scholarly. There's a window that looks onto a courtyard where several trees stretch their arms to the sky in supplication for a mild winter. Mel's office is on the outskirts of campus, in the College-in-the-Trees building. Its only furnishings are a beat-up pine rectangle for a desk, a refugee from a 1970s dorm room covered in the gouged initials of now middle-aged alumni, along with two chairs. There isn't even a bookcase in her office.

"How the hell did you get Abe's office?"

Ben grins sheepishly. "Tina sent me an email at the end of the summer asking me if I wanted to use it since Abe wasn't going to be around. Colton didn't want it because he says it's haunted."

"Hmm," Mel says, feeling both relieved and annoyed. Ben took Tina's weekend poetry seminar during the spring semester, despite having no interest in poetry. His descriptions of some of his classmates and their abstract work were biting though amusing, with Tina receiving the brunt of his satirical analysis—particularly her Sophia Loren Collection gigantic glasses. "Every time she walks into class, they're in some subtle new position on her face. Either tilted up on one side, or way down on her nose. Sometimes hanging from one ear." He'd shaken his head in disbelief. "And don't get me started on her lipstick. It's this bright red she draws around the vicinity of her lips in a Picasso-like version of a mouth."

Ben unpacks a few books and a binder from his bag and places them on his mahogany desk. "You remember that paper you helped me write for Townley's Restoration lit class?"

Mel nods.

"He emailed me the other day about submitting it to some journal he reads for."

"Must be nice," Mel says. She'd helped him figure out his topic, his argument, and the structure of the paper, not to mention find sources. "And you're buddy-buddy with Tina now, too."

"I wouldn't say that."

"She likes you, right? Knows your name. I've met her at least five times, and she never remembers who I am."

"That's why you should have taken her class with me. You're a terrific writer, but you gotta play the game, Mel. It's not all about how you write but who you know."

Mel rolls her eyes at him. "What do you think happened between her and Abe?"

"I have no idea, but I bet his refusing to pass her poets' dissertations didn't help."

Ben closes the door behind him, and they head over to this semester's graduate student reading. Melody has never signed up for a slot because she dreads reading her work in front of large audiences. Since this year's cohort of graduate students is skewed toward poets (Tina's choice now that Abe is gone), she also hasn't been to many readings. But Ben decided to make an appearance at this one and asked her to come along.

Inside the auditorium, attendees sit scattered in their separate cliques. The room gently slopes down to a stage with a podium. The predominantly orange scheme of carpet and wall color makes Mel feel as if she's inside a pumpkin. Ben goes to stand in a row in the middle of the room, casually surveying the turnout. When he waves hello to someone behind them, Mel turns and sees the blond woman who was in his office at the beginning of the semester. She's encountered her around campus several times since then.

"Who's that?" Mel whispers as they settle into the seats Ben chose for them.

"Elaina Longacre. She's a poet in the master's program."

"I see," Mel says, raising her eyebrow. She'd ask if he was dating her, but he'd only evade the question. Was it a poetry manuscript Ben was referring to in his Facebook post? Would he ignore the friend who'd helped him with his writing for the past four years to help the attractive poet he just met?

Prose poet Fiona Briggman-Young walks to the podium. She gestures for everyone to move closer together but is ignored and smiles at her failed attempt to herd the audience into a more tight-knit group.

"Hello, everyone," Fiona says. "Thank you for coming to today's graduate reading. It's my pleasure to introduce your first poet. I've been a fan of Wade Warder-Scott's work for years. When Wade writes of his childhood in Arkansas and the tribulations of growing up as the only child of a single mother, it speaks to me." Fiona's chin dips in several small rhythmic nods, her mouth purses, and she looks thoughtfully toward the side of the room. Her stance at the podium is relaxed and confident. Mel imagines herself in the same place, all twitchy and nervous, and grimaces. She realizes her expression could be misconstrued and replaces it with a blandly approving smile.

"Wade, if I can call him that," Fiona says, smiling at her own inside joke, "is making a name for himself as a poet." She turns a page of notes and looks back up. "He's won numerous awards, including the Humboldt College Chapbook Award and the *Suffolk County Literati Magazine* award for his poem 'My Mama.'"

"That's the journal Tina edits," Ben whispers. Mel nods. Since her appointment as the creative writing director thirty years earlier, Tina comes to campus only four weekends each semester. The rest of her time is spent working on this magazine and her own poetry, which focuses on the lives of second-generation middle-class Greek American women. Tina is also the poet laureate of Astoria, Queens. "You know my mom is a quarter Greek," Ben whispers to Mel.

She gives him her best squinty-eyed Charles Bronson look of skepticism. So that's how he'd wheedled his way into Tina's favor.

Fiona continues: "Finally, Wade has had his work published in such literary journals as *Grassgreen*, the *Endicott Review*, and his high school magazine."

"Not to mention his kindergarten newsletter," Ben whispers to Melody, who snorts.

"It's my honor to introduce a great man and a great poet, who also happens to be my fiancé."

As Wade walks to the podium, Fiona meets him halfway. He's sporting a goatee and a button-up blue shirt with tie, jeans, and a tweed blazer. The couple exchange a brief yet passionate kiss, and Melody looks away in embarrassment. She imagines Drake introducing her in the same way and their sharing a kiss like the messy-drunk first make-out session they'd had in the Belmar's parking lot.

Ben has an evil smile on his face. "Think of all the little Briggman-Young-Warder-Scotts that'll be running around one day," he whispers to Mel, who lets out a "psht" of amused approval.

Wade reads several poems, ending with "My Mama," a crowd favorite. Melody catches references to the sound of locusts, the smell of Mama's lemon cake, wearing worn-out sneakers, and a lot of rain. Afterward, Wade takes out a handkerchief from his pocket and wipes his eyes.

His soft gaze graces the audience as a sad smile crosses his face. "I must subscribe to the Tina Petrakis school of writing: if it doesn't move the poet, it won't move his audience."

Ben nods in solemn agreement but looks at Melody sideways. This is one of Mel's favorite traits of his, a willingness to burst balloons of pretension or self-importance that encase the process of writing. "It's a job," he'd once said. "Let's stop romanticizing it and putting it out of reach of normal people."

"You want to come over for dinner tonight?" she asks, almost forgiving him for his failure to start her novel.

"Why, I'd love to."

They listen to two other poets and one fiction writer, who reads endlessly from a rambling and incoherent piece he explains was influenced by Pink Floyd's album *Ummagumma*. The crowd shifts restlessly in their seats as he drones on, though he never looks up to note their impatience. Ben and Mel exchange a glance and sneak out like soldiers caught behind enemy lines.

"God, what a day," Ben says, getting into Melody's car. He cranks the heat to high and directs a vent toward himself. "I have so much work and all I want to do is write. Or read your book." He rubs his hands together, as if in anticipation of diving into Mel's novel.

Meanwhile, he teaches only two undergrad creative writing workshops, which are limited to fifteen students in each; his coursework and field exams are complete; and with his novel done, he has nothing else to do for his PhD but defend his dissertation in the spring.

"Yeah," she says. Since giving her diss to Ben, she's started and revised several short stories, but nothing feels like it has "legs," as Abe would put it. Only blog posts come to her. Perhaps because her mind is circling around her novel.

"What's for dinner?"

"I don't know. Drake's cooking tonight."

He frowns. "I like it better when you cook."

"You'll survive one night of Drake's culinary skills."

Mel and Drake's apartment is on the second floor of a two-family house off Riverside Drive in downtown Binghamton. The houses in this neighborhood, ranging from colonials to Tudors, have small front yards and narrow driveways. Once upon a time this area of Binghamton, and the city itself, had been more prosperous, with homeowners not needing to bisect their houses to include upstairs apartments they rented to strangers. As factories in Binghamton closed, and IBM's campus nearby in Endicott was sold, the town's fortunes and future diminished. Businesses fled downtown Binghamton for the Vestal Parkway, which passes in front of VU, stretching out for several miles in either direction, and is lined with retail plazas and megastores like Target, Walmart, TJ Maxx, Kohl's, and Lowe's.

"Smells good in here," Ben says in a singsongy voice as he steps inside. "What's for dinner, honey?"

"Chili and corn bread, son," Drake tells him.

Ben pats him on the shoulder. "You're going to make a damned fine wife one day."

"I come from a long line of fathers who cook," Drake tells him. "You should give it a try."

Mel kisses Drake on the cheek in front of the aged stove in their tiny kitchen, where he stirs a pot of chili. The box of corn bread mix sits on the counter next to the toaster, and the sweet odor of it baking mingles with the tomato-bean of the chili. So much better than urine and smoke, Mel thinks. Which reminds her to bring leftovers to her father's house after dropping Ben off at his apartment later that night.

"Did the head fit?" Drake asks Melody.

"Barely. You and Ben want to get that monstrosity out of my car while I set the table?"

"What head?" Ben asks, opening the fridge to grab a beer.

Mel looks at the bottle in surprise. At the Belmar, when he was once asked by a drunk graduate student why he barely drank, Ben said he wanted to contradict the cliché of the alcoholic writer. But given what Mel knows about his undergraduate drinking, is there more to this? And what about his summer bartending stint?

"There's a huge dinosaur head in my back seat," she tells him. "Didn't you notice it?"

He lets out a half-embarrassed, half-self-amused snort of laughter. "How did I not see that?"

"Because you're self-absorbed," Drake says, with a not-so-genuine smile.

"You're probably right. But I make up for it with my charming personality."

"Exactly," Melody says, shooting Drake a look.

Later, as they're eating, Ben puts his fork down and wipes his mouth with a paper napkin. "I have to tell you about one of my students in my creative writing class. We're workshopping her story the other day. First off, she refuses to read any of her writing aloud in class. Instead, she hands it to me and says . . ." He ducks his head, slumps his shoulders, and in a high, breathy, girlish voice continues, "Professor Howe, could you please read my story to the class?" The look he gives Drake and Melody is pathologically shy yet frighteningly coy. He comes out of his performance. "I say fine. Mind you, this student keeps all her work in a pink folder with a kitten on the front and she has a laptop screensaver of the Olsen twins."

Mel nods but Drake looks blank. "You know, those two little girls who played the baby on *Full House*? They're fashion moguls now."

"How do you know this?" he asks her.

"I keep up with the world." Melody sits up straighter and stares down her nose at Drake while pursing her lips, giving him her Anna Wintour look.

Drake shakes his head. "It has to be hard for new writers to share their work with their peers."

Ben's expression is one of exaggerated pity. "True. But she also drops by my office constantly and never makes appointments. I can't tell you how many times I've had to say, sorry but I can't meet with you right now. The expensive chocolates she hands out almost every class, those I don't mind," he adds.

"What was her story about?" Mel asks, while wondering if he minds Elaina visiting him in his office without an appointment.

"Get this. It's about this brilliantly talented artist named Lillian who has a love-hate relationship with her mentor, the handsome Monsieur Bowe." He says the name in a cartoonish French accent.

"Jesus. How's the writing?" Mel asks.

"It's readable but she's fixated on this story. She says it's a novel, and she could definitely use more knowledge of art, which I've told her." He shakes his head. "But she's not having it. Still, I could do without lines like 'Lillian contemplated stabbing her mentor through the heart with a dagger dipped in cobra venom.'"

Melody laughs but Drake looks at her in surprise. "Don't you think you should talk to someone about this?" he asks Ben. "Look at what happened at Dawson College."

Surely Ben's student isn't dangerous like that. Statistically, women don't attack or murder people. Men do. She'd be more afraid if Ben's student was male.

Ben waves Drake off. "If we talked to someone about every creative writing student who's a little off, we'd never stop talking. It goes with the territory."

"Speaking of being a little off, I saw Rob Arver lurking in the library a few weeks back. I think he lives in his study carrel," Mel says.

"Who's he?" Drake asks, taking another serving of corn bread.

"He's a lit guy who's been in the program forever. I don't know how he hasn't graduated yet. He can't be funded anymore."

"He wants to be a writer too," Ben tells Drake, "but comes from this hardcore evangelical background. A while back, at this open mic event, he read this piece on Hell Rides."

"The fundamentalist Christian version of Disney World, right?" Drake says.

"Exactly," Ben says.

Later that night, Melody drives Ben to his apartment near VU. The building where he lives features bare-bones one-bedroom apartments rented to graduate students at a reasonable rate. A couch, dining set, desk, and chair come with the deal, as well as a bed. Since Ben's primary home is on the Upper East Side, he doesn't care if his apartment in Vestal is monastic.

A tinfoil-covered bowl of chili, topped by a piece of buttered corn bread, also wrapped, sits in the back seat.

"I like Drake," Ben volunteers, nodding his head thoughtfully. "I was a little concerned when you two first started dating because he's younger than you. And then when you moved in with him, I was more worried. Hope you're being careful not to give up writing time because you're in a serious relationship. Or get sucked into being a permanent partner hire. You know those jobs are never great."

"Thanks for your concern, big brother," Mel says. "You don't know what it was like living with my dad. You want needy? Try him. Drake's dad is a househusband and his mom has always been the primary breadwinner. He doesn't need me to take care of him."

Ben looks skeptical. "Even still, romance can really screw up a writer's output. Don't get distracted and work less. You're too talented. And super funny, which not many women are." Ben delivers this last sentence in a self-mocking tone meant to defuse the insult to Mel's gender.

"Ew!" she says, giving him a repulsed look. "So only men are funny? Look at Aimee Bender and Lorrie Moore. How about Dorothy Parker if you want to go back some. You know better than that, right? Though I appreciate the compliment."

"You know what I mean. You're the only other serious fiction writer in the program."

Mel knows he means this as a compliment but also wonders if that makes Ben view her as his only competition.

Later that night, when Mel comes home from dropping off Ben at his apartment and the food at her father's house, Drake is reading a scholarly article on the couch in the living room. A blanket the color of the Caribbean is pulled up to his chest.

"How's your dad?" he asks her.

Melody groans and places her messenger bag down on the dining room table. She motions for Drake to sit up so she can recline on the couch next to him. Swift hops up to lie on her stomach, tucking his paws into his chest to form a cat loaf. She pets him absently as he purrs. "You know how he watches TV with that teddy bear? I'm in the kitchen heating up the chili and I hear him explaining to it something the news anchor said. It was bizarre."

"You think he acts like that when he's alone? Or is he doing it for your benefit?" Drake stretches his arm out behind her to grab her hand.

"It's possible. Did I ever tell you about the time he faked having a stomach virus to get out of going to a wedding with his girlfriend Claudia? He actually whipped up fake vomit from a partly scrambled egg and baking soda, then poured it all in the toilet to prove how sick he was." Mel is sure behavior like this must have contributed to Claudia's leaving her father.

"What if you video him during the day? You could put a camera anywhere in his living room and he'd never notice it."

"Hmm," Melody says, skeptically. "Sounds like teen sitcom hijinks. And what if he does something gross? I don't need to see that."

"But at least you'd know whether it's an act or not. Don't you want to figure that out?"

Mel admits to herself that a part of her doesn't, because thinking it's an act makes her life much easier.

11

On a gloomy gray Saturday morning with thick cloud cover blocking any possibility of a lone ray of sunshine penetrating through, typical for late October in Binghamton, Mel pulls into her father's driveway. She braces herself for the argument to come, rehearsing some of her best reasons for why he needs help from sources other than her. Three plastic Halloween pumpkins sit haphazardly arranged in the front flowerbed. In the brisk breeze, a witch on a broom flies at an angle from between two of the porch posts. The TV is on so loud inside the house, she can hear it from outside.

Oji's garage door opens and Mel stands on the front porch, watching him reverse his Jeep out onto the street. He stops in front of her father's house, and Mel walks over to him. The twangy vocals of a country song waft from his car stereo as he opens his window.

"Where are you off to?" Mel asks.

"My line dancing class."

"Ooh, have fun!" She gestures with her thumb in her father's direction. "Any news to report on Sir Laurence Olivier?"

"He's angry at me for telling you what he does. He called me Mata Hari Haruto the other day."

"I'm sorry, Oji. I don't have any excuse for him other than he's old."

"He is lonely but he pushes everyone away. Except you, who he tries to hold on to too tightly." Oji makes a strangling gesture, and Mel's hand instinctively goes to protect her own throat. "I'll see you later. Come for dinner soon, okay?"

"I will."

Mel creeps back up the porch to squat in front of the living room window. Through a tiny space between boxes, bins, and stacks, she sees her father sitting on the couch with his left elbow on the arm and his forearm straight up. Even at his age, he curls his legs in, sitting in a Z shape. When he picks his nose and lifts one buttock to release a fart, she rolls her eyes. Then laughs at herself as nostalgia washes over her for when it was the two of them arguing over what TV show to watch (her father and his damned detective series or black-and-white films on TCM). Melody is struck by a premonition that one day she'll recall this moment and weep for the loss of her father.

She takes the opportunity to witness his behavior while it's not a performance meant for her, noting the irony that she is the spy he'd accused Oji of being. Her father rises, holding the stuffed bear, which he bows to before slowly waltzing with it in the narrow aisle between the couch and coffee table. He sits back down with the teddy bear beside him and strikes a match to light his cigarette. Gesturing toward the TV with his cigarette in hand, he talks to the stuffed animal as though explaining something important. Then he pauses to listen to its response and laughs like the toy is the Oscar Wilde of wit. A tendril of smoke appears to his left, which causes him to rise from the couch. For several moments he studies something Melody can't see. More smoke appears. Her father has his hands on his hips like an architect surveying a building. He heads toward the kitchen just as Mel rushes into the house.

She finds smoke rising from a smoldering piece of paper on the side table next to the couch, and her father returning to the living room carrying a glass of water. In those brief seconds, Mel sees something on his face that she's never seen before—blank confusion—as he stares down at the glowing embers. She takes the glass from him and douses the tiny fire burning in the overflowing ashtray and the pile of mail beside it. If she hadn't been there, would the entire house have gone up in flames? Or had he heard her pull up over the noise of the TV and enacted this entire scene for her? She has to admit that seems unlikely.

"Jesus, Dad! You could have burned the house down. You can't smoke in here with all this mess." Even with the more prominent smell of burnt paper in the forefront, the radioactive odor formerly emanating from the garage provides a faint chemical background. With her nose leading the way like a cadaver dog, Mel tries to sniff out the source, venturing as far as she can into the perimeter of the crammed room.

"What are you doing?" her father asks.

"Trying to figure out where that smell is coming from." She tracks it to a heating vent near the door to the basement. The one thing her father won't block on his floors is his heat registers. As soon as the outside temperature drops to forty, he has the thermostat cranked to seventy-five degrees.

"Nope. Smells fine in here."

Mel gives him a skeptical look and abandons trying to find the source. A mouse could have died in some dank corner of his basement, under a stack of accumulated belongings, and he wouldn't know. Or it could be food he's forgotten in a bag somewhere that's rotting. She finds the remote and lowers the volume on the TV so she doesn't have to yell at her father to be heard over it.

"You need to clean up in here already. It's a damn fire hazard."

Her father tucks his T-shirt into his old Wrangler jeans and tightens his belt. He looks like he's gotten skinnier. How many times has she heard him say "I'm hungry," only to add "Never mind" when she points out recipes he can make from ingredients he has on hand. Her father would rather go hungry than cook his own food.

"Fine," he says sourly. "I'll grab some garbage bags."

She shakes her head at his retreating back. "You make it sound like I'm asking you to prostitute yourself on a corner downtown."

A short while later, the area to the left of her father's old brown recliner looks emptier, with the boxes on top of boxes, stacks of old manuals and magazines, and plastic supermarket bags of unidentifiable items mostly cleared away. The burnt surface of the side table is covered by a glass dish holding peppermint candies that are probably stale.

He plops himself onto the couch and surveys his domain. A fly emerges from inside the lampshade to circle his head and he bats at it.

"Damn fly must be practicing for the Daytona 500. It's been doing laps around my head all day."

"Maybe if you kept it cleaner in here, you wouldn't have flies."

Her father makes a face at her and then spits into his hands. He runs them through his wild white hair, but it remains as untamable as ocean waves during a storm.

"That's what gel's for, Dad."

"Don't have any."

"What you need is a haircut. Your eyebrows look like something I might have knit back when I was trying to learn how." She should write that down. No, don't bother. It sucks.

"I'm not paying for a haircut when I can save money by having you do it. Find a scissor and cut it for me."

Mel briefly considers the length of time it would take to find scissors in her father's house, let alone ones sharp enough to cut hair. "I'm not cutting your hair anymore. You look like Phyllis Diller when I do."

"What does it matter what I look like, at my age? No one's looking at me."

Melody squints at him. "And if they did, could you invite them over for a meal?"

Her father scans the living room. "Why not?"

"Because it stinks in here. I don't how you can stand it. And when did you start smoking again?"

He shrugs. "We could pick up some of those nicotine patches at CVS."

"Good idea." Mel sees an opportunity to mention a home care attendant. "You're in your seventies now. You need to take better care of yourself. Wouldn't it be a good idea to hire someone who can help with cleaning and cooking?"

"What do I need that for when I've got you?"

Mel smothers the growl that almost emerges from deep inside her. "But what if I find a job far away from here after I graduate?" She hasn't told him yet that she is staying local thanks to Drake. Her daydream of teaching creative writing students in an Ivy League classroom has evolved into accepting the reality of teaching whatever leftover (most likely composition) classes VU tosses her way. Winning the fellowship would be so much better than that.

He waves off her comment as though it's not worth contemplating, sending a pang of dismay through her. "I can take care of myself."

"How are you taking care of yourself when your house looks like this and you don't eat on a regular schedule? Did you eat anything today?"

He scrunches up his face. "Don't think so."

"How do you forget to eat?"

"Someone I know doesn't seem to have that problem."

"Nice, Dad."

"I was talking about Swift, not you. Today he woke me up at dawn, meowing to be fed. I couldn't find him anywhere."

Mel is taken aback. "Swift doesn't live with you anymore. I brought him over to Drake's after we took him to the vet."

"Right. I forgot. Must have been a dream."

Mel rubs her eyes. "All right, let's go run some errands and talk about it on the drive."

She hustles her father out of the house to prevent him from having his teddy bear join them. On Front Street, she turns in to the Subway parking lot.

"How does a sandwich sound?"

"It'll have to do since we're here."

"I thought you liked Subway."

"Eh," he says, shrugging. "It's like a salad on bread."

"Ask for extra meat."

"You can do that?"

"Yeah. You didn't know?"

He shrugs. "There's a lot I don't know, kiddo. Like why you're wasting what little money you have not living at home with your father who loves you."

Mel sighs. This is not going as planned. How can she force her father to contemplate a home care attendant when he refuses to let go of the idea of her moving back in?

Inside Subway, a young man wearing a golf visor that causes his hair to pouf up on top greets them cheerfully. "Hello, folks! How're you today? Great day, isn't it?"

Mel's father looks outside at the overcast sky. "Looks bad to me," he tells the young man, whose concrete smile remains set in place.

"True enough. So how can I help you folks today?"

They give him their sandwich orders as the man's co-worker, a teenage girl with multiple ear piercings and heavily lined eyes, determinedly ignores them. Compelled by a powerful force, her gaze repeatedly travels to the large clock stationed on the wall above the cash register.

"You folks have a wonderful day!" the young man says as he hands them their sandwiches on a tray.

"Sandwich artist," Mel whispers to her father as they sit down at a table. "That's what Subway's calling their workers in commercials now. Kind of like 'seafood experts' at Red Lobster. Is that supposed to make the job more appealing?" Her father shrugs and takes an enormous bite from his sandwich. A glob of mayonnaise clings to the corner of his lip, but he ignores it. Mel points at it and he turns to look behind him. "No, your lip." She takes a napkin and wipes his mouth the way she would a child's.

"Thanks," he says, through a mouthful of partially chewed food.

"But I suppose it's not that different from adjuncts being called 'lecturers.'"

"What are you talking about?"

Mel shakes her head. "Nothing. Never mind."

After eating, they drive to CVS. In the makeup section, Mel is surrounded by pictures of pretty young women staring at her vacantly or with sexual hunger—she hadn't realized how desirable she is. Mel gives one image an exaggerated wink. An elderly woman in the aisle notices and raises her drawn-on eyebrows. Mel turns the wink into a hard blink as though something is caught in her eye, which she rubs to solidify her performance, before escaping the woman's scrutiny to find her father at the prescription counter in the back. On her way through the vitamin and supplement section, she's accosted by images of older women and a few men, because the only people who exist in the world, according to CVS, are either young women desperate to look beautiful or old people hoping to escape death through homeopathic healing.

Her father pays the copay for his blood pressure, cholesterol, and prostate prescriptions with a ragged twenty-dollar bill he pulls out of a pink plastic Hello Kitty wallet.

"Where'd you get that?" Mel asks.

He looks down at the wallet as though seeing it for the first time. "This? Yard sale, I think."

The cashier, an older woman, smiles at them. "Your father's in touch with his feminine side," she says, throwing back her head to laugh while slapping her palm down on the counter.

"Maybe," he says. "More like my cheap side since I bought it for ten cents." He takes his receipt and prescriptions in a bag and heads toward the exit with Mel in tow.

"You remember how much you paid for that but not if you've eaten?" Mel asks him.

He waves her off and continues walking.

"What about the nicotine patch stuff? You should buy some while we're here."

"I'll quit on my own. It's all about willpower," her father says, flexing a bicep.

Mel puts up her hands. "Do you need any groceries?" she asks as they get back into her car.

"Probably."

In the Giant supermarket on Front Street, Mel pushes a cart through the aisles, watching her father fill it with processed food.

"Juice boxes, Dad? What are you, five years old?"

"I like them. Do I tell you what to eat?"

When her father finishes drifting through his favorite aisles in the center of the store, they head for a register. Their cashier is a tall young woman with thick tortoiseshell glasses and lemur-like eyes.

She rings them up. "That'll be $87.38," she tells Mel's father, who holds his checkbook open on the small raised counter across from the register. Why he insists on using checks instead of a debit card is beyond Mel.

He stares blankly at the paper, holding his pen poised above it like a dowser. Concern blossoms as Mel realizes he doesn't know how to fill out the check.

"Are you okay?" she asks him quietly, but he stares at her silently.

The cashier looks sympathetic but says nothing.

Her father blinks and shoves his checkbook over to Mel. "You do this. You know my handwriting's a mess." He smiles at the cashier. "You'll never be able to read it."

"Okay, Dad." Mel fills out the rest of the check while willing her eyes to not well up. She hands the pen back to her father. "Sign here." Mel points, and her father adds his signature with a flourish.

They're crossing the parking lot when she hears her name being called. It's her former boss at Kiddie Kare, Trisha Monroe, paused with her grocery cart near the entrance to the supermarket. Mel heads back to talk to Trisha, who has possibly the cutest baby Mel has ever seen snuggled in a chest carrier. This is saying a lot because she doesn't like infants. During her years of working at Kiddie Kare, she made sure to spend as much time in her office as possible.

"Well, as I live and breathe! Melody! How are you?" Trisha says.

"Hi, Trisha. How are you?" Her former boss zooms in to give her hug, squishing the baby against Mel, who steps back out of fear of hurting it.

"This is my niece Rhiannon. She's Terrie's," Trisha says. She pivots so Mel can better see the baby's face. "Do you want to hold her?"

"Boy, would I ever, but you know . . ." Mel lifts the bags of groceries to show how full her hands are. "Cute kid."

"She's the best! She never cries and can occupy herself for hours. The Lord has certainly smiled down upon my sister, despite all her sins. Of which there are many, as you may recall." She whispers this last part in case anyone else in the parking lot can hear her. "My own children were such a chore when they were this age. Took years and years to get them potty trained." Trisha smiles brightly. "But the Lord never gives us tribulations we can't handle."

"Yes, that is so," Mel says woodenly. She falls back into her old habit of agreeing with all of Trisha's insights into the Lord's behavior. If only she understood her father as well as Trisha understood her god.

"And how are you, Mr. Hollings? As handsome as ever, I see."

"Old."

The baby looks at Mel's father with curiosity. She reaches out a small hand in his direction, which he gently high-fives.

"Well, we should bring this home before the ice cream melts," Mel says.

"You bought ice cream?" her father asks. "What kind?"

"Chocolate," Mel lies, grateful for her father's diminishing short-term memory. "It was nice seeing you, Trisha."

"You too, Mel. Why don't you come to Sunday service sometime? Or since that's not your cup of tea, I take a Zumba class there on Thursday nights at seven. We can shake our booties together!" Trisha shimmies her wide hips. Mel tries to picture herself clumsily dancing alongside Trisha to salsa music. She'd only be able to do it if she pretended to be Bugs Bunny dressed in Carmen Miranda drag. Still, it would be smart to maintain a connection to Trisha, even if it means making a fool of herself in a Zumba class. One day she might have to ask for her old job back.

"I'll do that," Mel says.

On the drive home her father says, "Never liked that woman. All that religious, holier-than-thou horseshit. Reminds me of your grandparents. Then paying her employees the least amount possible. Didn't she try to stiff you out of all your vacation time when you quit?"

Mel nods. "She gave me two raises during the eight years I worked for her. For fifty cents each time."

"But soon you'll be a doctor and can work wherever you want," her father says proudly.

Mel laughs bitterly. "That's not the way it works, Dad. I haven't had one university set up an interview for the MLA convention in January."

"VU will hire you."

Once again, Mel considers telling her father about Drake's job at VU and what it means for her. But she decides against it to avoid hearing a lecture about her relying on a man too much. Better to deal with his reaction down the road. All she says is "Not likely on a tenure track," which is true.

"You can move back in with your dad. And teach at CCC. I can make a phone call."

Mel imagines this as her future and quashes a whimper. "Let's hope it doesn't come to that, Dad."

12

Mel returns to her and Drake's apartment and takes a seat at the dining room table, her laptop open in front of her. She will get some grading done, starting with providing feedback on Joshie Grubber's Nobel Prize–worthy argument paper that proposes requiring all public assistance recipients take financial literacy courses to lift them out of poverty. Despite her best efforts to steer him toward a more informed argument, he has forged his own path using sources like *The Nation* and Fox News, having slept through the class when they discussed the differences between peer-reviewed scholarly sources and popular ones. Her attempts to focus are interrupted by the recurring image of her father sitting at the kitchen table after they returned from running errands. He'd stared down at a notepad with a pen in his hand without making a move to write a single thing. As if struck by a profound writer's block, he'd looked baffled by the task of making a list of things to do to clean up the house on his own.

The back door opens and Drake strolls in. "Hey, you want to get some pizza for dinner?"

At the sight of him, all her sadness rushes to the surface. "My dad's really losing it. It's not an act."

"Oh, Mel!" Drake sits down and takes her hand. "I'm so sorry. What are you gonna do?"

Melody shakes her head and wipes her eyes. "I don't know. Take him to his doctor first, I guess. Find out what's wrong." The words "Alzheimer's," "senility," and "dementia" parade through her mind. "And hope there's something that can help him."

Several days later, Mel and her father cross a parking lot to Dr. Loomba's office near Wilson Memorial Hospital. The building it's housed in is as gray and industrial-looking as Mel remembers from her childhood, when her father would take her to Loomba, who is a general practitioner, instead of a pediatrician. Inside, the ashy walls blend in with the slate industrial carpet. Art prints of pastel landscapes and vases of flowers hang in cheap brass frames on the walls. Minnie, the ancient receptionist, sits behind a pair of sliding glass windows.

"How are you, Minnie?" Mel asks, ignoring the sign-in sheet because there's no one else in the office. It's a Monday, in between Mel's morning and afternoon comp classes at VU. She'd been able to persuade her father to come only by telling him it was what her mother would have wanted. Minnie motions toward the clipboard from behind the glass. Only after Mel signs her father in does Minnie slide one pane open.

"What?"

"How are you?"

"Getting old," Minnie says, a grudge against time furrowing her brow.

"Tell me about it," Mel says, pursing her lips, which earns a cocked eyebrow from Minnie. "How are your grandchildren?"

"Same as ever, I guess. I don't see them much."

"That's too bad."

"Is it?"

Mel considers what direction to steer the conversation in to avoid its leading to a dead end. "It's been a while since I've been here." She can catch Minnie up on the last few years of her life and how she's pursuing her dream, or at least trying to. She imagines telling Minnie, who she remembers used to give her gum (some awful mint kind, but still, it was appreciated), how she's a PhD candidate and a writer. But what business does she have calling herself that when she's barely written anything over the past few months and when her work consists of teaching nothing but composition classes?

"We have a lot of patients coming and going," Minnie says. "Hard to remember everyone."

Mel scans the empty waiting room, the almond pleather–covered metal chairs, the ancient magazines on worn side tables. "I'm sure that's true." Disappointed, she sits down next to her father.

A short while later Minnie calls, "You can go in now," and they walk through the only other door, which opens onto a narrow hallway. Mel turns in to the first empty patient room, which is small with an examining table set on the diagonal in the center. The antiseptic smell of industrial cleaner sterilizes the air.

Her father moves toward the only chair.

"Dad, sit on the table," Mel tells him. "Do you need help?"

He waves her off. "I'm not as ancient as that crone out there."

"Are you sure about that?" she mutters. Since when did her father develop an antipathy toward older women? She recalls the woman at the vet's office who was an "old bat," and now Minnie. Is this yet another sign of his mental deterioration? Mel plasters on a welcoming smile when Dr. Loomba enters.

"How are you today, Mr. Hollings?" Dr. Loomba says. He sits on a tall padded swivel stool, holding her father's folder open. "And Melody, you're a big woman now." Mel sucks in her stomach and sits up straighter in her seat, a blush suffusing her cheeks. Does he mean grown up or large?

"I'm fine," her father says. "My kid thinks there's something wrong with me."

"You're forgetful a lot." Mel doesn't mention the fire. She should find a moment with Dr. Loomba when she can tell him privately.

"That's normal at my age."

"Are you still taking your medications for your heart, blood pressure, and prostate?" Dr. Loomba asks, looking up from the folder.

Mel nods. "I think he is, mostly." Her father shrugs. "Could it be side effects from combining those or not taking them consistently?"

Dr. Loomba tilts his head and shrugs tentatively. "Not likely. How is your diet?"

"Fine," her father says, as Mel replies, "Awful."

They look at each other for a long moment before Mel continues. "I try to make my dad eat healthier, but he'd rather eat fast food than cook his own meals."

"How about alcohol? Do you drink?"

"A beer here and there."

"Are you angry more often? Do you have outbursts of temper?" Dr. Loomba asks.

"Definitely," Mel says, answering for her father. His scowl confirms her response. Mel gives the doctor a "See what I mean?" look. "He's changed in the last year. Since I moved out."

"That could be normal. Often when an elderly person's routine is upset, that can exacerbate any cognitive issues they may be experiencing."

Way to make me feel guilty, Dr. Loomba, Mel thinks.

Her father looks insulted. "I'm not crazy. I just need some help around the house."

"I offered to find you that, remember? And you refused." Mel notices that near the top of the colorful diagram of the male reproductive system pinned to the wall across from her seat someone has crossed out "penis" and replaced it with "peepee."

"I don't want a stranger in my house."

"Whoever we found wouldn't be a stranger for long."

Dr. Loomba watches them with a half-smile on his face. "Here's what we will do." He lifts his stethoscope up to his ears. "I'll check your vital signs, and then we'll need blood and a urine sample. This will rule out some issues."

"Then what?"

"I will refer you to Dr. Oberlin, who is a neurologist."

Her father gives Mel a look like this is a betrayal he will never recover from. "Now see what you've done? You won't be happy till I end up in a loony bin."

"Stop exaggerating. Besides, you already live in one of those."

"Mr. Hollings, the neurologist will only run some helpful tests. She will not commit you to a mental institution."

Back in the lobby, Mel tells her father to wait for her. She heads back to Dr. Loomba's office, where she finds him sitting behind his large desk. He squints at his computer monitor, leans forward until he's only inches away from the screen, and pecks out letters on his keyboard with either index finger, pausing to look down to ensure he's hitting the right ones.

"Hi, Dr. Loomba," Mel says, waving awkwardly. "Do you mind if I ask you a few quick questions?"

Dr. Loomba shoves the keyboard away. "Of course. Have a seat." He gestures at the chair in front of his desk.

Mel sinks into it. She takes a deep breath. "Should my father be living alone right now? I moved out a while ago and can't help but think I need to go back."

Dr. Loomba exhales thoughtfully. "Well, that's hard to tell right now, though certainly routines and having someone around to help him would be valuable, especially if you can establish them now, before any cognitive decline becomes more significant."

"That's what I thought." Mel's shoulders slump.

"We don't know that for sure, however. Dr. Oberlin will be able to tell you more. But it would certainly benefit you as well as your father if you could bring someone into his house to help him. The sooner you do, the faster he'll become accustomed to it."

In the days following her father's doctor appointment, Melody sets up interviews with several candidates for home care attendant. Now, Diana Lane sits in a dining chair across from her in her father's living room. Diana is her third attempt. The first two women had walked into the living room and walked right back out. Diana had looked around, shrugged, and sat down. Mel can't tell if she's reassured by this or nervous that it reveals a similar propensity for hoarding.

Diana is in her early fifties, with dark blond hair worn in two long braids that fall on either side of her neck, making her look like a Viking hausfrau. Her outfit consists of a white cardigan over periwinkle scrubs. Beside Diana is a stack of boxes with a basket precariously resting on top. When her chair nudges the boxes, the basket falls, and Diana's lightning-fast response in catching it belies her size. Her movement reveals a large Tinker Bell tattoo on her inner left forearm.

"Just so's you know, I don't do any heavy lifting," Diana says, putting the basket, which holds sewing supplies Melody can't imagine her father using, on the floor beside her chair. She crosses her tiny feet in front of her.

"That's fine." A sound coming from the guest room draws Melody's and Diana's gaze. "Cat," Mel says, to avoid explaining that her father refused to participate in the interviewing process and was instead hiding in the spare bedroom.

Diana nods. "I hurt my back a few weeks ago something terrible."

"That's too bad."

"I've had back problems for years. It's these," she says, gesturing to her breasts. "Imagine carrying them around all day, every day."

"I can't," Melody says, trying not to look at Diana's chest.

"You're lucky being on the small side."

Mel nods.

"I was taking care of my grandkids. Lord knows I love 'em, but they're bad kids." Diana shakes her head sadly. "I'm the only one they listen to 'cause I'm not afraid to show them what's what." She taps her leg with a hand that must be a persuasive deterrent, especially when combined with Diana's rattlesnake reflexes. "'Course they leave their toys everywhere, even in my kitchen. So what happens? I slip on one and fall right on my ass." Her disgust is tinged by glee—if her grandchildren are bad, then at least they're good at being bad. "Let me tell you, there was hell to pay once I got back up."

"There shouldn't be any heavy lifting working with my dad, though granted, he's a slob nowadays." Melody looks around the living room. More noise emerges from the guest room, along with the sound of bedsprings creaking.

Diana makes a face. "You got a mountain lion back there?" She chuckles at her joke.

"Something like that. I'm planning on getting some cleaning done during Thanksgiving, so it won't be as bad in here. But I have to warn you, Dad can be . . . a little abrupt. Tactless. Downright rude sometimes." Melody looks down the hall again, tensed up and waiting for a reaction, hoping her father hasn't heard her. She leans in to whisper to Diana: "He might be suffering from dementia. I won't know for certain until I take him for his next doctor's appointment."

Diana waves her off. "Don't you worry none. I've worked with lots of elderly people and I'm sure I've heard worse. My ex-husband George had a gutter mouth. Got sick of listening to him hollering at me while I paid all the bills. That's why we divorced. That and the fact he was screwing my neighbor." She shakes her head in wonderment. "Can't understand why anyone would want a skinny old sausage like George."

"No accounting for taste," Mel says. "About my dad. I'm hoping to have someone visit two times a week to start. To do some cleaning, keep him company, and take him out to run errands." She leans in again to whisper, "I'm not sure if he should be driving anymore." Mel thinks about the latest dent in her father's car, the one now caving in the left-side rear bumper. He told her someone must have hit it when he was buying birdseed at Agway, but without looking her in the eye.

Diana hunches forward conspiratorially, and the chair's rear legs leave the floor, nearly dumping her forward. With an abrupt movement backward to regain her balance, she puts the chair legs back on the ground. "Whoa. That was close. Don't worry. I'm a good driver." Her hand reaches around behind her when she sits up straight. "Damn," she says, with a pained expression. "I think I hurt my back again."

That night Mel meets Drake at Whole in the Wall, where she finds him already eating a dish of their penne with pesto. "Sorry, I couldn't wait. I was starving," he says.

"No worries. I'm late." When the server stops at their table, Mel orders a bowl of mushroom soup. After Diana Lane left, Mel asked her father if he wanted to join her and Drake for dinner at the natural food restaurant. He'd responded with a moue of disgust, like she'd handed him a mug of curdled milk to drink.

"How'd it go?" Drake asks, with one hand across his full mouth.

"She was great. The perfect match for someone like my dad. But he stayed in the guest room during the entire interview. And when she left, he vetoed the whole idea. 'I'm not having that woman in my house,'" she said, imitating her father's gruff voice and gangling posture. "He's perfectly fine having me spend hours doing everything for him."

"That's not fair. You're his daughter, not his housekeeper."

"Tell me about it." Mel steals a piece of pasta off his plate. "But how do I force her on him?" She pictures Diana Lane on the front porch ringing the doorbell, then peeking through the windows, as her father hides inside, before she gives up and leaves.

"I don't know, but I don't see your dad wanting to live in an assisted living place. Why not use what the neurologist says to convince him to hire this woman? It's a better option than having to move out. Maybe tell him that's his only choice, even if it's not true."

Mel tries to imagine her father's reaction to her telling him something like that. The scene he would make about her betraying him. When exactly had their roles shifted so that she is now the parent? It must have been a slow transition starting from way back. As a tween, she'd taken over all the laundry and cooking, and most of the cleaning, because if she wanted a semblance of order like she saw at her friends' houses, she had to create it herself. She stares out of the window at the traffic on Washington Street, worrying about how this will affect her future. Mel leans back, her face wrinkling in distress. "I need to figure this out. As if I don't have enough to worry about."

Drake takes another bite of his pasta. He reaches across the table to grab her hand. "With me taking the VU job, you can stick around for your dad. Plus, it's a good opportunity for me to get some admin experience."

When Mel first pursued graduate school, this was not what she envisaged for her future. She dreamt of all the books and stories she'd publish that would propel her onto a path to full professorship in a new city she could explore. Instead, she'll be fortunate to have an adjunct instructor position at her alma mater in her hometown, thanks to Drake. The job he's taking involves forging connections between governmental agencies and university paleontology programs, and requires only administrative work rather than fieldwork and teaching, something Drake seems lukewarm about. So how will he feel about her being the reason he's not doing what he's trained for? And how much writing will she be able to do if she's teaching four classes of first-year writing each semester?

She forces a smile. "I really appreciate you saying that."

13

Excited conversation punctuated by laughter from Ben's students can be easily heard in the small classroom next door where Mel sits surrounded by several of her peers in her weekly meeting with her composition unit. These meetings are designed to guide new graduate instructors on teaching first-year writing. It's Mel's sixth year teaching first-year writing, and her resentment over having to attend these required meetings grows incrementally each semester. The windowless room is also where she teaches her afternoon composition class.

Having sat in on one of Ben's classes when he invited her to read a story to demonstrate how to create strong dialogue, Mel knows he holds court at the head of the conference table in his room. His female students stare enthralled as he reads aloud in his deep voice, watching him as he occasionally brushes back a lock of blond hair that falls across his forehead. The young men in his class study him closely, hoping to pick up mannerisms they will graft onto their own burgeoning masculinities. Ben's favorite gesture when he reads his own work consists of a shake of the head along with a self-deprecating coy look that reminds Mel of an Oscar winner at an after-party.

Unlike other PhD candidates at VU, Ben avoided teaching composition to larger classes of captive first-year students. He'd walked into Professor Pollon's office before the start of his first semester, miraculously finding the chair of the English department seated behind his desk, and demanded that he be given two creative writing courses to teach, or he wouldn't teach at all. An emergency shuffling by the department's normally arthritic management resulted in Ben getting his way.

It's near the end of the hour-long C-Unit meeting, and they've team graded several student op-eds on topics ranging from steroid use in baseball, to video game violence, to one paper that, surprisingly, covers how Steve Irwin's death will impact interest in wildlife conservation.

"Hey, Mel!" Annie Sago shouts from her side of the table as though she's across campus. "Loved your blog post on NASCAR! It cracked me up!"

"That's so nice of you to say."

"I hate babies too!" she yells.

They all stare blankly at Annie, and then Jimmy Baethan, their C-Unit leader, quickly redirects their attention. "Any issues with your classes or students?" he asks the new instructors. Jimmy carefully enunciates every word, as if he's conversing with children who don't speak English. He has his laptop open in front of him, recording every response and comment from the group as part of the C-Unit's efforts to demonstrate the importance of these meetings.

Please, god, no one answer, Mel thinks, stealing a glance at the clock on the wall. She'd like to catch the recently elusive Ben and ask him for her manuscript. Several weeks have passed since he promised he'd read it, and she needs to finish revising it in time to apply for the post-doc fellowship. She winces at the sounds of enjoyment coming from Ben's room next door and wonders if this is what it feels like to be a freshly divorced woman trying to sleep in a hotel room next to horny newlyweds. What she wants to do is leave the meeting and loiter in the hallway outside Ben's class until it ends. She would also like to leap up on the table in front of her, kick everyone's laptop to the floor, stomp on their papers, and do a backflip dismount at the other end before running screaming from the room.

"Boy, they sound like they're having a good time over there!" Annie bellows, gesturing in the direction of Ben's classroom.

Mel smiles grimly, Lou Grant trying to dampen Mary's enthusiasm. The sound of drainage being cleared from the back of a throat catches her attention. She whips around to stare at the source, Joseph Sivolani, who rarely speaks during these meetings. He shrugs apologetically before looking back down at his laptop.

"I have a bit of a problem," Laurie Mills says. A large diamond engagement ring graces her ring finger. She stares at Mel with a passive-aggressive smile left over from their first C-Unit meeting, when Mel mentioned that these sessions are more beneficial for less experienced instructors. "I have this student who doesn't turn anything in and says nothing during class. I doubt if he does any of the readings." Laurie pantomimes throwing a lasso. "And I'm wondering how I can wrangle him into participating?"

Act like you're a monkey in a cowboy outfit riding a dog, Mel answers in her head.

Jimmy scans the group, his gaze lingering longest on Mel, who he relies on to answer most questions. "S-o-o-o-o-o, what do we think is the best way to deal with this situation?"

Laurie says, "I'm sure it isn't something more *experienced* instructors have to worry about, but for instructors like me who have *less experience*, it's helpful to hear how to handle things like this."

"Have you talked to him to find out what's up?" Mel asks, giving in to the role that's expected of her.

"He's a nice enough kid outside of class. He says hi whenever I see him. But of course, what do I know about 'difficult students' given how *little experience* I have."

Wrestling alligators, Mel tacks on mentally.

"Definitely fail him," Annie yells. "I have one of those too, but mine cops an attitude." She leans forward, her low-cut shirt exposing her cleavage. Her expression is confident. "He's always giving me these disgusted looks in class."

Ever the Swiss ambassador, Jimmy holds up a hand that counsels patience. His expression is one of gentle amusement. "I think that may be premature," he says.

Are you sure he's not checking out your boobs, Mel wonders, then feels ashamed. Sure, a young man fresh out of high school might be fascinated by Annie's twenty-something-year-old breasts, but it would be wrong for her to mention to Annie that if she wants to be taken seriously, her cups shouldn't runneth over. Male college students should be perfectly capable of ignoring Annie's body to gain from her greater knowledge of writing and argumentation, just as Annie can ignore theirs to teach them. Mel mentally pats herself on the back for this higher way of thinking.

"I'd talk to him before doing anything drastic," Mel says quietly, purposely lowering her voice in the hope this will force Annie to speak more quietly. "You never know what's going on in his life. It can be tough making the adjustment to college and living away from home for the first time. Some of these students don't know the first thing about managing their time and workload." As she speaks, Mel realizes her hands, which normally play a cameo role in emphasizing certain points, have been elevated without her approval to star. Spontaneously and without volition, her fingers twist and dance like Busby Berkeley chorus girls. Until she sits on them.

"Yeah, you could do that," Annie roars. "Give him a chance, I suppose."

"Well, if that's what *you* think I should do," Laurie says, looking only at Mel. "I'm so sorry for being so *inexperienced*."

At training gorillas to use computers, Mel finishes for her.

"Then," Mel murmurs softly, ignoring Laurie's tone and forcing her, Jimmy, and the ever silent Joseph, to lean in to hear her, "if nothing changes, you'll have to give a grade appropriate to his effort." By the end of this sentence, Mel's voice is a dying woman's whisper.

"WHICH WILL PROBABLY BE AN F ANYWAY!" Annie screams gleefully.

At that moment, Mel realizes the classroom next door is silent. Ben has dismissed his students early. He knows her C-Unit group meets next door; they've met for coffee afterward throughout the entire semester right before her afternoon class. She can't help but start to think he's avoiding her.

14

The Monday before Thanksgiving break, Melody sits at the dining table with her laptop. It's a little past 7:00 a.m. Drake is asleep, and the apartment is quiet and peaceful. She takes a sip of coffee. Several project folders are neatly organized on her computer's desktop. One is for her novel, another contains short story starts, a third is her master's thesis. There are several others, but none sparks the slightest interest. Her urge to write is in suspended animation. Instead, she plays Luxor on her cellphone, which has a player fire balls at other ones to make them disappear or cause chain reactions. She's warming up her brain, she tells herself, getting it ready to write.

After thirty minutes of gaming, she showers, dresses, gathers her teaching materials, and drives to VU through a light snow. The sky is the color of a storm-disturbed ocean. But VU's undergraduates never dress for the weather. On her way to her first class, Melody walks past young men in pajamas and socks with slippers and young women wearing what amounts to black pantyhose as pants.

A while before her second class, Melody shows up for Ben's office hours, which he holds twice a week before the two classes he teaches. She knocks on the closed door, but there's no response. She tries the handle, but the door is locked. On Friday she'd texted to ask how things were going with her manuscript. He'd taken two days to respond. "Terrific! I'm a big fan!" But rather than buoying her, as his compliments normally would, they'd made her skeptical. If he thought the book was so great, wouldn't he have finished reading it already? Melody presses her ear to Ben's door. After several moments of silence, she determines he's not hiding and has canceled his office hours.

She looks at all the surrounding closed doors of the English professors and wonders if any keep office hours anymore. Every time she walks down this hallway, regardless of what time it is, no one is here to interact with students. Gone are the days when she would stop by to hang out with Abe and talk about books, writing, and publishing. Abe was one of the few remaining professors who used his office to write in. He would post a sign, letting passing students know that he was working and was not to be disturbed, that he would come up for air at a certain time that day and would welcome any distractions. Now, it seems as if faculty members must all work at home, robbing the department of its vitality.

Mel heads to the nearby coffee kiosk and finds a seat. After using Ben's office hour to grade her students' op-eds, she returns to Ben's office door and takes out her Post-it note pad and a pen. "What's up, Ben?" she writes. Then she draws a smiley face next to it to soften the tone before adding her initials and affixing it to his door.

Mel takes the stairs back to Ben's classroom on the second floor, where she finds him already ensconced. She curses the multiple back stairs and routes that made it possible for him to evade her. Students enter, and she stands in the doorway until, finally, she has Ben's attention. Melody waves at him and motions for him to join her. Slowly he rises from his desk and meets her in the hall outside.

"How's it going, Mel?" he asks, smiling and relaxed.

Melody clears her throat. "How's my book coming?"

He nods enthusiastically. "It's going great! I'm making lots of progress. I have all kinds of ideas for what you can do with the characters and the plot."

Melody exhales. "Oh my god, you don't know how great that is to hear! I figured you hadn't started."

He waves her off. "What? You know I wouldn't do that. I've just been crazy busy. My book was bought by a publisher and the editor wanted another round of revisions. Now, the copy editor has it. Plus, teaching and everything else," he says, vaguely waving his hands around the invisible tasks consuming his time.

"Holy crap. That's amazing!" She lightly punches his arm. "Are you freaking out?"

"A little."

"We should celebrate. And now I really appreciate you finding time for my book. It means the world to me that you're reading it."

"I'll finish it during Thanksgiving break. Does that work?"

Melody calculates. This would give her approximately two weeks until the post-doc fellowship deadline in mid-December to revise the entire thing. It's possible to accomplish if all she does is work on it and grade the final portfolios for her two composition classes. Her regular visits to her father's house will have to pause, but this should be okay. "That would be great."

Mel heads to her own office in the College-in-the-Trees building but makes a detour to the dining hall adjacent to it, since she has no actual appointments with any of her students. She takes a seat in a booth on the second floor overlooking the cafeteria. With the holiday approaching, everything is quiet. Mel types up an email to Trisha at Kiddie Kare, feeling her former boss out to see if she might need her to come back at the end of the spring semester to take up being office manager again. It would be good to have another option for employment after graduating.

As she hits send on the email, Sherry Turner walks by, carrying a tray with a plastic container of cafeteria sushi on it. She pauses in front of the booth, staring down at Mel, who gives her a welcoming, if hesitant, smile.

"Do you mind if I sit with you?" Sherry asks, looking away.

"Sure. No problem." This is the third time this semester Sherry has sought her out. The first time she told Mel she was thinking about being a creative writing major. "My friend is taking Professor Howe's class this semester and I got to sit in on a few," she'd said. "He's amazing!" The second time, Mel was in the middle of a meeting with another student and Sherry had stood outside her office door, watching Mel with a smile on her face she couldn't characterize: stressed, confused, exhilarated? Mel had paused with her other student to give Sherry a concerned look. "Can I help you with something, Sherry?" she asked.

"I'm sorry," Sherry had said. "I don't want to interrupt, but I've been doing some creative writing. And I was wondering . . ." She stopped and stared at Mel for several awkward moments, then ducked her head, a shy teenager on her first date. "I was hoping you could give me some feedback."

"I'd love to read your writing, but my schedule's kinda hectic this semester."

"There's only one thing I want help with." Despite her timidity she sounded determined. "It's another personal essay."

"You have my email. Send it and I'll check it out. It might take a few weeks, but I'll give you some feedback on it."

Sherry had thanked her but then never sent Mel any of her writing, for which Mel was grateful.

Now, Sherry sits down across from Mel and opens her sushi, carefully covering it with pieces of pickled ginger and large chunks of Play-Doh-like wasabi. She picks up a piece with her fingers and dips it into a small container of soy sauce. While she's no sushi connoisseur, Mel could swear that's not the correct way to eat it.

"How are your classes going this semester?" Mel asks.

"I've got all these papers and exams and my time management skills aren't the best. Plus, I'm having a hard time finding research."

"Do you remember the library research tutorial I did in our class? There's also the reference librarian who can help. And the tutors in the Writing Center."

Sherry's expression makes Mel feels as though she's being stared at by a two-hundred-year-old tortoise. Mel offers her an encouraging smile.

"Right. The reference librarian. I forgot about her." Sherry eats another piece of sushi and chews on it slowly, perhaps counting each mastication to ensure she reaches a specific number. "So have you been hanging out with Professor Howe a lot this semester?"

"Not really. We've both been busy. He's been occupied with his writing a lot lately." And god knows what else, Mel thinks, picturing Elaina. Certainly not Mel's dissertation.

"That's awesome," Sherry says. "He's so talented."

"Yeah," Mel says. "Are you taking his creative writing class next semester?"

After a portentous minute, during which Sherry looks like she's considering saying something important, she closes her plastic container and rises. "I need to get to class," she says in an aggrieved tone that suggests Mel is keeping her there against her wishes.

15

Mel and her father stand in the doorway of a model room in the Oak Field assisted living and nursing home. The faint undertone of urine beneath the smell of commercial cleaning products depresses Mel. The halls are decorated with handmade Thanksgiving cutouts of turkeys, cornucopias, and pilgrims, making it resemble an elementary school rather than a home for the aged. Why are funeral homes decorated in a more appealing way than elder care facilities? After yet another argument between Mel and her father about hiring Diana Lane, she's showing him this option, hoping it will scare him into choosing a home care attendant.

She could be at Drake's parents' house right now instead. He'd invited her and her father to join them for Thanksgiving, but Mel declined. She could imagine her father asking for a table setting for his teddy bear and the exchange of glances between Drake's parents as they politely complied.

The guide leaves them to "get a feel for the room," and her father sits in the recliner, his oversized green Carhartt coat hunched around his neck. A twin bed holds a prominent central position in the space, while a long bureau with a mirror sits across from it. An older-model TV rests on the bureau. The walls are painted a pale salmon, with darker rose curtains. Mel feels like she's in a two-star hotel room.

"Why is it even called Oak Field when there isn't an oak in sight?" her father asks.

"There probably were when they first built it." As Vestal Parkway expanded, and the retail plaza next door was built, the trees were eradicated. "What do you think?"

He looks at her vacantly as though struggling to reconcile an image he has of her from the past with this one of her now, when she's older, larger, and trying to detach from him.

The day before, she'd taken him to the neurologist. After running tests of her father's reflexes, coordination, muscle tone, and strength, and digging into his medical history, Dr. Oberlin had spoken to Mel privately to share a preliminary diagnosis of dementia. The results of the exam and cognitive test were somewhat inconclusive, but she felt the best course of action was to treat her father as though he was beginning to exhibit signs of mild cognitive impairment associated with Alzheimer's. There were some medications she could start him on, the first of which could potentially slow the disease's progression. Down the road, there were others that could mitigate some of the symptoms. An MRI or CT could help with reaching a more definitive conclusion, but Mel was sure her father would refuse. Dr. Oberlin's receptionist had given Mel several brochures, designed to prepare families for what to expect and outline options for care as the disease advanced, and Dr. Oberlin had also advocated for Mel to arrange her father's "affairs," which caused her to picture herself as her father's pimp. Afterward, she drove him home and then went through the rest of her day as though nothing had changed. But now this room in this facility forces her to face the reality of her father's future. The incontrovertible knowledge that his behavior isn't an act designed to manipulate her fills her with grief. At a molecular level, his brain is eroding, the synapses firing inefficiently, with sections decaying at an unpredictable rate.

As he sits across from her in the model room in Oak Field, her father's gaze focuses, and he looks her up and down. "You gained weight."

Mel shakes her head sadly. "Not recently. But thanks." She doesn't have it in her to argue with him.

"Move in here and I bet you'll lose it right quick. It smells awful."

Mel considers the fact that his house smells worse. Yes, this place is depressing, but when she compares it to his house and how he chooses to live, Oak Field is an improvement. "If you lived here, I'd bring you food from the parkway or from Rolando's Diner all the time. A cheeseburger deluxe with French fries."

He waves her off. "You shouldn't waste your money. I know how poor you are."

"Don't be like that, Dad. You know I don't want you here. But I can't take care of you and your house. I have to teach and write and take care of my own place. What happens if I move away one day for a job? Do you really want me to stay in Binghamton forever?" Mel feels a twinge of remorse for using guilt to persuade her father.

He rises to look out the one window. "Can't barely see anything from here. Not that there's anything to see other than a parking lot. Is my car down there?"

"No, I drove. You shouldn't drive anymore, remember?"

"Why not? I've been driving since before you were born."

"I know, but now you can take a break from doing it. If you hired someone to help you, I wouldn't have to do it all. I'd have time to take you places. We could go antiquing on the weekends."

"I have to pick up your mother."

"No, you don't." Her father's mental state is worse in the mornings, as if the fog of sleep is denser.

He strides toward the door with purpose. Mel grabs at his arm as he passes her, but he jerks it free. "Dad, please."

"You want me to leave your mom out in the cold, waiting?"

"Dad, Mom doesn't need you to pick her up."

"Why? Did you already get her?"

Mel winces internally over the lie she has to tell. "Yes, I did. She's home now."

In the hallway outside, a woman who looks like she's in her early fifties carries a box into the room next door. Drawn by mutual curiosity, Mel and her father stroll past. It's the last room at the end of a wide corridor that ends at a large window.

"Mom, listen," the woman says loudly. In response, her mother mutters something Mel can't understand. "I live in California now, but I'll visit as much as I can," the woman says. "I'm sorry. But they'll take good care of you here, better than being home all by yourself all the time. You know it's not good to be alone so much." It's clear to Mel this woman's trying to convince herself as much as her mother. She exits the room and gives Mel a desolate look that assaults her. "It's so goddamned hard," she says and wipes beneath her eyes. Mel nods and her own eyes well up.

If her father ever ended up living here, would she be close enough to visit him? It would be terrible not to see him regularly. Not to know how he's being treated or adapting to his new lifestyle. What if they abuse him? Is that something that happens in nursing homes?

"C'mon, let's go," she says, heading toward the exit.

But they take a wrong turn and find themselves in another section of the facility. An elderly man sits sunken into himself in a wheelchair outside a room. With a lecher's wide grin on his bobbing head, he reaches out and takes Mel's hand, refusing to let it go until she uncurls his fingers with her other hand. They walk past a Jazzercise class held in a large room. Old women, some in wheelchairs, slowly cavort to Britney Spears's "Oops! . . . I Did It Again." Their bodies are stooped and bent as if gravity is stronger in this room. Two women bump their hips gently, perhaps in fear of breaking them.

Mel's father gives her a disgusted look.

After their visit to Oak Field, they head to her father's bank, where the large window to the left of the entrance has been shattered. The flattened bushes planted beneath it and the snow bank in front bear the unmistakable impressions of tire tracks.

A bank employee stationed at the entrance opens the door and greets them.

"What happened?" Mel asks, gesturing at the broken window.

The woman shakes her head, and Mel imagines that her neck is probably tired from every time she's answered this question. She leans in and whispers, "One of our customers. I guess he thought he was in reverse and not drive."

"Was anyone in the office?" Mel asks. The door to this office is shut to prevent the cold air outside from gusting into the building. Through the glass pane beside the door, Mel sees a woman measuring the window frame.

"No. Fortunately, Sandy's on vacation this week."

"Good thing," her father says.

"Worst part," the bank employee whispers, "the man had his children in the car with him. Luckily, no one was hurt."

All three shake their heads in a synchronized movement.

The interior of the bank is inexplicably decorated with a Hawaiian theme. Although the parking lot is covered by unrepentant patches of ice refusing to relinquish their hardened state, inside the building, leis surround posters advertising low interest rates on home equity loans and money market accounts. On the tall counter separating tellers from customers, several brown-skinned plastic figurines wearing bandeau tops and grass skirts frenetically shake their hips to a beat only they can hear.

Melody and her father sit in the small seating area, waiting to speak with a manager.

"I think it's a good idea if my name's added to your accounts," Mel tells him. "This way, if you ever need me to withdraw money for you, I can."

"Fine by me, kid. You're going to end up with everything one of these days." Her father watches a teller with long blue fingernails count out money for a customer. "How does she do that with those nails?"

"Who?"

He gestures toward the teller. "That Black girl."

"Woman, Dad. She's a woman. Not a girl."

He scowls at Mel. "To me, she's a girl."

"I'm pretty sure they wouldn't allow a girl to handle thousands of dollars every day, or even hire one."

"You can get off your high house, Mel."

"Horse, Dad. Not house."

"That's what I said."

"No, you didn't." His face settles into a grimace.

"What did you think of Dr. Oberlin?" Melody asks him, to change the subject.

"She's all right. I don't know why she spoke to you instead of me after she finished poking and prodding me and asking me all those dumb questions. Aren't I the patient?"

"Maybe that's how they do these things."

"What 'things'? What'd she tell you?"

"That you're getting older."

"That's obvious. How much did it cost for her to tell you that?" He snorts and goes back to gazing at the teller.

"Would you stop staring? It's rude," Mel whispers, elbowing him lightly.

"Ouch! Why'd you hit me?" he says loudly, clutching his upper arm and flinching away as if she's stabbed him with a red-hot poker, drawing the attention of the bank's patrons and staff.

Mel puts her hand on her forehead and takes a deep breath. A woman with short dark hair approaches them. Her name tag reads "Sue-Anne." "Hello there! How can I help you today?"

"I'm a crazy old man and my daughter needs to take over my money."

Sue-Anne's eyes widen, but her surprise is quickly masked. "I'm sure we can help you with that," she says with a hesitant smile.

After Mel provides numerous pieces of identification that prove she is her father's daughter and signs several forms, they leave the bank and Mel drives them to his lawyer's office, where they have an appointment to give Mel power of attorney, notarize her father's will, and add her name to the deed on his house. They sit in the waiting room for some time until the lawyer, Dan Jansenson, rolls in his chair out of a room down the hall from the reception area. Without rising from his seat, he glides toward them. The chair is wide and ergonomic, covered in brown leather that reminds Mel of a cockroach. It both swivels and tilts backward.

Still seated, Jansenson holds out his hand. "Morning, Collin. And Melody, right? How are you?"

"Could be better," Mel's father says. He looks as grim as a man picking out his own casket. The stuffed bear, which Mel didn't have the heart to tell him to leave in the car, dangles from one hand. Jansenson gives it a quick look but otherwise ignores it. Mel wonders what he's experienced with other clients to make him so blasé.

"I see," Jansenson says sadly. "Why don't you two follow me to the conference room and we can get started." He swivels his chair around with his feet and rolls back down the hall.

As they gather their coats, Mel touches her father's forearm. "He can't walk?" she asks him in a whisper.

Her father shakes his head. "He doesn't want to waste time getting in and out of his chair. Says when he's at work, he's at work."

Mel imagines doing the same thing on campus. She could wheel her office chair down the hall and out of the building, along the paths and sidewalks that crisscross the campus, though many have a steep up- or downhill grade. The fantasy ends with her rocketing down one of these hills, flying off the curb, and crashing into the side of a campus bus. They follow Jansenson into a large conference room with an oval table, on top of which are several neat stacks of paper.

"Take a seat," the lawyer says, gesturing toward the chairs. He rolls over to the door and closes it before swiveling around to face them. "Would you like something to drink? A bottle of water?"

"Sure, thanks," Mel says out of curiosity to see how he will retrieve the water.

Jansenson rolls around the far side of the table to a small fridge at the other end of the room. He returns to the head of the table and hands Mel her water.

"Thanks."

"I don't see why we have to do all this now," her father says. "Not that I mind giving Mel the house since it's going to be hers one day anyhow, but why the rush?"

Jansenson nods sympathetically. "Trust me when I tell you it's better to take care of these documents early on than wait till the last minute, when it becomes much more difficult."

He slides a stack of papers over to her father and points out the highlighted sections requiring his, then Mel's, signatures. On their second stack, Mel's pen rolls out from under her fingers, across and off the table.

"I'll get it," she volunteers, rolling her own chair around the right side of the table to where the pen landed. She leans over to retrieve it from beneath the row of chairs. When she sits up, she's hit square in the face with her father's disapproving look. Jansenson's expression remains blank.

"Sorry," Mel says, rising from her chair and pushing it back into place before sitting down.

The entire process takes less than an hour. Mel suggests they visit The Spot on the way home and get some lunch and her father grudgingly agrees. Both order breakfast instead—oval plates of omelets, hash browns, and toast. The Spot is an old-fashioned diner, with burgundy vinyl booths, faux stonework on the walls, and a large display case of beautiful but ultimately unappetizing desserts near the cash register.

"What do you want to do, Dad?"

"Go home and take a nap. I'm tired of running around."

"No. I mean what do you want me to do for you? If you could have your way when it comes to living arrangements, what would that look like?" Mel braces herself for the answer she doesn't want to hear.

"I dunno. I don't see what all the fuss is about. I'm a little forgetful. Always have been. You know that." He looks at her plaintively.

"Dad." Melody puts her hand over his. "It's more than that. Dr. Oberlin says it's probably going to get worse. I wish that wasn't true." Her voice cracks and she blinks back tears. "But it is. We have to decide what you want to do . . . with the rest of your life."

"I want things to be the same."

It's dark out when Mel arrives back at the apartment, having spent the rest of the day at her father's, cleaning and purging while contemplating her future. She sits on the living room couch with the lights off. She could call Cicely and go for coffee. She could talk to her about what's going on with her father. They have become better friends lately, and Cicely has spoken to Mel many times about her failing long-distance relationship. Or she could call her friend Ramona from her Chenango Forks elementary through high school years, who she hasn't spoken to in a few months, but she doesn't have the desire to confide in her either. What she wants to do, more than anything else, is fall asleep for a few days and wake up to a different world where everything is normal and leaving Binghamton is a realistic option.

Mel reaches for her laptop in her messenger bag and rests it on her lap. She opens it and checks her emails, ignoring the ones from literary journals rejecting her work. She clicks on the one from Trisha, feeling an odd combination of dread and faint hope. "Hi Melody! So good seeing you the other day and hearing from you by email. I wish I had better news about the office manager job but I'm giving my sister a chance at that. Cross your fingers she doesn't bankrupt me! But we always have openings for childcare attendants if you're interested. Don't forget about that Zumba class!" Trisha's signature at the bottom includes a Bible verse: "The righteous person may have many troubles, but the LORD delivers him from them all (Psalm 34:19)."

Mel stretches out on the couch and closes her eyes. A memory of Kiddie Kare's chaotic rainbow-colored playroom forces itself on her. She imagines being surrounded by screaming and crying toddlers needing naps, potty visits, or timeouts—and then pictures herself falling to the ground in a temper tantrum like an enormous baby. A small, desolate laugh escapes her.

She wakes up when she hears the back door open. Drake comes in, holding two paper bags from Wegmans.

"I thought you were staying with your parents till Sunday."

He shakes his head and places the bags on the dining room table. "We got into a fight, and I left early."

"About what?" Mel sits up and Drake joins her on the couch. He puts his arm around her and rubs her back.

"My folks decided to cut the umbilical cord, since I have a job already lined up after I graduate," Drake says, pretending his fingers are scissors. "Mom wants to retire early and needs to save more, so no more rent help. Which is fine except they just gave my brother a down payment on a house."

"That sucks."

"Yeah, it does. How did things go with your dad at the neurologist's?"

"She thinks he's showing signs of dementia."

"God, Mel! I'm so sorry." Drake squeezes her tightly to his side. "Did she say anything about how fast it'll progress?"

"No way to tell really. He has a prescription for a new drug that's supposed to help, but who knows?"

"Were you at least able to convince him to have someone come by a few times a week?"

She shakes her head.

Drake looks around the apartment. "I've been thinking, this place is kind of expensive, especially with my mom not helping me anymore."

Mel gives him a puzzled look. "Where are you going with this?"

With a sigh he says, "What if we moved in with your dad? Maybe we could save some money on rent and keep an eye on him at the same time. Then, when I start working at VU in June, and have a real paycheck, we can look for our own place."

Melody stares at him in surprise. "You'd do that?" Drake nods. Mel tries to read the expression in his eyes. Is it resignation or determination she sees there?

"I mean, how bad could it be if all three of us work to keep his place clean?" he asks.

16

An hour into the farewell party at Drake and Mel's soon-to-be former apartment and most of the guests they invited have arrived. Cicely, whose long-distance relationship recently ended, sits on the living room couch with her new love interest, Oscar Ozanam. Annie and Laurie from Mel's C-Unit group, along with Laurie's partner, Stella, stand around the dining room table and pick at the variety of dishes Mel and the invitees have provided. Drake's friend Ted tries to insert himself into their conversation, his eyes fixed on Annie, but is relegated to awkwardly eavesdropping from the periphery. Several of Drake's paleontology peers cluster together, while creative writing and literature graduate students form their own groups.

A few days earlier, Drake had asked if she wanted to hold their second annual end-of-the-semester party. Mel had considered that there would be little possibility of having people over at her father's house once they moved in with him. "I don't know if we should. I'm not in the best of moods."

Drake rubbed her shoulder. "I don't blame you. But you can't stop living because of what's going on with your dad. Maybe a party would cheer you up."

She sighed. Her father hadn't been keen on the idea of Drake moving in, though he was gleeful over Mel's return. But once he conceded, Mel brought Drake over to give him time to interact with her father and to start making the house more habitable for them. They stayed for a few hours, which allowed Mel to make a small dent in the hoard in the guest room she and Drake would be taking over. While cleaning, she studied her boyfriend, noting his neutral expression when she and her father squabbled over tossing or donating items.

"You're sure you're okay with moving into my dad's place?" she asked him on the drive back to the apartment.

"Sure I am," he replied. She'd scrutinized him to gauge what he was thinking. The reality of how her father lived had to be sinking in. Then there was the fact that whenever he spoke of the VU job he'd accepted, it still sounded like he was trying to convince himself he'd love it.

At the party, a carefully constructed playlist, including alternative music, the occasional up-tempo pop song, and hip hop, plays in the background. Swift rubs against guests' legs as if he's running for office and hoping to secure votes. Boxes of Mel's books take up one wall in the living room; Drake hasn't begun packing his belongings or putting his furniture in storage. Colton Russell, associate professor, poet, up-and-coming star in Black queer studies, enters the apartment. He unbuttons his long gray coat, revealing a turquoise turtleneck and form-fitting black jeans. He's the only faculty member in the English department to regularly socialize with graduate students and demand they call him by his first name. Mel had taken his course three semesters back, during which he allowed creative writing students to turn in a piece of fiction or nonfiction as one of their two papers. The story Mel wrote for his class won a contest.

"Thank you for inviting me to your party," Colton says, leaning in to embrace her. "Here's some wine. Where are the glasses?"

"Follow me." She leads him through the dining room into the kitchen, finds a glass for him, and opens the bottle of red he's brought. After she pours him one and a small amount for herself, they clink glasses and return to the dining area.

"So how are you, my dear? I haven't seen in you in forever. Nice work on that contest first prize, too. That was a strong story."

"Oh yeah, I'm practically famous now that the *Kansas Review*'s five subscribers have read it. But I appreciate you letting me write it. That was an amazing class. You really know how to put together a diverse reading list."

"That's why they hired me at VU. I'm Dr. Diversity."

Mel considers Colton's words and is mortified. Has she just spouted a microaggression or come off as patronizing? "Oh my god, I'm so sorry! I just meant it's great to read books that aren't written by a bunch of old white men. So many of my lit classes were like that, worshipping the canon. And Abe is great, but he's old school in his literary tastes."

Colton laughs and pats her on the arm. "It's okay. I know what you meant."

Elaina Longacre enters through the kitchen. Her white-blond hair falls straight down her back. Black eyeliner makes her eyes bluer. She's carrying a tinfoil-wrapped plate that she shifts to one hand to wave hello to Mel and Colton. "Hi, Mel! I made hummus."

"Thank you!" Mel says. Elaina places it on the dining room table and removes the tinfoil to reveal green sludge. "Wow, it's so green!"

"It's spinach hummus," Elaina says proudly.

"Cool." Mel considers asking her for the recipe out of politeness but doesn't think she has it in her to feign interest. She's relieved when Elaina wanders off into the living room to say hello to other poetry graduate students.

Mel turns back to Colton. "What about you, Mr. Big Shot? Second book of criticism published, third poetry collection! You're in the big leagues now. You'll be leaving VU soon, right?"

Colton smiles. "Do you want me to autograph something? If I do your arm, you can have my signature permanently tattooed onto your flesh so you're forever reminded of my greatness." He pushes back a dreadlock and Mel laughs. "Kidding aside, you know I'd be happy to write you a recommendation letter."

"I could use one of those. Want to be on my committee too?"

"I'd love to! Who's your chair?"

"I don't have one now that Abe's gone. I don't know who to ask. I thought about Professor Pollon, but he's a Shakespeare guy and I can never find him in his office to ask. I can't tell you how many times I've tried to chase him down."

Colton nods sympathetically. "His expertise in the art of evasion is legendary."

He's not the only one, Mel thinks. She'd exchanged texts with Ben a few days earlier, on the Monday after Thanksgiving break: "When can I pick up my book?" His response arrived the next day: "Plugging away! I'll have it soon." She'd looked at the calendar on her phone. The two weeks she had to revise were dwindling away. How much serious revision could she do? Didn't she tell her comp students that revision wasn't something that could happen at the last minute? Mel had opened the file of notes for the book on her laptop and started implementing them, few though they were. At least she could finish these while she waited for Ben.

"So, why did Abe leave last semester?"

Colton purses his lips. "I couldn't say."

"You're killing me. All this secrecy and for what?"

He puts a hand on her forearm. "Let's just say that he and Tina had a falling-out that was a long time coming. To be honest, I can't help but agree with Abe making some of the poets revise before they could graduate. Not my students, of course. I expect a lot from their dissertations."

"I heard they fought in the hallway after one defense."

Colton scrunches up his face. "It was more like a heated exchange."

Elaina returns to the dining table and Colton and Mel watch her fill a plate. Mel imagines herself as a zoologist studying the eating habits of a unicorn. Until Elaina uses her index finger to swipe hummus off the serving spoon and onto her plate. Colton shudders, but something about Elaina's action pleases Mel. She's imperfect, human.

"Remind me not to eat the hummus," Colton tells Mel after Elaina leaves. "Isn't your friend Ben dating her? I've seen them together around campus."

Mel shrugs. "He's not forthcoming when it comes to that stuff."

Colton leans in and says quietly, "Let me ask you a question. Don't you find him a little . . . macho?"

Mel snorts. She imagines Ben dressed up as the construction worker in the Village People, awkwardly going through the motions of "Y.M.C.A." But then she thinks about his writing, how he's never written anything from a woman's perspective or in a point of view other than first person. "First person's just my thing," he'd once said, as if he never wanted to take a vacation from his own mind. There are times when Mel wouldn't mind a long sabbatical from hers.

As if her thoughts have conjured him, he's now in her living room, standing beside Elaina. When did he arrive and how did he get in without her seeing him? Shouldn't he be taking every waking moment to work on her novel? Mel envisions running into the living room to deliver a kick to his solar plexus, along with several karate chops to his arms and head, then ushering him out of the apartment and back to her manuscript. She will corner him at some point and ask him how it's going.

"Maybe a little," she tells Colton.

"Hmm," he says. Then he leaves her to talk with a group of grad students standing in the living room perusing the few remaining titles in Mel's bookcase.

Over the next few hours, Mel looks for an opportunity to find Ben alone and ask him about his progress on her book, but he remains glued to Elaina's side, with a varying assortment of other students moving in and out of their orbit. He's avoiding her in the friendliest way possible—waving from across the room, toasting her with his glass, and mouthing "great party" in her direction, but without ever coming over to her. It's completely unlike his usual pattern of behavior at parties, which is to remain with her the entire time so they can talk about books and laugh at his comments about their peers.

From the living room, Mel watches him pick a grape from a tray of fruit someone brought, and she sends him a subliminal suggestion to eat the hummus. Elaina steals the next grape from his hand and pops it in her mouth. "Eat the hummus," Mel says aloud in a Darth Vader voice.

"What did you say?" Ted asks. He's given up on his pursuit of Annie.

"Just talking to myself. I need to eat more hummus. It's crazy good for you."

Ted studies her doubtfully before moving off.

Later, Drake sneaks toward the stereo in the media cabinet with a CD case in his hand. Mel's carefully constructed playlist has been a hit. She's overheard comments like "Holy shit, I love that song." Or "Man, I haven't heard that in ages." In pockets throughout the living room, guests have broken out into spontaneous and awkward academic dancing: prairie dogs periscope up and down out of their dens, bartenders use invisible cocktail shakers, and witches stir large cauldrons.

Mel cuts Drake off from reaching the stereo. "What do you think you're doing?"

He puts the CD behind his back, but Mel has already seen the cover art for Pantera's *Vulgar Display of Power*, which features a fist landing a punch on a man's face. "Nothing."

"You are not playing Pantera. Nobody wants to hear that."

"I do," he says, looking hurtfully stubborn, which tells her he's buzzed.

"Yeah, put on some Pantera," Ben says from across the living room. It's hard to tell if he's drunk, though Melody has seen him spiking his red cup with bottles from the liquor table.

"Seriously, Ben? Since when do you listen to them?" There's a hint of venom in Mel's voice.

"I grew up listening to them. Nothing like a little Slayer or Pantera to get a party started."

Mel shoots Ben a scowl and holds her hand out to Drake. "Give me that." She refuses to ruin the painstakingly established mood and have their guests' eardrums assaulted by Cookie Monster metal. He hands her the case and walks off pouting.

Near one in the morning, Mel carries a garbage bag out to the small back deck, where, despite the cold, Drake has a game of darts going. He and Ted are a team, while Ben and Oscar are their opponents. Oscar leans against the wall of the house next to Cicely, waiting for his turn. The glass patio table is covered with empty beer bottles and a few used plastic plates, stacked precariously with plastic forks between each layer. Mel shoves these in the garbage bag and then stuffs it in the can at the bottom of the stairs leading to their tiny backyard.

When she returns to the game, Oscar gives Mel a thumbs-up. "Good party," he tells her.

"Thanks."

"O-h-h-h yeah, motherfucker!" Drake says, high-fiving Ted. "That's two bulls and an eighteen closed out. Look who's getting their asses kicked." He walks over to the board and pulls out the three darts, before handing them to a grim-looking Ben.

Later, when the party winds down, Ben waves good night to Mel from the back door. Elaina passes him on her way out, holding her car keys, leftover hummus, and purse.

"Hang on a sec," Mel calls out to him. She's about to ask him about her book, but seeing the way he stands, one arm against the door as if he needs its support, stops her. Does she want to hear drunken excuses for why he's not done yet? "Are you two all right to drive?"

"We're fine. Elaina's driving. She didn't drink tonight." He salutes Mel good-bye and closes the door behind him.

With Cicely and Oscar's help, and as Ted and Drake play another round of darts, Melody cleans the apartment. She thinks about how much she dislikes parties. All the work of tidying beforehand, buying food and drinks, making up a playlist of music, and then the picking up afterward isn't worth it. She should leave the rest of the cleaning for Drake to do in the morning. He is not her father—that's part of what she loves about him and what helped her decide to move in with him—but now look at what she's doing. Dragging him and herself back to where she came from.

It's well past 2:00 when Cicely and Oscar leave. "That ought to do it," Mel says, putting another garbage bag out beside the filled can in the backyard. Through a first-floor window looking onto the landlady's kitchen, Mel sees the elderly woman standing at her sink, her hair wet with dark-brown dye forming peaks around her head. Mrs. McFadden had been surprisingly understanding when Drake explained that he needed to be let out of his lease early to move in with Melody so they could help care for her aging father. When she turns around, the thick smudge of dye coating her eyebrows calls to mind Groucho Marx.

In the living room, Melody finds Drake and Ted wrestling on the rug. Her boyfriend, who outweighs Ted by a good thirty pounds, has him in a headlock. The wood coffee table, a gift from Drake's mother, tips over, and an empty plastic cup catapults into the air.

"Would you two cut it out?" she says, standing over them. "You're almost PhDs for chrissakes. Act like it."

"He's concaving my nougin," Ted cries out. "And damaging my spline."

Drake looks up at Mel, laughing. He unhooks his arms from Ted's neck and rises awkwardly, then holds out a hand to help his friend up. They sprawl next to each other on the couch, sweaty and disheveled.

"We beated him," Ted tells Drake, a satisfied look on his face. "We almost didn't. But then you saved the day, Superman." Ted stretches his arms out as if flying through the air.

"What are you talking about?" she asks, as she returns the table to its upright position and picks up the cup.

"We kicked Ben's ass at darts," Drake says.

"We beated him at everysing," Ted says, head back and eyes closed, an exhausted Sugar Ray Leonard.

"You look pleased," Mel says to Drake.

He grins. "Feels good. Especially coming from behind." He cocks his right arm at a ninety-degree angle and flexes his academic bicep. "I don't like that guy. But he's your friend."

"Yeah, he is. And I need him. He can make a huge difference in how good my book is. I can't fix it on my own."

"I don't trust him. He's shady." Drake says this with conviction.

Melody laughs at him. "You're being dramatic."

Drake grabs her hand and pulls her onto his lap. "Well, he better do what's right because no one messes with my woman! We're a team. Wherever I go, you go. And verse visa."

17

At the end of the semester, Mel trudges through several inches of slush from the Science II building, where she held her last morning class, to the English department. Her joy over the semester being over is tempered by dread. She is determined to find Ben, who should be holding office hours before his first class. He has to know the deadline for the fellowship is only a week away. She knocks on his door, but no answer. It's locked. On her way to the English department at the end of the hall, light flooding out from an open door illuminates a small section of the otherwise dimly lit hallway. A bearded man Mel doesn't recognize as English faculty sits behind his desk eating corn on the cob.

She walks into Ben coming out of the men's room. His initial expression is unhappy, but he quickly alters it into a smile.

"Hey, Mel!"

"I was just looking for you. Got a minute?"

"I'm in a bit of a rush." He pulls his phone out of his back pocket to check the time, then shakes his head in disbelief at what he sees. "I have to meet a student before class."

"Did you have fun at the party?" Mel asks, falling into step beside him as he heads back to his office.

"An excellent time was had by all."

"I barely got a chance to talk to you. How was your Thanksgiving break?"

"Busy. Crazy busy. I had to do another round of revisions on my book."

"So . . . you didn't finish mine?"

Ben stops and sighs. "Listen, it's not that I don't want to, because I love your writing and I know how much you've always helped me, but I really could use a few more days."

Mel can almost feel her blood pressure dip dangerously low. Is this what people mean by having their "heart sink," she wonders. "I don't have a few days."

He stares at her blankly.

"Just give me what you have and let me start working on that."

"Okay," he says. But he pauses before unlocking his office door. Inside he retrieves a thin stack of paper from a desk drawer and hands it to her. "I promise to finish it up by the weekend."

"Great," Melody says, turning and walking away. This is all he has to give her after having had the novel since May? How much could he love the book if this is all he's read? Mel's hope plunges. Despite knowing she has a job at VU after she graduates, she still feels despair. Because winning the fellowship would be so much better in so many ways.

As Mel heads to her office across campus in the College-in-the-Trees building, she imagines the grueling course load lying ahead of her, teaching four first-year writing classes each semester that drain the life out of her. Winning the fellowship would let her be a writer, working on getting more publications. That could land her a better job, with a smaller teaching load that includes creative writing classes. A position based on her own independent efforts, not her boyfriend's.

A few minutes later, the alarmingly few pages of her book are neatly stacked on her desk. She skims through them one at a time, reading the comments Ben left in the margins in red ink. Occasionally there are style and mechanics notes where she needs a comma or semicolon, the kind of stuff she tells her first-year writing students to ignore when they're looking at developmental drafts. But she also finds remarks like "This character has no redeeming qualities" and "What a sex-obsessed idiot!" and "Why is she so dumb?" He's also written "Ugh" several times in the margins, in spots where Mel had thought she was revealing some deep truth about the struggles these women have endured. There's nothing related to the plot, because how could he have anything to suggest about the book's narrative arc when he's read so little of it?

Mel's eyes burn and acid wells up from her stomach into her throat, sensations she's never felt in response to feedback on her writing. There is not one useful piece of advice to be found in the pages Ben returned to her. Her worst enemy wouldn't have written such spiteful words about something she'd taken years to create and worked so hard on. Ben is a child asked to clean his room who does it poorly to avoid having to finish.

Melody stares blankly out the single narrow window in her office, which overlooks a barren courtyard. She considers the lies Ben's been feeding her to keep her off his back and recalls all the times she's had him over for dinner. All the car rides back and forth to her apartment, to meals they ate out and readings and parties. She sees him at her and Drake's party, eating the food she'd made, drinking her alcohol. She thinks about how often she's read his work, not just his novel but so many other stories and pieces of literary criticism he wrote for courses that he felt ill-equipped to deal with. How flattered she'd been that he respected her enough to ask her to become his reader and how much effort she put into the feedback she gave him. Each memory exacerbates the acid in her stomach. Blood rushes to her face, and her heart speeds up as violent thoughts fill her mind.

Mel stands facing in the direction of Ben's office. She thrusts a finger at him through the wall. "You cocksucking motherfucker, dickhead, douchebag, shithead jerk," she says through clenched teeth, emphasizing each word with an angry jab.

A creaking sound behind her causes her to whip around. Ed, the janitor for College-in-the-Trees, stands in the doorway, his cleaning and garbage-collecting cart in front of him. His straight brown hair reminds her of Keith Partridge. He's dressed in a green coverall.

"You got any garbage, Mel?"

Mel stares at him for several uncomfortable moments. She imagines what her face looks like: teary-eyed and marred by hurt and anger. With any luck, she's the spitting image of Joan Crawford in *Mommie Dearest*'s wire hanger scene. "Sure. You may as well take these," she says, manically gathering up the pages of her novel from her desk. She raises her arm high and drops them into the garbage bin, spreading out her fingers with a magician's flourish as they fall.

"That's not for paper," Ed says.

"Of course not," Mel reaches into the can and crunches the pages together. "I may as well keep them, then."

"Okay. Have a nice day." Ed pushes his squeaking cart down the hall.

Mel checks her phone. It's time to head to her second class of the day. She writes a quick note letting her students know she'll be back after her class for extra office hours, then tapes it to her door. As she leaves, she sends Ben a text: "Don't bother with the rest." She refrains from adding *"asshole."*

Quickly, she gets one in return: "I'm sorry, but I'm only telling you the truth. The book needs work."

"No kidding. But that doesn't mean you get to destroy it. I've spent hours reading your work. Do you think it was all great? Forget about the rest."

"I'll leave it in your mailbox."

And just like that, he avoids reciprocating all the help she's given him.

In her class, Mel has her students do peer reviewing to avoid interacting with them. She sends a text to Drake: "He completely screwed me over." Without her having to explain, Drake immediately knows what she means. "I'm so sorry, Mel! I hate that fucking guy."

After class, she shuffles back to the College-in-the-Trees building to do her extra office hours and help students frantic for last-minute feedback on their final portfolios. Her gait is slow and methodical to avoid slipping on patches of slush that have now become ice thanks to a drop in the temperature. The campus is barren of all but leafless brown trees, with gray icy sidewalks. Female students in black puffy jackets, deer-colored Uggs, and leggings as thin as onion skin plod past her. Young men dressed in jeans and hoodies slog by.

She finds Sherry Turner sitting on the floor outside her door and curses herself for leaving the note on it. Melody takes a deep breath and wishes Sherry would suddenly decide to take a vacation in Tahiti. Instead, she pops up with inhuman energy. She is of above-average height and prettiness, with large blue eyes and soft ash-brown hair that looks as though it has never been touched by harsh chemicals. The black leather tote she carries appears expensive and new, as do her knee-high black leather boots.

"Hi, Ms. Hollings. Do you have a few minutes to help me with some writing?"

"Sure. Why not?" Mel says, hiding the toxic sludge of emotions churning within her behind a friendly veneer. It's not like any of her current students are waiting for her.

She motions toward the fraying orange seventies-style chair in the corner. Her office reveals the impermanence of her position and her insignificant status. A VU calendar from the year before is pinned to the wall above her desk. The month it's turned to, the previous May, features a photo of the men's basketball team in front of the brand-new gym and event center.

"Thank you so much," Sherry says. "I always have a hard time finding your office. You're, like, totally hidden away."

"Tell me about it." Melody takes in her surroundings with the bitterness of an innocent inmate surveying her jail cell. "College-in-the-Trees? More like in the void." She shrugs. "But how can I help you today?" She sounds like a customer service representative, which is basically what she is. This is what happens when a university views its students as customers who are always right. Give them new gyms, recreational opportunities, massive health centers to make it feel like their four years pursuing a bachelor's degree is an extended visit to an all-inclusive resort. So many of Mel's students seem to have no interest in writing or reading. They're under the impression that first-year writing is an easy course, and that anything they dash off in a first draft is good enough work. Or is that just her currently miserable outlook contaminating everything?

"I've been behind all semester." Sherry lets out a self-deprecating chuckle as Mel recalls this was an issue Sherry had in her class as well.

"Poor time-management skills. It's a problem I need to work on." Her expression turns serious, a criminal talking to her parole officer.

Melody nods. Get to the point, she thinks.

"I was wondering if you can tell me what I need to do with this personal essay I'm working on. You have to submit a complete piece to be accepted into Professor Howe's advanced fiction class next semester and this one is my best. You probably remember it from when I took your class."

Mel barely prevents a growl from emerging from deep in her throat. First Ben avoids teaching first-year writing, then he lands Abe's office, and now he's being handed the chance to teach an advanced creative writing class. How interesting also that Ben is called "Professor Howe" while she's "Ms. Hollings" when they're both at exactly the same point in their doctorate journey. She recalls that Sherry had submitted her essay well after it was due. As with all her students, she'd provided her with a full page of typed-up notes on the first draft. "Do you have the feedback I gave you? That'll help me remember what your essay needed."

"Yep. Somewhere in here." From her tote bag she removes a blue folder with WRIT written across it. She rifles through it, finally pulling out the draft of her essay with Mel's notes stapled to it. Mel quickly scans through her comments to refresh her memory.

"Did you use my suggestions when you revised your paper for the final portfolio?"

Sherry inhales through her teeth. "Well, a little. I probably should have done more. But I was wondering if you could explain them again."

"As I mentioned here, you were jumping around a lot, which makes it hard for your reader to follow. Clearly, this lacrosse game was important to you, but I don't get why this one was different from any others. Also, try to make the people who appear in this essay talk normally. Most people don't say things like 'You are blessed with talents the likes I have never seen before.'" Mel points out the dialogue in the essay and tries to look knowledgeable, though the truth is, what does she know about writing? Nothing, according to Ben. "You also end with the line 'Things would never be the same,' which is a bit confusing. What 'things'?"

"I was trying to be mysterious."

"The better way to do that is with specificity and details that give the reader the information they need and make the writing more vivid. For example, if I say some guy was mean to me, that's vague and doesn't do much for the reader, right?" When Sherry nods, Mel continues. "But if I tell you he wrote vicious comments in the margins of a book I wrote that he was supposed to edit seven months ago and that in doing this he utterly destroyed my confidence and got out of helping someone who has been his personal chef, editor, and chauffeur for the past four years, that's much more specific, and therefore more engaging and persuasive."

Sherry looks impressed. "That makes sense. Do you have a pen so I can write that down?"

Mel digs into her messenger bag and feels wetness at the bottom. When she pulls out her hand, it's covered with ink. She upends her bag on the floor beside her desk and turns it inside out. A large suppurating black wound mars the cloth lining. Melody gives it and her stained hand a baleful look.

"Yikes," Sherry says.

Melody nods. In her desk drawer she finds a stack of brown paper napkins. She hands Sherry one, leaving a faint ink fingerprint on the top right corner. Then gives her a pen she finds in the drawer.

Sherry scribbles something on the napkin that looks like "Mack wore moo specs" before handing back the pen.

"I'm a little confused," Mel says. "If Ben's class is for advanced fiction, why are you submitting a personal essay, which is nonfiction?"

Sherry nods. "I figured I could add some made-up stuff and make it more fiction."

Mel holds her tongue. "Sure, that'll work," she says.

"Could you read it again and tell me what you think?"

"I'm not sure what that would do if you haven't fully revised it. Especially since you want to add made-up stuff."

Sherry concedes this with a nod, and it occurs to Melody that what Sherry wants her to do is rewrite the essay for her. She's meant to be everyone's servant, cleaning up their writing, their homes, their lives. "I suppose it wouldn't make sense for you to look at it again."

"No, it wouldn't. You have to do the work to fix your own writing first." As she says this, Mel resolves that she will never again help someone as much as she's helped Ben. She will put her own writing first from this day forward.

"Gotcha." Sherry smiles but makes no move to leave. When Mel had her as a student, she'd taken a vow of classroom silence, though she seemed to believe seeking Mel out during office hours compensated for all her late work and lack of participation. Melody leans back, smiles weakly. She is tissue thin with nothing left to give, and yet somehow more is expected of her.

Sherry rises to leave but pauses in the doorway. "I have a weird question for you."

"No weird questions in writing."

"It's not about that. You and Professor Howe are friends, right? 'Cause I've seen you two around together a lot."

"Right."

"You're just friends, right?"

Melody squints at Sherry. Of course, it's unimaginable to Sherry that someone as attractive as Ben would date a portly, average-looking woman like herself. Something ugly arises in Mel. She lowers her voice to make it Lauren Bacall's sexy rasp. "Actually, Ben can be quite a flirt." She sits up and pastes a sophisticated smile on her face, then crosses one leg over the other before leaning back in her chair, hoping the stubble on her shins isn't evident through her tights. "But that's how he is with everyone. And he has baggage." Mel coughs several times to clear her throat. Her voice is more drag queen than Lauren Bacall, so she archives it.

"What kind of baggage?" Sherry comes back into the room. "I'm not asking for myself, but I have a friend. She took his class last spring, and we went into the city during summer vacation to listen to him read at the bar he was working at. He was so cool to hang out with."

Mel studies her former student carefully, remembering Ben's expression when she saw him talking to Sherry. Concern mingled with disgust rises within her. How could he socialize with undergrads in a bar at his age and theirs? Alcohol, flattery, combined with his ego were the ingredients for a gross recipe. She leans forward with her hands clasped between her knees. A spot on the carpet draws her attention and Mel considers it while thinking of what to say. She looks up at Sherry's hopeful and innocent face. "Your *friend* should run for her life from Ben." She considers telling Sherry something unsavory, frightening her by hinting at deviant sexual practices Ben engages in. But will that be enough to combat Sherry's desire to hear what she wants rather than what she needs? "Ben isn't a good choice for someone her age. If he encouraged something like that, he's also a horrible human being. That's legitimate grounds for firing or expulsion or something," she adds, though she has no idea what the university has in place to prevent situations like this. Ben certainly wouldn't be the first male graduate student to act like this with an undergraduate. Does she need to involve Professor Pollon as the department chair or maybe the dean of students, whoever that is, given what Sherry is saying? "Tell her to stay away from him. He has nothing to offer her but misery because he's completely self-centered. The only person Ben cares about is Ben."

Mel inhales deeply and lets this truth sink in. She'd let herself be taken in by his need of her, a habit she'd learned from being her father's daughter. As though being important to Ben somehow made her important in general. Had their relationship ever been one of equals?

Sherry's shoulders sink at Mel's advice. "I suppose I should go. Thanks for everything."

When she leaves, Melody slumps in her chair. Now, added to her stress over her novel manuscript—she has a measly six days to revise it without anything of use from Ben—is concern over Sherry. Who should she talk to about this and what's the best course of action? Maybe Kelly, the graduate secretary, knows. Mel opens her laptop and types out a quick email. "Just had a female undergraduate student mention 'hanging out' with a male graduate instructor. What should I do about this?"

A short while later she receives the following response: "Define 'hanging out.'"

Mel runs through what Sherry told her about Ben. Without specific knowledge, how can she answer Kelly's email? She writes back, "I don't really know."

Outside her window, the campus trees are poorly executed stick figures. She spots the unmistakable Dr. Martens plodding of her office roommate, perennial PhD candidate Derrick Philson, heading toward the entrance of the building. She'd first met him when she received her office key and moved in at the beginning of the fall semester. He was already ensconced, having chosen the nicer desk in front of the only window and the more comfortable chair. His back was to the door, and a long, thin brown ponytail stretched down his back. Melody knocked on the door.

"Can I help you?" His smile was that of a stockbroker interrupted during a multimillion-dollar trade.

"Sorry? I was given a key," Melody said.

"Oh. I guess we have to share." Derrick sounded as if he'd been told that, along with his teaching duties, he'd have to empty out garbage cans in the building.

"I won't be here much. It's a little out of the way."

"That's what's good about it. If my students can't find me, that's their problem," he said. Melody nodded, considering this pedagogical method. "So what are you? English lit or creative writing?"

"Creative writing."

He pursed his lips. His eyes were the color of stagnant pond water. "I could tell."

"Really? How?"

"You don't look like the lit crit type."

Had she been insulted or complimented? "What does that look like?"

"They usually have a stick up their ass."

"Oh. What are you?"

"I'm lit crit. But I'm different." He leaned back in his chair and stretched out his feet, which were protected from the physical dangers of academia by his black leather boots. His faded jeans were tucked into their tops, and he sported a black Motörhead T-shirt. "What year are you?"

"Last year. Coursework and field exams complete. All but dissertation."

He smiled patiently, and Melody realized he was waiting for her to ask, "And you?" which she did.

"Well, that's a long story," he said. "I finished my coursework and field exams six years ago, but the diss is what's holding me up. Been working on that for a couple of years." Mel did the math. Given what Derrick said, he had been working on his PhD for at least eight years. "I was involved with this woman for a long time. I put her needs ahead of mine. Anything she needed or wanted, I gave her. But she was crazy, neurotic. A dancer. Stunningly beautiful." Derrick looked as though he was recalling a fond dream he didn't want to wake from. Mel had wondered what it was about her that invited confessions. Then she realized he had stopped talking and was staring at her strangely.

"Are you okay?" he asked her.

"Headache," she said, rubbing her temples and smoothing out the scowl triggered by her thoughts.

"Gotcha. You had this weird look on your face, like you were having a stroke. So anyway, here I am now, picking up the pieces. And hoping to graduate next year."

"Cool." Melody moved toward the door.

"Hey, maybe you could read this story I wrote and let me know what you think."

"I sure wish I had the time," Mel said, trying to look crushed that her hectic schedule wouldn't allow her to read his work.

"Gotcha."

"Well, nice meeting you."

Since then, Melody has avoided Derrick by never hanging up her office hours sheet. She thinks he's gotten the hint, because only once, not long after their meeting, did he leave her a note that said, "Coffee?" To which she replied, "Sorry, super busy."

Now, she watches him approach, his green-and-black flannel shirt peeking out beneath his black leather jacket. Run, she thinks, quickly gathering her bag and exiting.

A Pessimist's Hellish Diary: Musings from a PhD Student

Blog Post: Revenge in Aphra Behn's The Rover

For some reason lately, I've been recollecting Aphra Behn's play *The Rover*, which I read for a Restoration lit class a few semesters ago. It was first performed in 1677, and the character that has stuck with me the most is the libertine Willmore, who Behn based on the Earl of Rochester. His mistress, Elizabeth Barry, acted in many of Behn's plays, even taking the role of Hellena in *The Rover*. According to one literary theorist, "Behn must have known what kind of man Rochester was, at his worst as well as at his best. [And] Willmore ... suggests a kind of benign revenge on Behn's part" (Stapleton 77).

"Benign revenge?" I don't think so. *The Rover* is a full-on takedown of Rochester, which he probably deserved.

Here's why Willmore is so awful: he's the Restoration's version of toxic masculinity.

Starting with being a lecher. At one point in the play, Willmore tells the character Hellena, "I wish I were that dull, that constant thing/Which thou woud'st have, and Nature never meant me" (5:298–99). For Willmore, Nature is the perfect scapegoat to excuse his hypersexual behavior and inability to be faithful to one woman. Apparently the boy couldn't help it, or "boys will be boys," excuses we hear today when men do things they know they shouldn't.

As Payne puts it, "Willmore, for all his verbal grace and physical charm, also represents a darker element, a danger always just barely avoided and continuously threatened, even beyond the apparent manifestations of callous disregard of women's feelings" (47). He's a predator, who takes advantage of women to meet his needs without concern for theirs. If that doesn't describe today's toxic male, I don't know what does. How awful that we're centuries removed from Behn's play, yet characters like Willmore, and the man he represents, seem so familiar.

Willmore is also an idiot, who repeatedly needs to have things explained to him, most often by his friend Belvile. What's with these men who can't figure things out on their own? I know a few in my graduate program who rely upon a woman's help because god forbid they do the work themselves.

Then there's how Willmore acts, another way Behn criticizes Rochester. First, he seduces Angelica and has sex with her against the advice of his friends. Then he drunkenly almost rapes Florinda and gets into numerous fights over women, nearly killing the viceroy's son. It's hard to imagine how anyone could view Behn's portrayal of Willmore as a gentle critique when she "shames her rakes, making them appear foolish to the point of humiliating them" (Stapleton 83). Wouldn't it be nice if shame and humiliation could make a man like this behave better?

Through him, Behn argues that a man who is completely selfish will put himself first, to any friend's detriment. Willmore's actions throughout the play prevent "smoother social interactions" (Doody 62). In this way, Behn echoes what Thomas Hobbes argued, "that the truly simple and individualistic life resting on male individual power is unlivable and uncivilized" (qtd. in Doody 61). That's as much true in our own era as it was during the Restoration.

Given that gender during this period was considered "not fixed but mutable" (Doody 58), Behn is saying that identity is as much a performance as roles acted out on the stage. In other words, Willmore chooses to act as he does and was socialized to do so. A sensible male like his friend Belvile can maneuver within society. A "natural" man like Willmore can't. And yet, how often does today's version of Willmore/Rochester get away with harming others without consequences?

As a woman trying to earn a living as a writer, no easy task then or now, Behn was aware of the changes the English economy experienced during the Restoration. She could see firsthand that men whose sole concern was their own benefit and pleasure couldn't function in a more feminized economy and civilization based on more equitable exchanges. Behn was also a witness to how the Earl of Rochester treated Elizabeth Barry. Her revenge makes a fool of Rochester, lampooning his stupidity, ridiculing his hypersexuality and self-centeredness, and showing her audience that libertines like him have no place in a new society.

When I read *The Rover*, I imagined Rochester's response to the play and wondered whether Behn's punches landed any blows. I sure hope so.

Works Cited

Behn, Aphra. *The Rover*. Lincoln: University of Nebraska Press, 1967.

Doody, Margaret A. "Gender, Literature, and Gendering Literature in the Restoration." In *The Cambridge Companion to English Literature*. Ed. Steven N. Zwicker, 58–81. Cambridge: Cambridge University Press, 1998.

Payne, Linda R. "The Carnivalesque Regeneration of Corrupt Economies in *The Rover*." *Restoration: Studies in English Literary Culture, 1660–1700*, 22, no. 1 (Spring 1998): 40–49.

Stapleton, M. L. "Aphra Behn, Libertine." *Restoration Studies in English Literary Culture, 1660–1700*, 24, no. 2 (Fall 2000): 75–97.

18

After attending the theater department's winter production of Pierre-Marie Ventre's obscure resistentialist play *Les Choses Sont Contre Nous* Mel and Cicely go to Cyber Café West for coffee. As proof of Ben's betrayal—she's been trying out several words to describe what he did, and this one is in high rotation—Mel brings the pages he commented on. She hands the thin stack to Cicely as though they're condemning evidence at a double murder trial. The deceased? Her writing confidence and her friendship with Ben.

"Enjoy." Melody leans back to drink her coffee as Cicely flips through the pages and reads Ben's comments. The café's décor features a hodgepodge of cast-off couches and furnishings, mismatching chairs, and walls painted a variety of colors. It has the feel of an art school fraternity house. Playing at a low volume in the background on crackly speakers is Bob Dylan's "Subterranean Homesick Blues." What Mel hears are profound lyrics such as "bleep," "blurp," and "blap."

Each of Cicely's sharp inhalations causes Melody to nod emphatically. Occasionally Cicely adds a "Jesus!" and finally a "fucking asshole." Then she sits back and lets out a "phew." She rests her cheek in the V formed by her index finger and thumb and stares blankly down at the table, a monk deep in meditation. When she comes out of her fugue, Cicely seems refreshed, and Mel wonders if imitating her friend might do her good.

"See what I mean?" Mel asks her.

Cicely nods her head. "I thought you had to be exaggerating. But this is brutal. Clearly he's in the middle of a psychotic breakdown." Around her neck is a blocky primitive wooden necklace that looks like the creation of a tandem jewelry-making team of a beaver and a five-year-old. Mel would love to have the courage to wear such jewelry. "He's a misogynist, a living, breathing Willmore. Doesn't he date some of his students? No wonder you've been thinking about Behn's play. We read it in Townley's class, right?"

Mel nods as she thinks of Sherry. "He could be," she says, while wondering why her initial response is to defend Ben. "The thing is, now I think the whole book is garbage. And I'm a sucky writer."

"I'm sure it's not, Mel, and you're definitely a strong writer." Cicely pats her hand. "I've been loving your blog posts, especially their increasingly feminist slant."

Mel furrows her brow. "I don't know if that's what I've been trying to do with them. I've been hoping they're funny or a good way to put my lit crit papers to use."

Cicely cocks her head doubtfully. "Seriously? Reading them is watching you manifest as a feminist right before my eyes. Face it, you're a feminist now." Cicely opens her arms out wide. "Welcome to the club."

Mel considers some of her other more recent posts, like the one on a tabloid newspaper's front-page coverage of female celebrities not wearing makeup, or another about how women are perceived—by men—as being not as funny as men, whether as comedians, writers, or actors, because the male comedic palate is accustomed only to masculine humor. Then there was the lit crit paper she posted on how contemporary male writers can't write fully rounded female characters because they developed their craft reading canonical male authors who had the same issue.

She sees these posts from Cicely's point of view and realizes her friend is right. She is manifesting as a feminist. Manifest Feminist. Mani/Femi. That's what she'll call the blog.

Cicely interrupts her thoughts. "You can't judge your book based on Ben's comments. Everything he wrote is way out of line."

"I had so much respect for his opinion."

"I'm sure you did, but you shouldn't be surprised by how he read your book. I read a couple of his stories online and none are written from a woman's perspective. All his female characters are foils for his male ones. He's not your audience."

Melody nods. "You're right. But he was so helpful with my stories. I thought he'd be the same with the novel. How am I supposed to revise this in less than a week and come up with an entire committee for my defense?"

"What about Tina as your chair?"

"God, no. She doesn't know who I am, plus she's all about her poets. Colton offered to be on my committee."

Cicely nods. "Good. Try some of the lit people. They may not know as much about creative writing, but at least they'll be helpful, not destructive." Cicely taps the pages in front of her.

"But what if they think my characters are 'shallow' or 'boring'?" Mel asks, putting the words Ben used in air quotes. She knows now this is the reason why she's held off on reaching out to any literature professors. Their professional lives are devoted to studying the greatest writers of literary fiction, and she'd be handing them what Ben described as "chick lit."

"They're not going to think that. You don't have it in you to write stories with characters like that. I know, because I've read a lot of your work too."

Mel sighs and considers what's ahead for her. Tonight, when she returns to her father's house, where she's mostly moved back in, she'll do some cleaning and unpacking, then sit in front of her laptop and continue her feverish revision. And don't forget grading, because she has forty student portfolios to plow through in the next week.

"Are you going to MLA?"

Mel wrinkles her nose. "No one wants to interview me. How about you?"

"Yeah. I'm on a Latin American lit panel. Plus I have two interviews."

"Good for you!"

"We'll see what happens." Cicely sips her coffee. "What'd you think of the email from Mindy," the director of the C-Unit program, "about increasing the enrollment caps on our comp classes in the spring?"

"I didn't see that one. I was too busy deleting five rejection letters from a journal for the one story I sent them. I guess they really, really, really, really, really wanted to let me know they couldn't use it. Why the increase in students?"

"There's been a spike in enrollment, so VU wants us to teach five more comp students per class. And you know how much they want to pay us for the extra work?"

"How much?"

Cicely makes a circle with her thumb and index finger. "Zero. Nada. Zilch."

Mel makes a disgusted sound. "What does the union say about this?"

"Nothing so far. I'm sure they'll get away with it."

That Sunday, Mel wakes up early at her father's house, roused by the sound of a car horn from the street. Prior to this forcing her into consciousness, her mind had turned the sound into a flock of geese flying overhead. She was in a field where it was bitterly cold and the ground was frozen and ashy brown, like a prairie in Montana. She had on a pair of skis, though she's never skied before, but there was no snow. When she fully wakes, she sees that the blankets are a mountain range separating her from Drake, who sleeps with one arm above his head. His mouth is slightly open, and his breath is as soft as a baby's. Mel's legs extend from her gray shorts like corpse-colored branches.

The spare room where they're sleeping is mostly cleared of her father's things, except for some animal art pieces hanging on the walls, the buck's head, and the deer family curtains, whose recurrent graphic features a thick-necked fourteen-point buck guarding a doe and fawn. God knows where her father found these curtains. At a yard sale?

She could finish redecorating the room but feels no desire to do so. Trying to whittle down one extraneous object after another from her father's clutching grasp, making trips to the Salvation Army with trunkloads of items, and bickering with him continually isn't what she'd planned on doing over winter break. Mel had imagined the six weeks off between semesters as a golden time devoted to writing new material because her novel revision would have been completely done. Instead, the deadline for the Alumni Emerging Writer Fellowship is a few days away and she has only her own ideas to guide her. She reminds herself of how Abe encouraged her to apply and his faith in her writing. As one of the few fiction graduate students at VU with a decent publication record, she stands a good chance of winning, even if her novel isn't as advanced as it could be.

She rolls out of bed to avoid waking Drake, who slept over for the first time. Only a few of his clothes hang in the closet, and his sweatshirt is draped over the back of her desk chair. Is she only imagining that he's treating her father's home more like a hotel room than their future dwelling place? In the living room, she sits on the couch with her computer on her lap to sneak in a few hours of revision, but this opportunity is interrupted by her father, who's an early riser. He steps sideways down the hall, made narrow thanks to the floor-to-ceiling stacks of boxes on one side. He has on a yellowy once-white T-shirt and plaid boxers, whose gaping fly reveals the fish-tongue top of his penis.

"Dad! Shorts!" Mel yells, closing her eyes.

"Whoops! Cat's out of the bag!" he says, adjusting himself before disappearing into the bathroom.

Since moving back in, Mel has spotted her father's penis on several occasions. She has no memories of this happening before. Not that she's unhappy about it, but what changed? It's as if he's reached an age where he doesn't care about the visibility or state of his body because his mind is too busy trying to keep everything functioning as normally as possible.

When he emerges from the bathroom, he's wearing his green terry cloth robe, the one with a hole in the pocket and ripped seams on either side. He settles into the big chair across from the TV and breaks the calm silence with the press of a button. Commentary from the hyperactive announcers on ESPN SportsCenter, like frat boys given the opportunity to be on TV, fill the space. Mel's newly born alter ego, an impatient, easily angered version of herself she's dubbed "Mel Two," shouts internally, Calm the fuck down! You have a captive audience of sports fanatics, dimwits. You don't have to be maniacs to keep your viewer's attention.

A short while later, Drake emerges yawning from the bedroom to sprawl on the couch next to Mel, close enough that her father gives him several sidelong looks beneath his shaggy eyebrows.

Drake rubs his scalp and grimaces. "Man, do I have a headache." He stretches his neck side to side before slouching against her thigh. When he catches Collin's disapproving look, he sits up. Mel smiles apologetically at Drake.

"Is that your stomach growling?" her father asks his stuffed bear, while rubbing at his own belly.

"Didn't hear a thing," Mel says, refusing to look up from her computer. At least if she can empty her email inbox, she can free up time to write later without distractions.

"Whoa. There it goes again. That one was loud," her father says, patting the stuffed animal's stomach the way a cowboy would reassure a testy horse.

"Nope. Didn't hear it," Mel says. She gives Drake a look to see if he's following this, but he's engrossed in a book.

"That sure looks good," her father says about a Jimmy Dean sausage commercial.

"Jesus F. Christ," Mel Two mutters under her breath. "Dad, I get it. You're hungry. But can you give me a few minutes? I'm trying to get some work done."

"No problem, kiddo. Why don't I drive down to McDonald's and pick something up?"

"You don't need to be driving or wasting money on that garbage. I went shopping two days ago and there's plenty to eat in the fridge."

"Are there eggs? And bread for toast?"

"Yes. Why don't you make some?"

"Your eggs always come out better than mine." He says this sadly.

Mel stares at him unmoved. "How is it possible that a man your age doesn't know how to make scrambled eggs?"

"I break them up too small."

"So don't." Father and daughter lock eyes for several moments. "You have to be patient with eggs. Don't put the burner on high and turn it down. Put it on the temperature you want, which is medium-low for eggs, and wait for it to reach that."

"See. It's too complicated."

Mel's shoulders sag. Should she ask Drake to make breakfast? But how would he find anything in her father's still chaotic kitchen? "Fine. You win. How about I make us some breakfast?"

"Sounds good, kid," her father says. "Your mother can help. I'll wake her up."

Mel nudges Drake, who's now listening with wide-eyed wonder. "No, Dad, I'll cook."

"You want me to make the toast?" Drake asks, stretching out on the couch when she rises. He rests the book on his chest.

"Sure."

"I could go for some fried eggs with runny yolks," her father tells Drake. "Go good with that ham I saw in the fridge."

She shoots him a Jackie Gleason glare. Clearly he remembers what groceries she bought.

In the kitchen, Mel unearths a large frying pan from her father's sizable collection that he stores in the oven. She gathers the ingredients from the fridge—eggs, ham, and butter—and waits patiently for the pan to heat up. With the butter melted, she adds several slices of deli ham, letting them bend and settle down onto themselves like collapsing ballerinas in pink tutus. The meat sizzles and the aroma of salty pork wafts upward. She'll let it brown up the way she knows her father prefers it. As the ham cooks, Mel works on unloading the dishwasher and reloading it with dishes that magically reappear in the sink regardless of how often she asks her father to put them directly in the dishwasher. When the ham is done, she pops four pieces of bread into the toaster for her father and Drake. She'll make her eggs and toast after theirs. She sets the table with napkins and forks, glasses, salt and pepper, and orange juice. Afterward, she surveys the table with grudging pleasure and imagines how Martha Stewart must feel. House-proud probably. The table was the first thing she completely cleared of her father's things when she moved back in. "I want us to eat together like a family again," she told him when he started to resist her going through his months-old mail and packing up the herd of cow creamers he'd assembled on the table. "Remember how we used to do that every night?" He'd nodded, his eyes welling up, and helped her whittle the cows down to the five he liked best.

After removing the ham and adding more butter, Mel carefully cracks four eggs into the frying pan, making sure to keep the yolks intact. They cook quickly, and she flips them over carefully. Grabbing two plates, Mel arranges the eggs and ham for her father and Drake. She butters the toast and places the slices next to the perfectly fried eggs and brown-edged ham.

"Here you go," she says, setting the two plates on the table. The men rise from their reclined positions in the living room, two male lions approaching the kill a lioness has brought down.

"Looks good," Drake says. "How come you didn't tell me to do the toast?"

"Didn't realize I had to tell you since you volunteered."

Mel moves back to the stove, adds ham to the hot pan, and then cracks two eggs near it, in a rush now to cook her food quickly so as not to eat alone. There isn't enough time to brown her ham. But then the minor kitchen gods conspire against her. The hot pan, which she forgot to re-butter, cooks her eggs too quickly, and when she tries to flip them, to create the same perfect over-easy eggs with runny yolks that Drake and her father are now dipping their golden-brown and buttery toast into, they stick and the yolks break. A miniature lahar of yellow spills like thick paint onto the hot surface of the pan, cooking instantly into a rubbery mat. She mashes the eggs with the spatula, manically pushing them into the ham and over the top of the pan onto the stove below. The smell of burning toast means that the toaster is too hot from the previous batch. She presses the button to end the cycle, and dark-brown bread pops up with a lively ding. This is what happens when you put yourself last, she thinks. Everything is ruined or less than. Mel turns the stove off and shoves the pan off the burner.

"What's wrong?" Drake asks her, looking up from his eggs. A yellow dot sits at the corner of his lip. Mel has an urge to wipe it off with a swing of the frying pan. What a dumb question. Who is sitting and who is standing? Who is eating and who is not?

"Nothing. I'm not hungry," she says, walking out of the kitchen.

"Might be her time of the month," her father stage-whispers to Drake, which stops Mel in her tracks. "She gets a little cranky right around it."

She turns around, her face heating up, and scowls at his back. Once, when Mel was in her teens, they'd gone on a hike at Buttermilk Falls in Ithaca. Halfway up the trail, she'd suddenly gotten her period. Rather than have her walk all the way back down bleeding through her clothes, her father raced to the park entrance, where he entered the women's restroom to purchase her a maxi pad. Breathless but triumphant, he'd waved it at her like a flag when he returned up the trail. Thankfully, no one was around to see him—or to see her shoving the pad in place. But this memory doesn't dull her anger.

"Actually, Dad, it's not. Cook your own damned breakfasts from now on. You're a grown man who's perfectly capable of that. Stop acting like a spoiled baby." She looks at Drake, who can't hold her gaze. He stares down at his plate, nods to himself. They both know how much she has to get done in the next few days. Mel grabs her laptop off the couch and throws on her coat over her pajamas. As she slams the front door behind her with a satisfying crack, she thinks of her office on campus. She'll barricade herself behind the door, hope Derrick doesn't randomly show up, and finish her damn book. She needs a long break from dealing with men and their constant neediness.

Two days later, right before the 9:00 a.m. deadline, Mel hits send on the email to Tina submitting her novel for the fellowship. She lets out a long breath and sits back in her hard office chair. She's been there since 6:00 after going to bed the night before hours past midnight. A flood of relief washes over her, temporarily extinguishing her exhaustion. She did it—and without Ben's help. It may not be perfect, and there are many more rounds of revision the book needs, but it's better than it was, and that's a huge step to be proud of. A buzz in her purse announces a text. "He's here. Hurry," it says. It's from Kelly, whom Mel bribed with a patchouli oil candle as a Christmas present to let her know as soon as Pollon hunkered down in his office. She closes her laptop and runs across the nearly empty campus to the English department.

When she arrives, Mel carefully closes the door to prevent it from slamming shut with the report of an M-80 firecracker. She passes Kelly's desk with a finger to her lips. Then she leans in to listen at Professor Pollon's door and hears a low voice saying "Sit!" several times. She knocks and waits for his cue to enter before opening the door. The chair of the department sits at his desk, his curly-haired dog standing across from him. Mel imagines that it was Gertie commanding the man to sit and stifles an exhausted laugh.

"Professor Pollon," she announces loudly from the doorway, a bounty hunter confronting a wanted criminal. He looks at her, but it's hard to pinpoint whether his perturbed expression is for her or the Labradoodle. Mel takes a seat and pulls the chair toward the entry to block his exit in case he considers hurdling over her to escape. "I'm so glad I've finally caught up with you."

"Yes. Well. Busy. Actually, on my way out," he tells her, nervously pushing his frames higher up on his nose. His glance slides off her like water on glass. Behind the cloudy lenses, his eyes look trapped. Mel resists the urge to remove his glasses, spit on each lens, and clean them on her shirt before restoring them to his face.

He stuffs papers from the top of his desk into a worn brown leather briefcase. A Norton Critical Edition of *Hamlet* follows. Pollon is wearing loose jeans that reveal his bare ankles above a pair of short black socks emerging from his scuffed hiking boots. The skin peeking out has a gray pallor.

"This won't take long," Mel says. "I need to know about next year. If I can secure one of those lecturer jobs."

"Possibly. Hard to say right now. Fiscal situation. Tough." Pollon shakes his head sympathetically. "Budget cuts."

He speaks as though he's been caught doing something embarrassing. This is contrary to how animated he was during the class Mel took with him years earlier when he was discussing Hamlet's need for revenge despite his doubt over the righteousness of his anger. Mel glances at the dog, who's still standing and staring her owner down. Possibly feeling Mel's gaze, Gertie gives her the side-eye, while refusing to look away from Pollon.

"I don't know if I'll have a job lined up for next year," she says, not mentioning being a partner hire with Drake, because it's becoming apparent to Mel that her boyfriend is compromising his own professional future to fit her needs, and that can only lead to him resenting her at some point. "I have zero interviews set up for MLA. Plus, there's my dad. He's not doing well. He's starting to show signs of dementia, and I need to stay local to take care of him."

Pollon sits back and studies Mel, rolling a pencil on his desk. "That's too bad. I'm sorry to hear that."

Mel nods. "Thanks. He started acting strange, well, stranger than normal for him, a few months back. You should see what a mess his house is. I've had to move back in with him. That's why sticking around after graduating would be super helpful."

Professor Pollon's hand stops moving and he picks up the pencil and writes a note Mel can't decipher on a pad. But he says, "I'll see what I can do."

"Thanks. I really appreciate it." She rises and holds out her hand to Pollon, who shakes it gently.

On her way out of the English department, Mel mouths "Thanks" to Kelly. She stops in the small room across the hall, where the copy machine is located, to print out a few copies of a story she wants to submit to some journals that accept only snail mail submissions. The printer isn't supposed to be used for personal jobs, but she's on campus and no one's around, so why not? The large copier is out of paper, paused mid-print. The document waiting to be duplicated and collated is Ben's syllabus for his advanced fiction class in the spring. She skims the reading list and finds a lone female author: Flannery O'Connor of course. Her anger at him, an ever-present seething below the surface, bubbles up, and Mel Two has an idea. She locks the door.

First she considers photocopying her middle finger and inserting it into Ben's syllabus. But it would be too easy to identify her hand. Then she cancels the copy job and drags a chair over to the copier. She opens the top to reveal the glass and adds one sheet of paper to the machine. Unbuckling her belt and unzipping her pants, Mel sits bare-assed on the cold glass and presses "copy." Surely it would be impossible to know it was her rear end in the photo. She imagines a police lineup of several women, including herself, with their pants dropped for Ben to identify.

The figure of a man appears outside the only window to the copy room and Mel recognizes Ed, the janitor. Quickly she folds her upper body down onto her lap, surprised at how flexible she can be under the right circumstances, and prays she's invisible. But Ed pays her no mind and instead turns away from the window to smoke a cigarette. Silently, Mel slithers down from the copy machine and pulls up her pants. She tucks the photocopy into Ben's syllabus before adding paper to the copier and restarting his job, then listens with satisfaction as each syllabus is stapled together with her contribution tucked within.

When Ben's and her copy jobs are done, Mel unlocks the door and peeks out. Sherry Turner stands in front of Ben's door up the hall, staring at it intently. She leans in and presses her upper body against the wood and places a kiss on the office hours sheet. Then she walks back up the hall, turns at the end, and disappears.

Mel exits the copy room and heads up the empty hallway, her boots sounding like a dry squeegee on glass on the tiled floor. She arrives at Ben's door and studies Sherry's kiss print. Grimacing, she imagines Ben being fake-embarrassed by this sign of worship. But why is Sherry on campus when classes are over for the semester? Doesn't she have a home to go to during winter break, parents who want to see her, and friends her own age to socialize with? A wave of empathy washes over Mel.

She looks up and down the hall, digs out a marker from her purse, and considers her options. What would hurt Ben's ego the most? She could scratch out the "w" in "Howe," which is written in a large font at the top of the sheet. But the resulting word doesn't sit well with her manifesting feminism. She could turn Sherry's kiss imprint into a semi-flaccid penis, with a Storm Trooper head, a throbbing vein running up the shaft, and drips of semen trickling from the meatus of the urethra. An oozing herpes sore near the base would add to the picture. But would any of that make a dent in Ben's confidence the way his comments had destroyed hers? Or did she want to hurt his reputation instead?

Mel Two decides. She uses the bold black marker to write two words and an exclamation point below the stamped version of Sherry's mouth, changing it to mean something much less flattering.

A few days later, Mel is at her father's house, processing rejections from jobs when an email to the graduate and faculty LISTSERV for the English department from Professor Pollon appears in her inbox. The subject line causes her to shrink into herself: "Copy Room Prank Under Investigation." She tries to imagine what this inquiry entails: Ben presenting the offending copy to Pollon, Kelly detailing when the transgression must have occurred, all three dressed in late-Victorian-era clothing, with Ben playing the role of Sherlock Holmes to Pollon's Dr. Watson, and Kelly as Mrs. Hudson. They sit around a tea service comparing notes on who was in the office at that time and whether the image was that of a male or female behind. Mel can't recall whether the photo can be construed as either. Certainly her rear is not small. Will Professor Pollon put together the clues of her meeting with him to when the copy was made and realize it was her? She should go on a strict diet right now so that when the trio of sleuths see her walking down a hall on campus, they'll turn to one another and say, "By George, that's certainly not the culprit!"

Professor Pollon's email ends with a warning that this type of childish behavior is unacceptable and can lead to firing or expulsion from the university. Mel imagines herself being handcuffed during one of her classes and having to do a perp walk out of the room, her students both aghast and gleeful to witness such a scandal. In his email, Pollon adds that because of the immature actions of one foolish individual, the room will be kept locked. Copies will now have to be requested from Kelly, who is probably overjoyed to have yet another task added to her duties.

Mel rubs her face with her hands and whimpers. Wouldn't it be just her luck if her attempt at revenge backfired and created animosity toward her from people who can help her, like Kelly and Professor Pollon? She sends out a prayer to the universe: Please don't let me get caught for this. Please let something go wrong for Ben that doesn't require anything from me.

19

Cicely, Oscar, Drake, and Mel stand outside the entrance of Brandywine Bowl, where they've spent the past few hours drinking pitchers of weak draft beer and listening to crackly disco piped through the aging speakers that hang precariously from hooks in the ceiling. It's an hour before midnight on New Year's Eve. They flip up coat collars and wrap scarves a little tighter to protect their vulnerable necks against the biting cold. Their breath sends out puffs of fog into the frigid air, and Mel imagines some of her soul escaping with each exhalation.

"Let's go to the Belmar," Cicely says.

"Can't," Mel says. "Gotta go hang out with my dad."

Drake sighs and links arms with her. "You want me to come with you?"

The fact that he asks tells Mel his preference, but can she blame him? Who would want to spend New Year's Eve in a messy house with a senile old man? Mel and her father's tradition of eating popcorn and drinking Boylan's black cherry sodas, watching the ball drop on *Dick Clark's New Year's Rockin' Eve* celebration while playing a board game, which they've done for as long as she can remember, can't be that appealing to a twenty-six-year-old man. Except Drake had also used his brother flying in from Chicago for Christmas as an excuse to go home for the holiday, leaving Mel to spend it with her father watching a marathon of Christmas Claymation cartoons and the original *Grinch Who Stole Christmas*. Drake had asked them to join him, but bringing her father wasn't an option. Nor was leaving him alone, and Drake knew that.

"No, that's okay. Go ahead without me," she says.

"Why don't you meet us after?" Oscar says. "We'll be there late."

"I don't think so." In her current state of mind, alcohol beyond the few beers she's nursed over several hours will act as an instantaneous depressant. Better to be miserable alone than drag the others down with her. That week, she'd gotten several letters and emails rejecting her stories and job applications. And she's confirmed through several comments Drake has made lately that he's clearly not enthused about the position he accepted at VU. If Professor Pollon doesn't come through with a lecturing job, all her hope will rest on winning the fellowship. And that's if she doesn't get caught for desecrating Ben's syllabus copies . . . "You guys have fun without me. But only a little bit," she tells Drake with a smile.

He leans in and kisses her on the lips. She can feel relief radiating off him. "I'll call you at midnight."

Her father's neighborhood is lit up for the holiday season. But his house stands out because of the combined Christmas and Halloween decorations. From outside, she can see all the inside lights are on—in the living room and bedrooms—as if a child had been left alone there. Plastic Halloween pumpkins peek through the snow in the front flowerbed. The witch on her broom is still hanging between two of the porch posts, while between two other posts, a large plastic Santa dangles by his hat. But inside the house there's no sign of her father. His bear sits forlornly in the center of the old couch, watching the blaring TV, a teen abandoned by her prom date. The unmistakable smell of burnt popcorn immediately greets her along with the underlying sweet chemical smell she's come to associate with her father's home. In the morning, the odor follows her out of the house, clinging to her clothing and hair, until later in the day when it dissipates.

"Dad?" she calls out, taking off her coat and wedging it into the crowded closet near the front door. She puts her keys in her bag and throws it on the recliner.

Mel wanders into the kitchen to turn off the light. Sitting in the center of the table is their Christmas tree, a one-foot-high ceramic version with an electric cord and multicolored lights at its tips, most of which no longer glow. Her father bought it after she'd moved out. His hoarding made it impossible to fit a real tree in the living room. Once when Mel was seven, they'd gone to a tree farm in Endicott.

After trudging through the snow and up and down the tree-covered hillside until they found the perfect specimen, Mel had to pee. The woman who owned the place refused to let them use the bathroom in her house. Her father dropped the tree right in front of her without paying and stalked off with Mel in tow. "You can keep your damn tree if you won't let a little girl go to the bathroom," he'd said over his shoulder, before adding, "Shameful." This was the first appearance of The Rebuker that Mel recalls.

This Christmas, Mel had woken up to find several presents from her father surrounding the ceramic tree—a $100 Bookery II gift certificate because he knew she'd prefer to patronize a small, privately owned bookstore fifty miles away in Ithaca rather than the mega-bookstore on the parkway; a Whitman's Sampler box of chocolates with a price tag on it from a store in downtown Binghamton that had been out of business for several years; and a large brown leather purse in the shape of a western saddle, complete with stirrups and horn. "I remember how much you used to love horse stories, kiddo," he'd said proudly.

Mel had bought her father a large picture frame with multiple sections in it for individual photos. "I thought I'd put together a collage of photos of you, me, and Mom," she said. "We used to have a bin full of them. Have you seen it anywhere?"

Her father's expression had turned strange in a combination that was part guilt and part something Mel couldn't identify. He'd probably moved the bin and was now embarrassed that he couldn't remember where it was. "Don't know where it went. Must be around here somewhere. I'll keep an eye out for it."

The frame still leans on the back of a kitchen chair, a multitude of fake family photos of strangers staring back at Mel whenever she sits down to eat.

Milk rings on the tabletop resemble a Spirograph drawing. Her father had probably eaten a bowl of cereal for dinner. Mel looks at the sink, and her suspicion is confirmed by the bowl and spoon resting there. Eating Frosted Flakes as a meal is common for him, and tonight that fills Mel with a heavy sadness. She turns off the lights in the bathroom and bedrooms before circling back to find her father coming through the basement door in the kitchen.

"What were you doing down there? I was calling for you."

He freezes for a moment before speaking. "Thinking about your mom."

"Oh, Dad." She wraps him in a big hug, her cheek pressed against his chest, and he squeezes back. She feels his big bony hands patting her back reassuringly and breaks down. What if he gets to a point when he doesn't know her anymore and there are fewer hugs in her future? Mel tries to absorb the feeling of her father's arms comforting her for later when she might have to imagine it and inhales deeply. The chemical odor fills her nostrils and she leans back away from him. What has he been handling to cause his clothing to smell this way?

"What's this about?" he asks her, tipping her chin up to see her tear-filled eyes. "How come you're not with Drake and your friends bowling?"

"Everything is horrible," Mel mutters.

"Did Drake do something to you, because I'll set him straight. Remember that boy who used to tease you about your weight when you were in middle school? The nerve of that pork chop."

Michael Norbutt, how could she forget? Forever known to the entire middle school as Michael Nobutt when his football jersey arrived with his name misprinted. Her father never revealed if he'd had a hand in this, but Mel is certain there was a connection. The Rebuker wouldn't let an opportunity to right a wrong pass him by. She can understand that compulsion now.

"No, it's not Drake. He's fine. We're fine." Though Mel wonders if this is true. "It's just, nothing can go right." Or is it also that nothing can go wrong for Ben that bothers her just as much?

"Don't worry, kiddo. It's the winter blues. Wait till spring and you'll feel better."

Mel takes no comfort from his words. They are the inane clichés of someone who exists in a different reality from the one she inhabits.

The only good thing she's seen in her father since his diagnosis, and maybe due to the meds he was prescribed, is a continually positive outlook. Rather than being depressed, he seems to be liberated, as if he doesn't have to apologize for his behavior or moderate it now. What would it be like, Mel wonders with some envy, to act however you wanted with no regard for how you were perceived?

"Why don't we make some more popcorn, because mine was kinda burnt. We can watch an old movie. Think you can find a good one on Netflakes? Maybe one with Audrey Hepburn. I know she's your favorite. Or is it Katharine Hepburn that you like." He looks surprised. "Were they related?"

"No, I don't think so, Dad. And yeah, sure. We can do that."

20

A week after the January 2007 MLA convention in Philadelphia, the entire English graduate student and faculty LISTSERV receive an email from Tina that causes a snarl of disgust and anger to emerge from Mel. The message notifies them that Ben's "brilliant manuscript" *The Stinkfist Chronicle* won the Alumni Emerging Writer Fellowship "despite competition from other gifted writers." Mel closes her eyes. The dickface-asshole-bastard submitted his manuscript, the one she'd helped him with that was then also edited by an agent, an actual editor at a publishing house, and a copy editor. How is that fair? How much better would her book have been with all that professional help?

Not long after, Mel receives a text from Ben asking her to call him. She suppresses the urge to write back "Fuck off" and tosses her phone on the bed.

Unlike Ben's, her manuscript is a steaming pile of horse manure because her attempts at revision were rushed and insufficient. Plus, Abe, who would have been her ally, hadn't stuck around to be on the selection committee. Then there's Ben's conquest of Tina, which Mel imagines involved a sycophantic insinuation of his person into her circle of favorite poets. He most likely mentioned his mother was a quarter Greek, if that's even true, while fondly recalling Sunday dinnertime feasts of lamb and spanakopita. Mel pictures him asking Tina for the best way to make tzatziki. He probably learned a handful of Greek words and ended his emails to her with a *Yiasou!* In starless-void moments, Mel pictures Ben with his eyes glued shut performing sexual acts on Tina's frail frame as she holds her oversized glasses in place.

No way is she calling him. Their relationship has hit an abrupt end, like a pier on a rocky coast.

But staring at her phone, the cliché "keep your friends close and your enemies closer" occurs to her, and isn't Ben her enemy now? If she wants to get back at him, which she does despite the close call with the "Copyroom Caper," as she's dubbed it, she'll have to at least appear to maintain their friendship. It's the only way justice can be served. She imagines herself proudly accepting the mantle of The Rebuker from her father. But does she have this in her, to pretend they're still buddies while plotting revenge?

As she remembers Ben lying to her face, telling her he wasn't applying for the fellowship, she diabolically strokes an imagined goatee on her chin and decides yes, she does have it in her. She texts him, cloaking her real intentions beneath a façade of forgiveness and fake congratulations.

He writes back immediately, asking her to meet him at Lost Dog Café so he can explain. She agrees.

That night Melody arrives first at the restaurant. She stands in front of the black counter near the entrance as the host looks at her chart and finds a table for two. Lost Dog hums with conversation from the busy Friday night crowd. Mel follows the young woman to a table. Artwork for sale hangs on the maroon-painted walls. The high ceiling reminds her of a converted loft space in New York City. She doesn't see anyone she knows. When the server stops by her table, Mel orders a pitcher of beer. Not long after, Ben arrives.

The server places a pair of menus, two icy cold glasses, and the pitcher of beer on the table as Ben sits down. He fills her glass before reaching for Ben's.

"No thanks. None for me," he says.

"Come on. You deserve to celebrate." Mel smiles widely to show that there are no hard feelings, only soft ones.

Ben hesitates, then nods. He takes a sip, followed by a gulp. He wipes the foam from his lip and sets the glass away from him, a determined look on his face. "About that. I want to apologize. If you only knew what's going on in my life right now, you'd understand."

"Why are you even in Binghamton right now?" Ben normally left for Manhattan as soon as he could at the end of each semester, though with his dating Elaina, Mel shouldn't be surprised he stayed in town. She thinks of Sherry. That must be why her former student was wandering the English department hallway after classes ended, because she knew Ben had remained upstate. But she wouldn't know that unless he told her. That's messed up, Mel thinks, while considering how little she really knows about Ben's romantic life. Would he be so secretive if all his relationships were aboveboard?

"That's part of what I need to tell you about." He takes another drink of beer, and Melody knows he's weighing how much to reveal. Even with her, there's always been a parsing of information to put the right spin on everything. He's his own public relations executive. "You remember how I had to revise my book so many times?" Melody nods. "Well, my agent liked my revisions but she wanted more changes. There I was thinking I was done, and I had to go through it one more time before she thought it was ready to be submitted."

"Tough break," Mel says, trying to keep the bitterness out of her voice.

"This was all last semester, and I barely had the time to work on it and teach and have office hours."

Mel considers the two sections of creative writing he taught, capped at fifteen students per class. He is utterly oblivious or has selective amnesia, forgetting that her teaching load consists of two sections of composition and forty students with five assigned papers, while she also has to hold office hours, apply to jobs, and take care of an elderly parent suffering from dementia.

"Then the book went to auction and we really thought Simon and Schuster was going to take it. But that fell through." He looks disappointed, then fortifies himself with another drink of beer. "I can't tell you what a roller coaster this whole experience has been. One minute you're thrilled and the next despondent."

"It's not being published?" Please, by all that's holy, let something turn out badly for him, Mel thinks.

"Graywolf took it." He shrugs. "I'd hoped a big trade publisher would pick it up."

If they were on the edge of a cliff, she could easily provide the back slap of congratulations that would push him over the edge. "I would be doing cartwheels down the bar if that happened to me. It's Graywolf, for fuck's sake, one of the best independent publishers."

"I know, you're right. But you know how it is."

Not really, Mel thinks. "We should toast your good luck then!" She raises her glass and he does the same. She takes a small sip and puts down her beer.

Ben drinks down a long swallow of his. "I've also been seeing Elaina, who's completely different than anyone I've been with before. That's why I wanted another year up here."

"No wonder you didn't leave her side at the party." Of course Elaina is the reason why Ben applied for the fellowship. She's in her first year of the master's program, which takes two years to complete. "How's her writing?" Mel asks nonchalantly.

"Great. I read her poetry collection. Pretty solid work."

"So you two are hot and heavy?" Mel assumes that Elaina's collection was the manuscript Ben was talking about on his Facebook feed since he certainly didn't think of her own book as "solid."

"We were, but then somebody screwed around with my syllabus and office hours sheet and Elaina thinks there must a good reason for someone to do that to me."

Mel keeps a carefully bland and attentive look on her face while mentally toasting Elaina for her sound conclusion. "What happened to your syllabus and office hours sheet?" she asks, as though she didn't receive the email Professor Pollon sent out to everyone, but it wasn't like Ben's syllabus was mentioned in it.

Ben waves her off. "Plus, she heard some rumors. Completely untrue of course."

Mel recalls Sherry's molestation of Ben's office door and their conversation during her office hours. She considers asking him about her former student, but the thought of violating the young woman's trust stops her. "I hope they are. Untrue that is. You know they've been going around for a while now."

"And you never told me?" It occurs to Mel that Ben expects that she should always have his best interests in mind. But has he ever had hers?

The server stops by to take their order. Ben quickly glances through the menu and asks for a large, fancy salad. In public he often eats food that will make him appear health conscious, while gulping down huge portions of whatever meal she's cooked for him when they're alone. Mel requests a cheeseburger with sweet potato fries. When the server leaves with their menus, she says, "If I didn't think they were true, why would I bother saying anything to you about them? I figured it was people being jealous of you. You know how shitty grad students can be."

"Right." He drinks from his glass.

"Oh, come on. We're all grown-ups here. So you flirted with a student—that's all you did, right? In France that's like the rule," Melody says, picturing herself wearing a beret and walking past the Eiffel Tower with a handsome undergraduate on her arm, though she's never been to France, doesn't own a beret, and has zero desire to date an undergrad, regardless of how attractive they might be. "Americans are so . . . , " she searches for the right word, "provincial." She leans back, adopts a sophisticated expression, but inwardly cringes. She's going straight to hell for this one, but maybe he'll reveal more if he thinks she's not judging him. "As long as flirting is all you did," she repeats.

Ben watches her performance with raised eyebrows. He takes a drink and weighs what to say. Then he lets out a small, embarrassed laugh. "It wasn't anything serious. The problem is with Elaina. She wants nothing to do with me now." He puts the empty glass down and looks crushed. Melody refills it. "She's an amazing person. Just beautiful. But she thinks I'm 'shady.'" He puts the last word in air quotes.

"I don't know how she could think that of you."

Ben squints at Mel but she keeps her face blank. "Then there's an ex-boyfriend in the mix complicating things. Or maybe she thinks I'm too old for her." Like Mel, Ben is older than the rest of their cohorts, who entered graduate school straight from receiving their bachelor's degrees. He'd adjuncted at NYU for many years, in comparison to Mel's years as an office manager. Where might her publication record be if she hadn't worked a nine-to-five job, with only two weeks' vacation and some holidays off throughout the year?

"What makes you think that?"

He shrugs. "She's only a year past getting her BA at Vassar. And I'm good at picking up on what women feel."

Mel suppresses a snort of laughter. She stares at Ben with her head cocked. "Why not act younger?" Since you like young women so much, she thinks. He looks at her questioningly as she tops off his glass then continues. "Do what young people do. Go out a lot. Have fun. Drink and dance." She pictures Ben at The Rathskeller, a downtown bar patronized by VU undergrads, dancing a scholarly jig with twenty-year-old students.

He shakes his head and Melody knows he's not considering this one. "I thought I'd write her something. Since that's my thing."

"You could do that. Be all witty, which you're good at. Tell her what she wants to hear to win her over."

"I wouldn't want it to sound cheesy or desperate." He takes a deep drink and scopes out the attractive Asian waitress taking the order at the table next to theirs. Mel recalls how Ben had written "cheesy" and "desperate" in the margins of her book.

"Definitely not." What is the most off-putting thing Ben could write in a letter to Elaina? Not that Mel knows her, but she's beautiful and a poet. She'd probably want her writing to be taken seriously and her looks ignored. "Tell her how gorgeous she is and that you're consumed by her beauty. She'll think it's flattering as hell." Mel taps the table. She refills his glass before taking a small sip from her own. The waiter comes by with their food. Melody sprinkles salt on her fries and Ben digs into his salad.

"Let me buy dinner, because I owe you big-time," he says.

"You really, really do."

He nods, and Mel wonders if he realizes the damage he did with his words in the margins and between the lines of her novel, a palimpsest that destroyed her writing confidence. They're well into their dinner and barely a word from him about it. Or anything that justifies his behavior.

"What are you working on, writing-wise? Are you still writing stuff for that blog?" Ben looks down as he cuts up his lettuce, grilled vegetables, and tomatoes into smaller bites.

"Yeah. But I have a couple of new story ideas. One's about two babies who fall in love," Mel says, watching his face closely. "Another's about turning the Khmer Rouge killing ground into a tourist attraction."

Ben looks impressed. "Love it."

"Then I have this script concept about a little person who abducts a rich old lady. I'm thinking Peter Dinklage would be perfect for the part."

"Fantastic stuff," he says nodding, his eyes feverish with enthusiasm. He takes a mouthful of food, chews. Then a long swallow of beer.

She stares at him silently for several long moments.

"What?" he asks, wiping his mouth.

"I call bullshit. Those are all crappy ideas. You're agreeing with me because you feel bad about what you did."

He exhales and looks away from her. "You're right."

"You couldn't find someplace in the middle, where you're not trashing my writing or praising me for crap?"

"I can definitely do that. Not a problem. It's what I used to do, right?'

"Yeah," Mel says, but now it's too late because she would never let him read another word of hers.

"You know that I was super stressed over everything happening with my book. Now all this stuff with Elaina, it's been rough," he says, a look of resolute martyrdom on his face.

"Yeah, sounds it." Mel takes a vicious bite out of her burger, ignores the juice dripping down her fingers. They eat silently for several minutes before Ben leans back.

"Look, I am sorry about the fellowship."

"So much for not applying."

"I don't remember saying that. But I really didn't want to submit my novel. Tina practically made me do it."

"Really?" Mel shoves several fries into her mouth.

"She's my diss chair now, so I sent it to her to read at the end of November." Ben takes a bite of his salad.

Conveniently right before the deadline for the fellowship, Mel thinks, and after it had gone through several rounds of professional editing. Smart move on his part to have the chair of the department also chair his defense, though she's a poet. It's not like he needed her feedback to improve the book. "I see."

"Teeth," he says, baring his teeth at Mel to ensure there's nothing stuck in them.

"Good," she says, not telling him about the green foliage sprouting out from the whitewashed picket fence of his upper row of teeth. Mel weighs what he says against the fact that he must remember the reasons she wanted to win the fellowship—to stay near her father and gain more time to write and actually teach creative writing. The acceptance of his book for publication almost assured Ben of employment post-graduation. He didn't need the fellowship.

"Are we good? Because I'd hate to mess up our friendship. You're like a sister to me."

"You remember my dad was diagnosed with dementia, right?"

Ben's shoulders drop. "Holy shit, you told me that."

"Yeah. But it wouldn't have made a difference since you were basically forced to submit your book." Unable to look at Ben, Mel watches a gay couple at the bar, flirting with each other over their drinks.

"Listen," he says, sounding as serious as Kennedy during the Cuban Missile Crisis. "I'm going to talk to Tina and Pollon, see what they can do for you next year."

As if that'll make a difference, as if Ben has that kind of pull. "I've already talked to Pollon. And Tina's Tina. She doesn't know who I am." She arranges her face into a facsimile of a smile, takes a salty sweet potato fry and knocks it against the edge of her plate, like tapping ash off a cigarette, before shoving it into her mouth. "No worries, I'll just be Drake's partner hire. It'll all work out in the end. Have some more beer."

21

The ceiling and walls in the guest room are tongue and groove pine. Melody told Drake the last time he stayed over that it was like waking up in a casket. But on this late January morning, she's alone because Drake stayed at his apartment. The guest room, which Mel chose over her own former bedroom since it shares a wall with her father's, fits only a full-sized bed, which isn't as comfortable for Drake as the queen at his place. There also isn't a weird smell for him to wake up to every morning at the apartment. Mel has searched for the source throughout her father's hoard on the main floor and in the garage but hasn't been able to track it down. It springs up in random locations like a materializing ghost.

She stares up at the knots in the ceiling and sees moth wings, breasts, gynecological diagrams of vaginas. One knot resembles a cowled woman whose mouth is open wide in a soundless wail, her hands pressed against her ears. Mel calls her the Howling Madonna. There's also a bashful owl, who holds one wing across her torso. A sad lioness stares down at Melody from another board. The golden retriever appears resigned to being a two-dimensional creature stuck in a ceiling. The worst face of all, though, is the grimacing clown. As Mel groggily stares up at it, its mouth moves yet no sound emerges. It seems to be saying, "Get down," as though commanding her to dance. But that doesn't even make sense. Mel blinks hard and sits up. She must have fallen back asleep and slipped into dreaming.

It's a Saturday and she has nowhere to be, a state she would normally enjoy. She leans her pillow against the headboard. Even with a cushion acting as a buffer between her and the thick horizontal branches of wood, it's uncomfortable. The nightstands are made from the same pine as the walls. The two paintings she left hanging depict forest scenes in faded greens, grays, and browns. Clearing the room of all her father's "collections" only revealed the hideousness of what was left behind. Melody recalls with longing the Sheetrocked walls in Drake's apartment.

The previous night, after lying awake for hours and finally drifting off to sleep, she woke to the sound of her father walking down the hall, on one of his many bathroom trips. It was after 3:00 a.m., so she decided to get a drink and some aspirin to knock out the headache that was preventing her from sleeping soundly. Outside her door, her father was edging past the motion-detecting night-light she'd plugged in. His back and palms were pressed against the opposite wall as he inched by with his eyes fixed on the red blinking night-light, an elderly ninja on a dangerous mission.

"What're you doing?" she whispered.

He jumped. "I didn't want the light to come on and wake you two up."

"Too late for that," Mel said, following him down the hallway. "And Drake's not here."

He stopped short, blocking Mel from entering the living room. "I forgot why I came in here." One of the side effects of the medication Dr. Oberlin prescribed for dementia was sleeplessness. Or the dementia itself could be the cause of his insomnia.

"Bathroom? Drink?"

"Right." He edged around her and disappeared into the bathroom.

Later that morning, Mel sits on the toilet, jeans around her knees, belly fat folding over onto the tops of her thighs. Her toenails are painted in chipped red polish. She doesn't remember when she painted them. She is tired. What should have been a good writing day has been cut short by a persistent headache and sleep deprivation brain fog. Outside the bathroom she can hear her father walking, creeping, pacing, wandering. She presses her fingers against her eyelids and feels her mouth open, not in a scream but in mourning for the life she briefly lived separate from him. When she rises, she flushes and strips off her clothes. She stares down at her legs. When did they become so stumpy? Whose legs are these? Is she developing that weird psychological disorder where a person believes a part of their body doesn't belong to them? Will this progress to an overwhelming compulsion to amputate her own limbs?

A knock on the door is followed by "Mel? You in there?"

"Yeah, Dad. Give me a minute."

"Take your time. No rush. Just wanted to ask you something."

"Okay. I'll be right out." She waits to hear his steps recede from the bathroom but doesn't and pictures him leaning against the door, with one ear pressed to the wood. "Dad. Can I have some privacy here?"

"Sure, kiddo. I'll be in the kitchen."

Finally she hears him walking away and sighs. With her right big toe, she eases out the bathroom scale from under the vanity, hits the button to turn it on, and then tentatively stands on the cold metal, repositioning her feet several times in the hope the number will be auspicious. It is not. She winces and hops off, not wanting the digits to be imprinted in her mind. This is her future, her weight and age increasing, correlating to a diminishment of all sorts of non-measurable aptitudes, like her desire to write or socialize. She and her father can create their own Grey Gardens of Chenango Forks. He probably has a moldy and balding fur coat somewhere she can wear to complete her transformation into Edie Bouvier Beale.

After dressing, Mel looks for her father in the living room and kitchen but he's nowhere to be found.

"Dad?" No answer. "Dad?" A little louder and nothing. Mel shrugs and retreats to her bedroom to try and write. She opens her laptop and finds herself browsing Facebook postings instead. A former high school friend has shared a chart covering the stereotypical ways women with their periods behave. Hilarious. Mel unfollows him. An image of Ben with his new car, a black Altima sedan, comes up. He stands leaning back against it, hands folded across his chest. The caption reads, "Feeling like an adult with my new ride!" He must have purchased it with the advance on his novel.

Mel scowls and reads the comments on his post, of which there are over 105. Really? He buys a car and this many people feel the need to congratulate him? Mel clicks on Ben's name, which takes her to his Facebook. Beneath the car posting, she finds another self-congratulatory one. "An embarrassment of riches," it says, and below it, a link to a story he's gotten published. After this is a photo, cropped to show part of the letter he received from Tina on behalf of the creative writing program at VU announcing his win of the fellowship.

Mel compares Ben's last few posts to her own, which are infrequent. A recent one was an ode to the joys of cleaning a cat litter box and another was a link to an article covering why women should only buy books written by other women, people of color, and members of the LGBT community. She'd tagged Frederick Schultz to this post, but her former peer at VU who "can't relate" to female characters and therefore didn't read women writers had commented only with a lukewarm "like" without adding the article to his timeline. So much for her changing his perspective. But she is stubborn and will continue rebuking him until he either blocks or unfriends her, or changes his ways.

When was the last time she had good news to announce? Right before the farewell party at the apartment, when she'd won a small award from a tiny literary journal. She's stopped herself on several occasions from posting something that would amount to a complaint because who wants to read that? Instead she's gone silent. Not that anyone has noticed.

Her father knocks and then opens the bedroom door without waiting to hear whether she's invited him in. A "Do Not Disturb" sign she created dangles from the doorknob. Mel turns to him. "Where did you go? I left the bathroom and you were MIA."

Her father looks guilty. "Around and about."

"Didn't you hear me calling you?"

"No."

"Were you outside?"

"Maybe."

"Do you even know where you are right now?"

Her father holds something small and metallic that Mel sees is a toenail clipper. He waves it in her direction.

"I need some help."

She rests her fingers on her keyboard. She unearthed her childhood desk, a reproduction Louis XIV piece her father found on the side of a road, from beneath stacks of boxes and piles of clothes in her old bedroom. He'd been thrilled when he showed it to her in the back of his old van. "Look what you can get for free if you just keep your eyes open. It's exactly what you wanted, right, kiddo?" It hadn't been, but Mel didn't want to diminish his satisfaction over his find. "A desk fit for a future writer!"

He sits on her made bed and gazes around, taking in the neat perimeters, the ornate desk clashing with the rustic bedroom furniture and walls, and nods in approval, as though this is the first time he's seen the room since Melody cleaned it. It is not. He visits several times a day whenever she's home, intruding on her quiet time, reading, or work to request help, tell her he's hungry, or chat about inconsequential things. "I like what you've done in here. You should do it to the rest of the house."

Mel Two, who she's been hearing in her head for several weeks now, echoes a resounding "Fuck off!" Mel One frequently has to remind herself that he's old and suffering from dementia. "If you'd help me, and if I had time, I would," she says slowly. "Now, what do you want?"

He grabs one pant leg to hoist his bare foot into the air.

"Holy Mother of God!" Her astonished gaze moves from her father's toenails, which resemble a bald eagle's talons, to his face. "What the hell, Dad?"

He looks both gleeful and sheepish. "Can't reach 'em."

Mel's face stiffens into the angry resignation of a Kamikaze pilot. "Hand them over," she says, palm out. He slaps the clippers into her hand and leans back on the bed, holding his foot out to her. Mel twists her chair around and takes it into her lap. When her fingers graze the skin of his heel, which feels like the bark of a pine tree, she shudders. On closer inspection, she realizes his toenails are yellowish, surely not a good sign.

"Just bought that clipper," her father says. "Other one was stolen."

"Yeah, sure it was," Mel mutters. "I don't think this is going to work. They're too thick." She tries futilely to fit the clipper's opening around a nail. "I have to take you to a nail salon or something." Melody imagines one of the women at Nail Heaven on Upper Front Street dealing with her father's feet and her expression as she contemplates what her life has become. She cringes at the thought.

"I'm not going to no nail salon! That's for ladies."

"No it's not. Besides, if you don't, we'll need a podiatrist."

"That's a kid doctor."

"You're thinking pediatrician."

He stares at her, looking baffled. "Whatever. Make an appointment and I'll go. Shoes are starting to hurt."

"I bet." She makes a note on her growing to-do list, which has been taken over by her father's needs. She'll have to research which podiatrists accept his insurance, make him an appointment for when she's available to take him, and then chauffeur him to it. At least she's had practice being someone's personal driver and assistant with Ben, and the demise of their friendship has decreased her workload. But she's replaced one needy man with the original and ultimate one.

He rises from the bed and straightens out his lanky frame, pats down his long flannel shirt over his baggy jeans. "That reminds me. I need to buy some clothes when we go out because all my pants and shirts keep disappearing."

"I did a ton of laundry yesterday and put all your clothes away. They're in your bureau in your bedroom."

"That's not my stuff. Everything's too big."

"That's because you've lost weight from forgetting to eat."

"No I haven't. I weigh the same as always."

"Then whose clothing is that?"

"Hell if I know. You must be doing someone else's laundry." He shakes his head at her foolishness and walks out, leaving the door open behind him.

Mel turns back to her computer and rests her forehead on the keyboard. Surely whatever words form from this random pressing of keys will be better than anything she's been able to write in a long time.

22

Right before the spring semester starts, Mel drives to campus for a program-wide C-Unit meeting. The song playing on KGB radio ends and a man who sounds like he smokes Marlboros, boxes for a workout, and may have spent significant time in the military delivers the station's self-promotional ad: "Wishing there was a live webcam in your bathroom so we could look at your girlfriend's rack! KGB!"

"For fuck's sake!" Mel says, turning the radio off. She looks for a parking space while wondering how the voice actor drums up enthusiasm for such awful writing. She imagines a classically trained thespian, down on his luck and disheveled, being handed the script. He reads the lines and gazes sadly at the bromeister radio producer, who's deeply satisfied by the words he's crafted. The actor thinks about the rent he owes and covers his integrity with a sheet so he doesn't have to look at the corpse.

The sky above is an all-encompassing white cloud the same color as the patches of icy snow covering the ground. It's so cold that Mel's nostril hairs freeze on contact with the air. The concrete walkway leading to the overpass to the library is littered with seedpods, which resemble strips of beef jerky so hard she could chew on them for an eternity before they broke down. A crow caws three times in what Mel can only view as a portent of ill tidings.

The conference room where the C-Unit meeting is being held is also the one Abe Pater used for all his creative writing classes. Filling the center of the room is a large table constructed of smaller tables, surrounded by chairs of various makes that have been scavenged from other eras. The only window is barred. Across from it are two large paintings. The one on the left depicts a gray table on which a liquor bottle, a revolver, and the skull of a horse rest. The painting on the right is a Jackson Pollock imitation in reds, oranges, and yellows splattered on a white background.

Mel takes a seat in the back where she can survey the other graduate instructors. What good memories this room holds for her: of lively discussions of the merits and challenges of the classic (read: white male) books Abe assigned, workshopping student stories, looking up from reading her own work to see the fully engaged expressions of her peers and knowing she was doing this writing thing right. And Ben's once helpful criticism. Were his previous compliments all a lie to get her to be at his beck and call? If so, she'd fallen for it. How she misses Abe. She could have gone to him for advice on this whole situation. Hell, it wouldn't have happened if he was still here. Ben wouldn't have asked Tina to be his diss chair and she wouldn't have compelled him to submit his novel. Abe would have recognized the unfairness of having an agented and professionally edited book competing with those of graduate students.

Mel's not sure which of her problems is the worst: losing confidence in her writing, Ben's betrayal of what she thought was a true friendship, fear over her future in her profession, living at her father's and his mental deterioration, or her powerlessness to change anything. If only she could get back at Ben in some way, then maybe she'd feel as though the scales of justice were starting to tip toward balance.

Sitting near the head of the table by the entrance is Smith Townsend, bearded and with rings on his pinky fingers. Next to him is the poet Valerie Amilio, whose pigtails provide an interesting contrast to her thick black glasses. She places a take-out bag on the table in front of her and the unmistakable aroma of Mexican food wafts through the room. She stares at the bag intently for several moments, as if the smell has conjured lines of poetry requiring contemplation.

Across from her is Manfred Horlycott, who spews his opinions in aggressive academese Mel can barely decipher, littered with words like ontology, hegemony, epistemological, and hermeneutics. His Facebook cover photo is a Bertrand Russell quote: "The whole problem with the world is that fools and fanatics are always so certain of themselves and wiser people so full of doubts."

Like Manfred, Winston P. Fredericks dominates discussions in literature classes. He lounges next to his peer. In his too small white leather motorcycle jacket with sleeves that end a few inches above his wrists, he reminds Mel of a member of a Good Samaritan biker gang. Newer instructors Mel doesn't know well fill in the seats around them.

White-Leather Winston tells Manfred of his recently received chili pepper on his GradeYourProfessor page. Mel perks up, recalling that Ben evaluates his ratings on this site at the end of each semester. "To make sure I stay on track," he once told her, though now it occurs to her that it's more to bask in the adulation of his students. Ben may shrug off all the positive reviews and chili peppers he's accumulated over his years of teaching, at both VU and NYU, but his compulsion to read every one contradicts his nonchalance.

"It doesn't count if you added it yourself," Smith volunteers, and Mel resists the urge to kiss him on top of his head.

Then she wonders, could an instructor add a rating? She shuffles over to an empty seat in the back corner of the room so no one can see her computer screen. A visit to the site quickly reveals that all she needs to leave an anonymous review is a .edu email address, which of course she has. But she'll have to be careful to make the writing resemble an undergrad's. What she wants to achieve is something that will prick Ben's ego and give him a taste of the crushing doubt she now lives with.

The door opens and Mindy, the C-Unit program director, rolls in on a scooter. Her left foot is covered in a black Aircast that rests on the scooter's elevated seat as she uses her other foot to push herself to the head of the conference table. She's wearing a paisley button-up shirt hanging all the way down to her knees in a kaleidoscope of colors that would offend even a Woodstock attendee.

"Hello, everyone! How was your break?" Mindy asks the group unwillingly assembled before her. Her enthusiastic demeanor is half motivational speaker, half prison pastor. It's part of the contract for all graduate instructors' teaching in the C-Unit program that they cut short their winter and summer breaks to attend these meetings held at the beginning of each semester.

"Not long enough," someone spouts, generating a "Hear, hear," from Manfred. Mel pictures him slamming down a tankard of ale in an Olde English tavern.

Pasting an interested look on her face and nodding occasionally, like her students do in her classes, Mel tries to make it seem as though she's taking notes on this ever so fascinating meeting. She fixes her mouth into a vacant half-smile while finding Ben's VU reviews on the GradeYourProfessor website. They're written in text-speak and with misspellings, but with an adoring and worshipful tone that causes her pleasant expression to devolve into revulsion before she wrestles it back into order.

"As you all know," Mindy starts, "the C-Unit program was initiated five years ago to standardize the teaching of first-year writing at VU."

Manfred raises his hand. "I find the reasoning behind the process of standardization deeply flawed." He inhales, and Mel knows this is going to be a long meeting.

But Mindy cuts him off with a smile and a held-out hand, palm forward. Mel stores this gesture for future use when she needs to cut off a man interrupting her. "We're all aware of your feelings about that, Manfred, but that's not what we're here to discuss."

Manfred settles back into his seat like an angry toad, and White-Leather Winston punches him in the arm.

Mindy continues: "Unfortunately, there are going to be some changes to our classes that I couldn't prevent."

Valerie opens her take-out bag and pulls out a wrapped burrito. The crinkle-crinkle of paper unwrapping is accompanied by the layered smell of spiced meat, beans, and cooked peppers, which fills the room.

Pausing only to give Valerie a raised eyebrow, Mindy goes on: "For graduate instructors who are course complete, classes are going to be larger by an additional five students because of increases in enrollment." Muted boos and groans erupt from the crowd, and Mindy grimaces sympathetically. "I'm in talks with the dean to see what can be done about this, and I wanted you to know that I will fight on your behalf to make sure you're treated fairly and that this change isn't permanent."

"Does that mean more money?" White-Leather Winston asks.

Mel looks up to see Mindy's reaction, but her face maintains its pained sympathetic expression. "I can't make any promises. But I'll do my best."

Mel knows what that means. Nothing. Great, now she'll be teaching fifty students to Ben's twenty since his advanced fiction class is capped at ten students per section.

She returns her attention to his GradeYourProfessor reviews and tries to imagine the types of comments Joshie Grubber would leave for him, in light of his end-of-semester evaluation of her. They're supposed to be anonymous, but she recognized his distinctive handwriting on the form. "Confusing class. Hard grader who wants it all done her way. Have to rewrite your papers a million times. Don't take it if you want an A." Given Joshie's tendency to fall asleep in class, no wonder he found the course confusing. Students like him thought their writing was perfect with the first draft. They were often indignant at any criticism.

She types: *Easy class if you show up and act interested. Pretensious teacher. Likes writing only like his own. Don't take him if you want help on your writing, unless you're a girl.* She rereads it but pauses on the last clause. Does she want to put that out there? Mel hesitates for several moments before deleting the last four words and hitting submit. She knows how much being told he's "easy" and "pretensious" will perturb Ben, especially alongside the average rating. Hopefully the seed she plants that his students only pretend to like him will grow into crippling doubt about his teaching persona. When they were friends, he would have come to her looking for consolation. He'd require her to stoke the fire of his ego with compliments and expect her to cast aspersions on the mental capacity, parentage, and moral compass of a student who would write such horrible things. But now, who does he have to talk to about it? No one. Because there's no way he will reveal his vulnerability to Elaina. Mel's fear that she could be discovered is overshadowed by her pleasure in imagining her words festering in his mind.

23

A few weeks into the spring semester, Melody wakes up in the middle of the night from a dream that VU's campus is infested with fleas and ticks the size of pit bulls. She'd been standing on the roof of the fifteen-floor Library Tower trying to find the bell—as though an actual metal bell existed—because it had the power to sonically repel the bugs, which were scaling the building to reach her. Noticing several dead does on the ground below, she backed away from the edge. They looked caved in as if the hematophagous creatures had sucked them dry. A group of fleas fluttered in her direction, their tube mouths inching toward her. Their laterally compressed bodies made them look absurdly thin head-on. The sputum of the ticks was shiny and hard like the roof of a car. Unengorged and hungry, they waved their forelegs at her to sense her location. If she moved the slightest bit, they would find her.

Relief fills Mel as she processes this is a nightmare, while a headache pulses behind her eyes. But the hallucinatory vividness of the dream maintains its grip on her. She pets Swift, who's curled up at her side—unlike Drake, who is not. Carefully, she slides out from under the blankets to avoid waking him and plods to the kitchen to nuke a mug of milk in the microwave. A crusty yellow substance is splattered on its interior walls, and a smell that reminds Mel of burnt cake wafts out of it. She adds honey to her milk, then sits down at the kitchen table. After sniffing at the air like a dog, she realizes the odor isn't coming from the microwave but from the entire kitchen. The night before, she'd noticed her father emerging from the basement, his clothing stained an oily black, with the same scent clinging to him.

"What are you up to, Dad?" she'd asked him.

He looked cagey. "Just the furnace. Needs a little TLC."

Had he brought something downstairs from the garage, where she'd initially thought the odor was emanating from? Or was he working on something in the basement that caused the smell? The one place she hasn't looked to track down the strange odor is beneath her, because of the chaos and gigantic spiders she knows she'll find there.

Mel opens a kitchen drawer that's packed with of an assortment of unopened mail, menus, rubber bands, and miscellaneous other items and finds a pen. On the back of an unopened envelope, she lists the sources of stress keeping her awake at night and causing her anxiety-filled dreams. Her classes are too large this semester, the ten extra undergrads making it harder to get to know each student and stay on top of grading; Ben has not only gotten away with being a terrible person but has also been rewarded for his behavior with the fellowship she needed; her father requires her near-constant care; her student loans will go into payment mode when/if she graduates in May. Mel pauses and exhales. She hasn't had a single invitation to be interviewed for an assistant professor position; and how will she graduate if she can't fix the myriad of issues plaguing her dissertation or round up the necessary members of her committee? What if Tina decides to be as hard on the fiction PhD candidates as Abe was with the poets the previous year? Mel's only option for employment rests on being Drake's partner hire, except she knows how he feels about the administrative position, and they've spent barely any time with each other since New Year's Eve.

She grabs her keys and throws her coat on over her pajamas, which consist of gray sweatpants and an oversized faded black sweatshirt. She drives over to Drake's apartment through empty streets and lets herself in. Every room looks as neat as it did before she moved out, with all of Drake's belongings in their place.

Outside his closed bedroom door, Mel pauses to consider what she'll say. She knocks a few times before going in, for a moment imagining she'll find Drake in bed with another woman. But no, he's alone, sprawled diagonally across the queen-sized bed. Is this how he prefers to sleep when they're apart?

"Hey, wake up," she says, shaking his shoulder. Nothing of her is left in the bedroom. But how much of herself had she even put into the apartment, other than her books and clothes? Just a few decorative touches that were easily transportable back to her father's.

Drake blinks awake and sits up. He glances at his clock and squints at Mel. "Is something wrong with your dad?"

She sits on the side of the bed and takes a deep breath. "He's fine. We need to talk about us. I'm getting the feeling you'd rather stay here than with me."

Drake reclines back on the bed and pulls what was once her pillow over his face. "I'm sorry, Mel," he says, his voice muffled. "I thought I could do it, but I can't. Your dad needs professional help, and maybe more meds, because isn't hoarding associated with depression? And you two bicker all the time. It's not healthy. I don't know how you can stand it." He peeks out at her, looking ashamed. "I never get headaches, but damn, staying at your dad's place gave me a ton."

"I know. I don't want to be there either, but what choice do I have?" Mel exhales hard. "It wasn't fair to put you in this situation. My dad is my problem."

"Why don't you hire someone to help him?"

"You know I tried." Drake strokes her back and she tries to remember the last time they had sex. Probably before the move, because her father's house is as conducive to an intimate encounter as a funeral home. She leans away from his touch.

"I get it. It's like having a kid."

And our relationship isn't ready for that, Mel thinks, staring down at her shoes. She has to be a single parent.

"You don't want to stay at VU after you graduate, do you?" she asks him.

Drake looks down at the pillow he's holding. "I have to tell you something. I was offered a job in Wisconsin as an assistant professor. It's one semester of classroom teaching with the other half of the academic year doing fieldwork and on-site teaching at the Florissant Fossil Beds."

Mel nods. "It's perfect for you. When were you going to tell me?"

"I'm not gonna take it."

"Stop. You know you have to. You can't stay at VU just to make my life easier. That's not fair to you."

"But what if I want to do that for you?"

"Nope. We're not doing that." She won't let Drake be sucked into the whirlpool created by her father's needs. He is not going to sacrifice his future to care for her. There's only one way to prevent this, and it fills her with sadness. "Look, I don't think I can be your girlfriend right now. I'm pulled in so many directions and so stressed out."

"You're breaking up with me?"

"Let's just say it's mutual, okay? Because the timing isn't right."

"I think this is a bad idea. What are you gonna do?"

Mel waves him off. "Don't worry about me. I'll be fine."

"Can I ask you a question?" Drake's expression is mournful. "Did you move in with me to get away from your dad?"

Mel scrunches up her face. "Maybe a little. Moving back in with him has made me realize how much I wanted to be out of there." And now she doesn't have a choice. Karma, she thinks.

"You know you're welcome here any time," Drake says. "Come spend the night whenever you need a break."

"Sure," Mel says, though she knows she won't. She takes Drake's key off the ring and gently places it on his bedside table before kissing him good night on the forehead.

Mel drives home, feeling the weight of her breakup with Drake but also a small sense of relief she can't trace. Maybe it's because being honest with Drake has alleviated some of her submerged guilt. But then a wave of worry crashes over her. Her most promising route to employment is now closed.

Back at her father's and unable to sleep, Mel sits at the kitchen table to study her list. A *Clipper* coupon magazine rests on the kitchen counter. Mel flips through the ads for sunroom additions, carpet cleaning, and an assortment of discounts at fast-food restaurants before landing on an advertisement for a telephone psychic reading. It's 3:43 a.m. She reaches for her cell phone and calls the number. The recorded voice of an extraordinarily cheerful woman answers:

"Welcome to the Psychic Network! All psychics are with other callers, but if you hold on, we'll be right with you!"

A song plays that reminds Mel of "The Little Drummer Boy" if it was performed by the Bee Gees. It's interrupted by a boisterous "Hello!"

"This is Chess Stelson with the Psychic Network! How may I help you?"

"Hi," Mel says, surprised to hear a man's voice. She'd much rather confess her woes to a woman right now. Even this can't go her way. "I was interested in learning about psychic readings."

"I can definitely help you with that!" Chess's voice is beyond cheerful; he is a true believer, and Mel wonders what time it is wherever he's at. She pictures him sitting in a small square cubicle, whose carpeted walls are decorated with mementos of his successful career in psychic reading. An "Employee of the Month" certificate hangs where he can always see it. "What do you want to know?"

"How exactly do they work, 'cause I've never had one before?"

"Well, psychics come in all types, but we all tap into psychic energy!"

"I see. But if you're far away from where I am, how is that possible?" Mel says, proud to have come up with such a reasonable question, despite her brain's sluggishness.

"First of all, can I have your name?"

"It's Mel."

"Mel! Is that short for Melanie?"

"Sure. Why not?" Melody says.

"Mel, I happen to work with spirit guides, otherwise known as guardian angels, and their energy is everywhere! So regardless of where you are, I can give you an accurate reading!"

Spirit guides and guardian angels—if only she had one of them. Mel instantly thinks of her mother wearing a pair of angel wings and floating above her. Her face is recalled only from photos; the real one is blurred by time. When did she last see a picture of her mother? Where has her father hidden them? "Sounds good to me."

"I also happen to be clairaudient and clairsentient, which means I'm super well suited to doing telephone readings!"

"You lost me, Chess." Mel puts her cold feet over the heat register pushing up warm air from the furnace in the basement. The sweet smell wafts up from the duct. Her purple leopard-print socks have holes at the heels.

He laughs. "Clairaudient means that I can hear things from the other side and clairsentient means that I can feel things!"

"Okay, then. The other side of what? Town?"

An indulgent chuckle—Mel is a clever child. "No! The other side of existence!"

"Gotcha. So, what's next?"

"That depends on you! I can give you two minutes of free advice and after that I'm going to need a credit card or recorded permission to bill this phone number!"

"Okay. I'll start with that. Tell me what you hear or sense about my life."

"W-e-l-l-l-l-l!" Chess says, drawing the word out, because he's either thinking hard or trying to use up her two minutes of free psychic advice. "I can feel that there's a great deal of negative energy in your life right now! And that energy is centered between your shoulder blades."

"You got that right," Mel says, imagining Ben stabbing her in the back with a pen. "But I wouldn't be calling a psychic if my life was awesome, right?"

"True!" Mel swears she can hear the clicking of a keyboard in the background. Or is that the aging furnace below her? Maybe it's the house, buckling under the weight of her father's thousands of belongings.

"I sense you're having some issues with your parents! Are they elderly?"

"Maybe," Mel says, impressed. But it's probably common for people to have this type of problem.

"You're in school, aren't you?"

"Could be."

"Life isn't fair for you as a woman. You'd like to get back at someone who's wronged you."

"Possibly." Too close to be legit, Mel thinks. How difficult is it to reverse-lookup her number then google her name? "Are you reading my blog?"

"Of course not! I don't know what you're talking about!"

"Then what's my name?" she asks.

"It's Mel . . . anie?"

"Right. Listen, Chess, if that's your real name, let's cut to the chase, Chess. What do I do to make my life better?"

"Whatever you have to. You have to do what's right for you before anything else.'"

Is that what you're doing, Chess? Mel almost asks. Is this how you imagined your life would play out, enclosed in a plastic cubicle—an adult-size playpen—figuring out what people want to hear and giving it to them with an audible smile? "I don't know how to do that."

"Yes you do."

Melody hangs up, guessing she's reached the end of her two free minutes. She empties her mug of milk and honey in the sink, which, as usual, is already filled with other dishes and pots. She will not wash them or put them in the dishwasher. In the bathroom, she takes two PM aspirin, knowing they'll make her a zombie in the morning. Back in bed, her mind drifts across the border into dreamland when a knock on her window startles her. She peeks past the blankets and sees a hand emerge from a gray jacket to knock on the glass again. Would a burglar knock?

Melody rises to look out her window. A current of terror travels up her spine at the sight of a gray-robed ghost standing on the other side.

24

"Professor Pater?" Mel asks. Happiness at seeing her former mentor fills her—if he's back, then he can offer her good counsel on how to proceed with her revenge against Ben. "What are you doing here?"

Abe pushes the hood of his gray coat off his head. His skin is the color of the moon. "There is something threatening eruption that you needs must know. You have been borne in hand, abus'd, and griev'd."

Mel looks at the alarm clock on her bedside table but can't decipher the numbers. "That sounds about right. We should meet in your old office and talk about it. You can kick Ben out."

"It's too dangerous for us to be seen together. We must not be coted but must keep close." Abe looks around as though suspecting he's being surveilled. He smooths back his hair, which is out of its usual ponytail. A large twig emerges from the back of his head and arcs out over his left ear. Several leaves intertwine with the long gray strands. And now he's wearing a beard dyed pink at the end like Dimebag Darrell's, the murdered guitarist for Pantera, Drake's favorite band.

"Dangerous how?"

"Psychologically." He nods knowingly.

Mel squints one eye, hoping this will help her make sense of what Abe is saying. When this doesn't work, she squints the other one. Professor Pater doesn't comment on the oscillation of shuttered eyes. "Not pickin' up what you're layin' down," she says in a country drawl.

He shushes her then looks behind him. "Be not credent of former friends who are co-leagued now in their cautel."

"What the what?'

"Tina and Ben are in cahoots. They plotted to have me killed off from the department on trumped-up charges. Tina used her connections in administration to push it through, while Ben was her go-to guy." Abe's manner is now remarkably similar to Jerry Orbach's from her father's favorite TV show, *Law & Order*.

Mel imagines herself as Ed Green, Orbach's partner. "It fits. But what am I supposed to do about it? I got other open cases to investigate, a book to revise, and a committee to put together."

"I can avouch it. You know it, too; 'tis not fantasy. You must take any occasion to watch them together. Be familiar and vulgar. See if they are the same to each other."

"'Course they are. She anointed him king." Mel grimaces and shrinks her head into her shoulders. She is Caliban on a miserable island surrounded by her father's collection of castaway belongings. "Benjamin the Great," she says, in a monster's voice.

"She did? Why didn't she pick you? Did you submit your book?" Abe looks and sounds as though he's about to cry.

"Sure did. But it was stale and antic."

"That's too bad." Abe's expression of condolence quickly alters to one of cunning. "But be not vailed, my unvalued friend. This only means you have a grudge against them both and that makes us rivals."

Mel stares blankly at Abe.

"Spy on their unrighteous crimes," he clarifies. "Send me a harbinger when you have impartment to approve."

"A who?"

"A signal of sorts. When you know something."

Mel now stands in the backyard, where she's tending a fire. She waves a blanket over it as she recalls learning certain Native American tribes may have done to communicate across long distances. But who knows how accurate any of her elementary school education was on this topic? They stopped teaching anything about Indigenous peoples in America beyond second or third grade, when they butchered the story of Thanksgiving.

Then she's back in her bedroom, watching Abe slink away from the window. "When we discover our enemies, we will not wear a brow of woe or be sick at heart but instead be galled! In fine, we shall bruit their unproportioned marriage to the body. And then general censure shall make the condolement only theirs." He reaches the road in front of Mel's father's house and runs away, far more quickly than Mel would have thought possible for a man of his age and apparent lack of fitness.

The sound of a man's and a woman's laughter and the aroma of cake end Mel's lucid dream. Her last thought before the eclipse of heavy sleep occurs is to wonder if it's her birthday.

25

The next morning, Mel stops at the red light before the intersection where Route 12 turns into Upper Front Street, which leads to the exit to Route 81. The heat in her car is on full blast, but only cold air emerges from the vents. The road is dusted with salt, turning it the color of driftwood. Mounds of dirty snow shrink down on themselves along Front Street's shoulders. Mel's thoughts are preoccupied by her dream of Professor Pater visiting her in the middle of the night. It had felt so real and yet impossibly odd. Most likely this was thanks to the two PM aspirin she took. But still, what could it mean? She read somewhere that the trick to understanding dreams was to analyze the emotions felt as they occurred, and not the bizarre images and scenes the brain created to accompany the feelings being processed. If that's the case, what she felt during her dream was relief at having an ally. Finally, someone in the form of Professor Pater, her beloved mentor, was on her side and saw things the way she did. She wasn't alone.

The clock on her car radio hasn't changed its mind about the fact that she's running late. Her thoughts travel to breaking up with Drake. He was the one bright spot in her life, there to console her and listen to her vent. But what right did she have to use him as her personal therapist? Or her means of securing local employment after graduating?

Bleary from a lack of sleep, she glares at the dark-green Chevy sedan in front of her at the light. The driver has been traveling five miles below the speed limit since Melody turned onto Route 12. Its bumper sticker reads "Beam me up, God." Is this some type of death wish? Small, colorful stuffed animals stare at Mel through the rear window of the Chevy: Beanie Babies, My Little Ponies, and a few gnomes in a rainbow of colors, reminding Mel of fish behind glass in a crowded saltwater aquarium. Or is Mel behind the glass and the stuffed animals are staring at her? When the light turns green, the sedan moves forward only to stop short when a truck pulls onto Front Street ahead of it. The stuffed animals shift. A purple My Little Pony forces itself forward. Its mouth opens wide. "Save me," it begs.

Mel closes her eyes. When she opens them, she slams on her brakes, but it's too late and she thumps the back of the other car. She catches the stunned eyes of its driver through the woman's rearview mirror and mouths "I'm so sorry" at her.

She follows the green Chevy into the empty parking lot of Humdinger's ice cream, where she gets out to survey the damage to both cars. A hand-sized square of metal protrudes from the Chevy's bumper, like an emerging tooth in a teething baby's mouth. The other driver, a middle-aged woman wearing baggy gray pants and a brown aviator jacket, takes in the damage with both hands on her head.

"What were you thinking? Weren't you paying attention?" she says.

"Your stuffed animals distracted me."

"That's no excuse. I bet you were on your phone, texting."

"I don't have a smartphone," Mel lies.

"So?" The woman removes her hands from her head. Her hairstyle reminds Mel of an older Frank Sinatra.

"You can't text unless you have one."

The woman gives her a skeptical look. "Whatever. Now your insurance can fix my car."

Mel nods, while feeling herself stiffen at the woman's derisive tone and the assumptions she's making about her. "I don't understand why you randomly stopped a second time after that truck turned onto Front Street. Or why you were going so slow to begin with."

"I follow the law, and if you'd done the same and not rode my ass the whole way down Route 12, we wouldn't be in this pickle."

"How are you 'following the law' driving forty the whole way when the speed limit is forty-five? Would it kill you to drive a little over the speed limit?"

"Maybe it would," the woman says as if this is a real possibility.

Mel notices a wet stain engulfing the front of the woman's thighs. "What's that all over your pants?"

She looks away. "I spilled my coffee."

"Ah-ha," Mel says, pouncing on a possible way out of this mess. She points a finger at the woman. "That's what made you stop short the second time." She glares at her, Perry Mason catching a witness in a lie. "Are you sure you want to get the police and our insurance involved?"

"'Course I do," the woman says. She stares longingly at Humdinger's, as though an early morning cone would improve her day, but the ice cream shop is closed for the season. A sharp breeze whips up a crumpled white paper bag along with dried brown leaves. Mel pulls her coat closer around her.

"Do you want a police officer to see all those stuffed animals blocking your rear window? You know that's illegal." Mel doesn't know if this is true. Had she seen one move and mouth actual words? She shudders. She must have fallen asleep at the wheel, which has never happened before, though god knows she hasn't been sleeping well since moving back in with her father. Or, worse, did she hallucinate? What if she's going crazy? Would she wonder about it if she was?

"Leave my babies out of it."

"Babies?" A flush warms Mel's face. She's tired, and will have to call Kelly and cancel her class because of the accident. The woman's face is pursed around the mouth like a rotting peach. "You're a damned grown-up. Don't you think it's time you put your stuffed animal away?"

When Mel hears herself using the singular form of "animal," she realizes her comment is meant for her father and his stuffed bear.

The woman rubs her cheek as though trying to remove a stain. She appraises her car with the bitter disappointment of someone discovering that the scratch-off card they thought was a winner isn't. "Oh, never mind," she says. "Some days it's not worth getting out of bed." With that, she climbs into her vehicle and drives off. Mel watches the car until it disappears. She sits in her Sentra, whose front bumper has a corresponding dent in it, and heads to VU. Her misery is Ebola-like. Yet there's also relief that this situation hadn't turned out worse. She's lucky her rhetorical skills helped her talk her way out of it.

When she arrives on campus, Mel heads for the English department library. Still thinking about her dream, and now on edge thanks to the accident and the unpleasant encounter that followed, she pauses to clear her head while scanning the extensive shelving system. When she catches sight of *Hamlet*, she stops. It sits next to an enormous *Riverside Shakespeare*, a copy of which resides in her library from when she took Professor Pollon's class. This *Hamlet* edition is an older paperback, fraying at the edges. Its cover features a blond Hamlet clutching a cross to his chest, dressed in dour black with a white collar, with an ethereal Ophelia in the background staring at something in the distance. Mel looks around to make sure no one can see her before tucking the copy into her messenger bag.

As she's leaving, a stack of familiar hardcovers hidden on a low shelf behind one of the chairs near the entrance catches Mel's eye. In particular, the title of one brings her to an abrupt halt: *Surrounded by Idiots*. What are Ben's discarded self-help books doing in an academic library? The other hardcovers are also here. She takes *Surrounded by Idiots* off the shelf and reads the marginal comments, which now fill her with resentment. There are asterisks and underlining, phrases like "cool idea" and "good thinking," the types of comments she would have appreciated receiving on her novel, along with helpful criticism. Mel looks through the other books and finds Ben's handwriting in every one. She sets her messenger bag down on the chair to retrieve the thin stack of her novel from the bottom, where she'd crammed it to soak up the ink spill. A black Rorschach blotch that could be either a bat in flight or a malformed heart stains the pages. She flips it open to a longish handwritten note at the end of a page to confirm what she already knows: that this collection of self-help books definitely belongs to her archenemy.

Now, given all that's passed since her first encounter with these books, her interpretation of why King Ben would read them has been altered. Maybe his life before VU wasn't as successful as he's hinted. But Mel Two wonders something else. What if Ben is more Machiavellian than that? Hasn't he managed to avoid teaching composition for the past four years? Didn't he end up with Abe's office and the fellowship after inserting himself into Tina's coterie? Wasn't Mel the idiot he surrounded himself with to chauffeur him everywhere, feed him countless meals, and help him with his creative and literary work?

Mel grabs one of the books and leaves. In a bathroom down the hall, she takes out the copy of *Hamlet* and decides to prop it up against Ben's classroom door—a small gesture but one that might unnerve him if he has any familiarity with the play and its themes of deception and corruption. But in case this is too subtle for him, she'll need something bigger to expose him for who he really is.

Mel rests the copy of *Surrounded by Idiots* on the edge of the sink and writes "Ben Howe thinks he's . . ." above the title. She uses her left hand to ensure the handwriting doesn't look like hers. If she had a trench coat and a tweed trilby hat, she'd pretend to be Inspector Clouseau. Henry Mancini's *Pink Panther* theme plays in her head as she exits the bathroom. The hall is empty. Mel props the self-help book against Ben's office door before walking upstairs to do the same with *Hamlet* at his classroom door. Now he'll know someone is on to him.

26

Several days later and there's no word whether or not Mel's minor attempt at revenge against Ben has had any impact. She can only imagine him finding the books and wondering who dislikes him enough to leave them and what message they are trying to send. Now Mel sits with two other women behind a table in a large room located in VU's University Union building. It's 8:00 a.m. on a Tuesday, a day when she doesn't teach. She yawns and rubs her eyes, trying to clear away the perpetual brain fog she suffers from every morning she wakes up at her father's home. Mel has been invited by a former student to moderate this panel at VU's Women in Leadership conference. The rows of chairs before her are sparsely occupied by young women sipping from coffee cups while dressed in their pajamas and winter coats. Mel agreed to participate at this ungodly hour on a day when she could have stayed at home because she needs something service oriented to add to her CV. She figured she would show up, keep the conversation moving through any lulls, improvise her responses to whatever questions the audience asked, and call it a day.

The other two women have laptops open in front of them, and both appear to be reviewing extensive notes on the questions they were sent by the leadership committee prior to the event. Melody had ignored this email. The brilliant purple shirt worn by Professor Gail Swinden hurts her tired eyes and makes the woman's mashed-potato-colored skin look even paler. The other participant, Professor Maria Gammatopoulos, wears her hair pulled back in a severe ballerina bun. They sit at ease chatting with each other. Both are full professors.

When Mel arrived, she'd said hello to the two other panelists, then sat down beside them and stared out at the audience, wondering how she arrived at VU and at this room, because she had no recollection of the drive to campus or the walk from the parking lot. She'd woken up late to the sound of her alarm, in the middle of a lucid dream that featured a tarantula farm she owned that she was trying to sell. Even now, what little she recalls of the dream distresses her. There was a sense of hopelessness to it because who in their right mind would want to buy her tarantula farm? She was going to be stuck with the damn thing forever.

Mel's former student, Clarissa, approaches the table, smiling and holding a clipboard. "Good morning, professors! I'm so glad you could make it! Thanks so much! This means a lot to the committee and everyone who came." She gestures toward the small audience, most of whom look as if they've just emerged from lengthy comas. "I'm going to introduce you and then hand it off to Professor Hollings. Is that okay?" Melody doesn't correct Clarissa's misunderstanding of her title because she appreciates her student not calling her "Mrs."

Clarissa turns toward the audience. "Good morning, everyone! Welcome to the Women in Leadership panel." She looks down at her clipboard and reads from the bios the panelists provided. Mel scolds herself internally, wishing she'd made more of an effort to submit an up-to-date and grander-sounding one for herself as the moderator. The two professors' introductions are lengthy, with detailed information on their various degrees from prestigious universities, multiple publications which include actual books, the awards they've received and professional organizations they lead. "And last but not least, our moderator, Melody Hollings, is a graduate student here at VU, where she also received her master's and bachelor's degrees." Mel grins in what she hopes is a welcoming way but is certain is more maniacal than friendly. "Professor Hollings has had some short stories published at literary magazines. And she teaches first-year writing." Clarissa, brought up short by the lack of information, turns to her former instructor, a sailor on a sinking ship looking for guidance from her captain. Mel shrugs.

The discussion begins with Mel asking the first question Clarissa has provided. On several occasions she opens her mouth to volunteer her own answers as well but is beaten to it by one of the other panelists, leaving her looking like a baby bird waiting to be fed. There are many questions Mel is incapable of answering, such as how she got her job, how she achieved tenure, and what it's like working in her department as a professor, all of which conspire to make her feel more microscopic. Why is she the moderator? Why does she even exist? Who is she and what is her name?

Professor Swinden instructs the audience to close their eyes, though Mel feels this may cause them to fall asleep. "Picture a professor. What do you see?"

"An old guy. Definitely white," a young woman calls out.

"Wearing a tweed jacket with elbow patches," another says, to laughter.

"He's smoking a pipe in front of a fire, with an Irish setter at his feet."

"His glasses are held together with tape and his breath is kickin' 'cause he smokes!"

"All right, all right. Take it easy. We get it," Professor Swinden says, trying to restore order. "Now open your eyes." She pauses as she gathers their attention. "I'm the only female professor in the business administration department. There's not a single doctorate in my family. In fact, most of my family has only bachelor's degrees." She says this proudly.

Professor Gammatopoulos nods appreciatively and chimes in. "My own parents were born in Greece during the Second World War and barely completed the fifth grade. I'm the only person in my family to graduate from high school let alone receive a doctorate." She looks at Professor Swinden with an expression that says, "Top that."

The young women in the audience turn their expectant gazes on Mel. This is her chance. The two panelists also pivot toward her, finally giving her an opportunity to speak, certain she can never surpass them in competition over "life challenges to overcome on the way to a professorship."

"My mother dropped out of middle school to have me," Mel lies. Surprise on several young women's faces spurs her on. "My father has an IQ of eighty-five." This last part, given his recent diagnosis, may one day be true. "I'm the first person in my family who can read."

The two professors look at her with disbelief but are too polite to challenge her.

Mel sits back pleased with her small victory. Why bother with the truth when it gets you nowhere, she thinks? Look at Ben. What lies did he tell to get everything he wanted?

The panel moves on to the question-and-answer portion. A young woman in the back, wearing thick black glasses, stands up to ask a question. "I was thinking of going to graduate school in the humanities and was wondering what kind of advice you could give me."

Mel begins talking before the other panelists have a chance to answer. "Don't do it, is my advice! Kidding. Sort of. Just expect to work with a lot of cutthroat people who are looking to stab you in the back so they can succeed. Then, top that off with how hard it is to find a job after you graduate. In other words, it's a goddamn picnic."

Mel stares fixedly at the young woman as she slides back down into her seat with fear on her face. Out of the corner of her eye, she sees Professor Gammatopoulos's hand reaching for the microphone, but she holds it tightly to her lips.

"I think I'm the best one here to answer that question since I'm in the trenches, trying to survive the war, bayonet in hand, ready to storm the enemy's bunker," Mel says, her free hand thrusting forward in a stabbing motion. "But here's the longer answer to the wonderful question asked by the lovely young lady who seems to be hiding right now."

Mel rises from her seat, holding the microphone. She feels the gaze of the two professors follow her as she moves to stand in front of the table. With a hand over her heart, she begins, "I don't regret going to graduate school for one minute because it changed who I thought I was. You have to understand, with my family background"—she clears her throat to cover the awkward pause as she remembers what she told them about her mother and father—"making a living has always been more of a priority than becoming educated. Except I wanted to write and have a career, not just a job, so after graduating with my bachelor's degree and working for years doing something I hated, I quit and went back to school. Sure, the past six years have had their ups and downs, recently more of the latter, which I won't get into here because it's not an appropriate venue, but that doesn't change the most important thing." Mel waits several beats, nods with each one, slips on an impassioned expression: she's Pat O'Brien giving his Knute Rockne speech. "Which is that one good day of writing is more fulfilling than years of doing a job you hate." She gives her audience a few moments to let these golden drops of wisdom penetrate. Mel tries to recall what this feeling she's described is like, but instead a void stares back at her. She drops the microphone on the table and puts her hands up in a gesture that says, "My work here is done!"

"What about getting a job after you graduate from grad school?" an audience member calls out.

Mel snatches the microphone before Professor Swinden can reach it. "They're creating too many of us, my friends, because we're cheap labor teaching undergrads. Then they punt us out into the world to fight over a limited number of tenure-track positions." Mel kicks an invisible soccer ball across the room. "We're a huge school of piranha, swimming after a teeny-tiny school of fish," she says, making her voice babyish on these last five words, "by which of course I mean assistant professor jobs instead of the crappy 'instructor' or 'lecturer' adjuncting ones that have no security or benefits, and pay for shit. I'm going to have a PhD, for chrissakes, and several years of teaching experience under my belt by the time I graduate, plenty of publications, but more than likely I'll be living at the poverty level, without health insurance, cobbling together as many adjuncting gigs as I can at colleges hours away from each other just to pay my bills and student loans." Mel takes a deep breath and wipes the sweat off her upper lip with a finger. She senses the moisture in her armpits and wonders how the audience would respond if she flapped her arms to dry them out. "Do you have any idea how many PhDs are on food stamps nowadays?" Mel makes her face resemble a disgruntled baboon's. "Is it any wonder that we sometimes turn on each other?"

She stares out at the audience, takes in their shocked glances. Good, she thinks. At least they know the truth now. Pleased with her performance, Mel sits down, leans back, and lets the professors take over the discussion, abandoning her role as moderator.

As the meeting wraps up, the school's photographer appears before the panel members to take a picture that captures the moment. Mel grins widely, open-mouthed, the way celebrities do, and as far from her usual close-mouthed smirk as she can get, in an effort to become someone else, anyone else, because who she is is a failure. But maybe this smile is inappropriate given the depressing news she's imparted to the audience. She sinks her face into a more somber expression, but it's too late. The photo is taken mid-grimace.

When the panel wraps up, Mel races out before having to talk to the two professors or Clarissa, her former student.

Later that day, Mel arrives at Professor Gibson's women's literature graduate class, which she's auditing. It's held in the same room as the C-Unit meeting she attended before the semester started. She takes a seat at the far end of the room to watch everyone and avoid turning her back on the skull painting. Professor Gibson enters the room and the class begins. Only a few weeks into the spring semester, it has already turned into a theory-heavy slugfest. Manfred is in full pontificating mode over something he finds "problematic" in a Joyce Carol Oates story. He doesn't talk but espouses and orates in a breathy voice with pauses in strange spots as though he's in love with commas. The names Foucault, Derrida, and Lacan are inserted into his commentary, which instantly causes Melody's mind to veer into a daydream about these three heavyweights in literary criticism standing behind Manfred arguing among themselves over who's smartest.

Professor Gibson listens to Manfred with a look of patient kindness on her tanned but wrinkled face. Gibson has a reputation for going out of her way to help English literature graduate students, reading the papers they're trying to publish, critiquing curricula vitae, cover letters, and statements of teaching philosophy. But how is she with creative writing students? Melody imagines sitting on Professor Gibson's lap like an enormous baby and being rocked to sleep.

"Jesus," Mel mutters to herself, closing her eyes to banish this image.

"Excuse me?" Manfred breathes in her direction.

Her eyes fly open. He glares at her as though she questioned his knowledge of postcolonial theory. Mel is sure her being a creative writing major combined with her occasional theory-free comments in class have made her as worthy of respect in his eyes as a high school student.

"Sorry. Just remembered I forgot my oven's on," she says.

He looks at her skeptically before picking up where he left off.

Mel's glance travels across the faces of her classmates as they ponder, disagree, or agree with Manfred's lecture. White-Leather Winston, a self-styled contrarian, pushes up the sleeves of his too small leather jacket and wades into the argument. Others join in as Manfred smirks in proud amusement over the heated debate he's triggered.

When the class ends, everyone rises to leave. If Mel shows Professor Gibson Ben's comments, will she take pity on her and sign on to be part of her committee, or the chair, although it's last minute and she's probably already on so many others? "Chick lit!" Ben had written in one spot, a damning phrase applied to fiction written by women whenever relationships or families are themes. But that's never a problem when a male writer takes on these topics. Melody had read a recent interview with a big-time agent who wondered why, even today, male authors are praised for writing novels about families but when a woman does it, her work is called chick lit or domestic writing.

She approaches Professor Gibson before leaving the classroom. "Professor, I was wondering if I could talk to you about something?"

"Of course, Melody. And call me Katherine."

They head over to Katherine's office, taking one of the back staircases down to the English department hallway. Once behind a closed door in Professor Gibson's office, Mel takes a seat across from the older woman and tells an edited version of her story, alluding to Ben without saying his name and only hinting at the extent of his comments, making the loss of Abe the primary issue. Even now, she finds herself protecting Ben, though she's also protecting herself should any of her efforts at revenge be discovered and attributed to her.

Professor Gibson sits back in her chair with a troubled look. "It is a bit last minute for me to become your chair, especially since I haven't seen previous drafts of your work. But I can understand how Professor Pater's absence has created this issue. Still, you should have come to me earlier."

"You're right, I should have months ago." Instead of being preoccupied with the expectation of getting her novel back from Ben, she should have been putting her committee together. But then her father's situation and her fear that any literature professors she asked would hate her writing had paralyzed her. She has Ben to thank for this last part as well.

"Tell you what. I'll do it. Send me your manuscript and I'll read it as fast as I can. That should give you a few weeks to revise it before your defense."

Mel is filled with a strong desire to sit at Professor Gibson's feet and have her stroke her hair. "I'll do that, and thank you so much!"

"Why don't you talk to Professors Zeigler and Russell? I'm sure they'd be happy to serve on your committee."

"Professor Russell's already on it, but I'll talk to Professor Zeigler. So that makes three, including you. Who could I ask for my fourth?"

"Let me think about that and I'll get back to you. Sig might have time."

"I don't have much luck getting in touch with Professor Pollon."

"I'll ask him for you."

The relief Mel feels at hearing these words brings tears to her eyes. Someone in real life is on her side.

At the end of the week, she sees the photo from the Women in Leadership panel in the school newspaper and, as she feared, the photographer had captured the precise moment when Mel most resembled Baby Jane Hudson—eyebrows arched so high her forehead is halved, mouth open to show all her teeth, though not in a smile. But this isn't the worst of it. While the two other women's front yards are neatly landscaped and tastefully decorated, Mel's is like her father's. The two top buttons of her shirt must have popped open during her crazed speech, before the picture was taken. Fortunately, her beige bra prevented her from being indecently exposed. The caption reads, "Professor Gives Impassioned Speech on the True State of Graduate School." At least they called her a professor.

27

Before leaving for her Friday morning class, Mel sits at the kitchen table eating a bowl of Lucky Charms, her father's second-favorite cereal, while browsing WBNG-TV's website on her laptop. Finally she finds the headline she's been looking for: "Police: Man Arrested for Shooting at Squirrels." It's datelined "Thursday, 3/15/07," followed by a brief article:

> BINGHAMTON. Officials lifted a lockdown for schools in the Chenango Forks district after shots were fired near the complex of buildings encompassing the elementary, middle, and high schools. Binghamton police responded before 9 a.m. Wednesday to a home on Maplewood Drive after receiving reports of an elderly white male firing a rifle at his roof. The police arrested Collin Hollings, 73. They recovered the .22 caliber rifle he allegedly used. According to police, Hollings had been shooting squirrels he believed had taken over his attic and were invading his home. Officials said Chenango Forks students were safe throughout the ordeal. Hollings, who is believed to suffer from dementia, may be charged with reckless endangerment, which is a felony.

The sickness Mel feels is like having a severe but headache-less hangover. She wishes she could call Drake and tell him about the latest episode in the Collin Hollings saga, but her vow not to use him as her counselor prevents her.

But at least what she feels now is better than the panic that nearly overwhelmed her when she received the phone call from Oji that her father had been arrested. He called Mel early on Wednesday, right in the middle of her morning class.

"Mel, you must come home right away. Your father has a gun. The police are here." The note of terror in Oji's voice was unmistakable.

Mel dismissed her students and raced to her car, imagining several awful scenarios. Just off campus, she took Murray Hill Road to go around VU and save some time but immediately came up behind a dark-gray Prius. Was there even a driver behind the wheel navigating this automotive turtle precisely ten miles below the thirty-five-mile-per-hour speed limit? Seeing an opportunity to pass, despite the double line separating the two lanes, Mel floored her Sentra and veered around the Prius, making sure to shoot the driver a scowl. But instantly she saw it was Professor Pollon and spastically rearranged her face into a friendly smile, waving as she sailed by.

When she arrived at her father's, three police cars were on the premises. His house, with its peeling paint and slush-gray exterior, looked especially seedy with law enforcement vehicles surrounding it. Mel had the disorienting feeling that she was stepping into an episode of *Cops*, a show her father insisted on watching even though she repeatedly pointed out to him how racist and classist it was. "I see what you're saying, kiddo," he'd answer. "Hadn't thought of it that way before. Good thing you're getting an education for the both of us." And then he'd go on watching. Though finally, after her repeated rebukes, she wore him down. "Thanks a lot for taking all the fun out of watching that damn show," he told her morosely.

Two of the police cars with lights noiselessly flashing sat parked in the driveway blocking in her father's car, with the third situated alongside the curb in front. Mel parked her own car hurriedly, noting later that it was on a diagonal on the front lawn. She quickly spotted her father's wild white hair in the police car parked curbside—not the ambulance that was also on-site—and exhaled in relief. He was in custody but not hurt.

"That's my father," she told the officer who tried to keep her from running over to him.

Another man approached her. He waved the officer away. His wide shoulders, combined with his short stature, reminded her of a silverback gorilla, but his eyes were kind. "Hello, miss. I'm Officer Donnolly. You say you're this gentleman's daughter?"

"Yes. That's my dad. Oh my god, where did he get a gun?"

"That's what we'd like to know since it's not registered."

"My dad's a hoarder," Mel explained. "You can go inside and see that for yourself."

Officer Donnolly nodded. "We've seen it. Do you live here with him?"

"God, no," she lied. "How could anyone live there? I don't even know how my dad does it." Mel's anxiety was further fueled by a burst of adrenaline caused by having to speak to a police officer. A torrent of sentences poured out of her. "He used to be cleaner, though granted, never a neat freak. Then I moved out, with my boyfriend, because, well, I mean, I couldn't live with my dad for the rest of my life. Being his housekeeper and cook and launderer. Of clothing, not money, because there is absolutely nothing illegal going on here, unless messiness is a crime. Which it should be, if you ask me." Mel considered stopping there, but the officer's blank stare made her even more nervous. "So, I'm a graduate student at VU, almost done with my PhD, which is awesome but hard. And it seemed about time for me to not live with my dad, because I'm getting older, you know. You can't stay with your parents forever, or in my case, parent, since my mom died when I was young. It wasn't murder or anything like that. Because my dad definitely didn't kill her. A deer did. I mean it didn't actually murder her, not with a knife or anything. It ran out in front of her car on 88. So she died in a car accident. You can probably read the report. Anyway, I'm not as young as I used to be. And it's been a downhill slide ever since. With my dad, I mean, though granted my life isn't great right now either. But that's a story in itself. Jesus. What am I supposed to do with him now?" She gestured toward her father.

Several moments of silence followed as Mel tried not to look at Officer Donnolly. It occurred to her that she would instantly confess to any crime she'd committed if she was ever interrogated. Or greeted in a kindly manner by an officer of the law.

"Well, I don't know exactly," he said, looking nonplussed. "But I know with the house being such a mess, someone your father's age shouldn't be living in it. Imagine if emergency personnel ever had to enter the premises, say, if he fell or had a heart attack."

"Believe me, I know. But every time I clear out parts of it, he brings new junk in. I have no idea where he finds the stuff since he's not supposed to be driving. I think he sneaks out when I'm teaching."

"I understand. But if it isn't cleaned up, I have to report the house and its condition to Adult Protective Services."

Mel glanced at Officer Donnolly's notepad, where all manner of incriminating things about her and her father were probably written, and considered how they'd gotten on the wrong track. Unless she took charge of the situation, who knows how much trouble her father would be in. She took a deep breath and adopted what she imagined was a lawyerly demeanor. "What are the charges, Officer?"

Donnolly explained the situation, pointing out Oji, who stood on his front porch talking to another police officer. She waved at him tentatively, and he smiled back, his expression tainted by guilt. So it was Oji who'd called the police on Mel's father when he'd refused to put away the gun. As the police officer continued explaining, Mel paid only partial attention because the sight of her father's neighbors, who were standing on their porches watching, attracted her notice. She did, however, hear the phrases "illegal discharge of a firearm" and "restricted area."

"Does your father suffer from Alzheimer's?" Officer Donnolly asked.

"Has my client . . . *father* received a clinical diagnosis of Alzheimer's?" Mel responded cagily, still in lawyer mode, using the tactic of asking a question in response to a question (as seen on *Law & Order*) to buy her time to come up with a good response that revealed little. She rocked back and forth on her feet with her hands shoved deep into her coat pockets and elbows sticking out in a "power pose," having recently watched a TED Talk on how posture conveys authority. She lowered her voice to make it sound more masculine, because according to an NPR piece she'd listened to, male spokespeople were viewed by the public as more effective in product advertisements.

"Not per se. But can we assume he suffers from some form of dementia? Perhaps."

Officer Donnolly watched her closely. "If you can provide me with documentation of some sort—"

"A doctor's signed note, notarized of course?"

"—that your father suffers from some sort of mental issue associated with his age, we might be able to reduce the charge from a felony to a misdemeanor."

"I'll see what I can do, Officer . . . that's Donnolly, correct?" Mel typed Donnolly's name into her phone with a flourish while silently mouthing the letters.

"Right," he said, giving her a wide-eyed stare. "By the way, is your father on any medications?"

"Just the usual ones an elderly male would take, for his blood pressure and prostate. I can show you them." She didn't mention the other pills Dr. Oberlin had put her father on.

"Are you sure that's it, because his speech was impaired when we arrived," Donnolly consulted his notes, "and his pupils seemed dilated."

"Are you saying he was drunk or high or something, because there's no way that's the case. My dad rarely drinks. Hell, he won't even take aspirin."

Donnolly nodded. "We'll still need to bring him down to the precinct to process him, but you can follow us and take him home after you pay his bail."

Never in a million years when her father added Mel's name to his bank accounts could she have imagined needing to withdraw funds for bail. "Can I talk to him right now?" Her concern that her father would have to be taken to the station in the back of a police car, fingerprinted and photographed for a mug shot, all parts of what she imagined being "processed" involved, eroded her act.

"Sure. Go ahead." Donnolly gestured toward the police officer standing beside the vehicle. As Mel approached, the officer opened the door but motioned for her father to remain seated.

"Howdy, kiddo," he said cheerfully. Her father was in his boxer shorts, a T-shirt, his green robe, and a pair of slippers. This is how he would appear at the police station.

"What the hell, Dad?"

He gives her an unrepentant scowl. "Damned squirrels. Don't you hear them in the attic at night? It's like a disco up there. They keep me up with their shenanigans."

"But a gun? I didn't know you had one in the house."

"Neither did I! Found it the other day when I was looking for rattraps in the garage."

"Do you remember where you bought it?"

"Nope. Probably been there for years from back when I took up hunting. I want to hang it up in the guest room, your room, to add to the rustic feel."

Mel grimaced. "Not happening. Besides, they're taking the gun away from you. You can't have an unregistered one, I think," she added, the legalities of gun ownership a mystery to her.

"That's stupid. Didn't used to be that way. Now government wants to get involved with everything you do. Pretty soon . . ."

"Dad, stop. You can't stand in your yard in this kind of neighborhood and start shooting at squirrels. This isn't the country, you know."

"I don't appreciate your tone, young lady. You don't talk to your father like that."

"I do when he does something as craz— . . . bizarre as this."

"Fine. I won't do it again. Satisfied?" He looked past her, at Oji standing on his porch. "That one," he said, gesturing with his chin in his neighbor's direction, an accusatory look on his face. "He's been in the house. Must have made another key when he had one. Officer, I want you to arrest that man on charges of breaking and entering and theft."

Mel looked at the police officer standing near them and gave him a small shake of her head. "Cut it out. Oji didn't break into the house or steal anything from you."

"Yeah? Well, where's my orange juice squeezer, huh? It's been gone for days. And I know he used to admire it. Said it was the fanciest one he'd ever seen."

"I threw it out because it doesn't work anymore. Don't you remember?"

"I could have fixed it." Her father turned away from her then, to stare through the grate separating the front and back seats of the police car. The conversation was over, according to him. "I'm cold," he said, motioning for her to shut the police car door.

Mel stared at her father's profile. His condition was far beyond having a home care attendant visiting him daily. Or even her living with him, because she couldn't be with him every moment of the day and teach. But what was the next step? Could she get him to move into an assisted living facility and give up his home? Or would there come a time when she'd have to force him to do it? The thought filled her with dread.

Mel pushes aside the empty bowl of cereal and closes her laptop. She wonders how much to tell her students about why she ended class early. Or whether she should share this article with her father, who is napping on the couch, his teddy bear tucked into the crook of his arm. Maybe it'll convince him that he needs more help than she can provide. She remembers his smiling face as he was processed at the police station, his joking with the officers as if this was nothing unusual. His mood had flipped from morose and angry at her to this forced cheerfulness. Mel contrasts this to the moment when no one could see them, when her father turned to her and whispered, "Help me."

28

A week later on a Friday night, after a long nap intended to help Melody catch up on several weeks' worth of disturbed sleep, she leaves her father's house to attend Professor Pollon's annual "March Madness" party. Every year, prior to the gathering, the English faculty spring-clean their personal and office libraries and transport the books they've culled to Pollon's house, where graduate students can pick through them. The party was first held years earlier by Pollon's ex-wife, the chair of the history department, and he now continues the tradition out of grudging habit. His frequent disappearances during the festivities are the subject of speculation ranging from meeting with his alien overlords to finding a prostitute to scoring marijuana to canoodling with his dog, Gertie.

Mel had gone back and forth about attending, partially out of fear of leaving her father alone. After bringing him home from the police station, she'd spent hours rummaging through boxes and bins, searching for firearms and throwing away as much of his general hoard as she thought she could get away with. There was even more she could get rid of in the basement, but Mel still refused to venture into that cavern of chaos. She preferred to keep pretending it didn't exist. Her father was probably retrieving items from down there to replace the ones she eliminated from the main floor.

Though she turned up no weapons, she did fill two large black garbage bags with papers, books, and magazines that either were out of date or reeked of mold. Rather than leaving these on the curb where they could draw her father's attention, she drove them down to Front Street late that night, where she hoisted them into a dumpster behind Lowe's.

In the end, she decided to attend Pollon's gathering because (a) he couldn't entirely disappear at his own party, which meant she'd have an opportunity to talk to him about a job for next year and ingratiate herself with him so he'd serve on her committee; (b) all of her attempts to ding Ben's ego seemed to have failed, as far as she knew, but maybe he'd mention one of them and give her the satisfaction of knowing he was aware that someone disliked him; (c) she wasn't going to give Ben the satisfaction of thinking she cared that he won the fellowship; and (d) she could fulfill Dream Abe's command to watch how Tina and Ben acted around each other. While Mel knows this Abe is a figment of her imagination fabricated from disordered sleep, he has a point.

Pollon's home on Drexel Drive is situated in a hilly area south of VU. The well-maintained neighborhood boasts spacious split-levels, ranches, and colonials, many of whose backyards adjoin undeveloped woods. This is the first time she'll see Ben since their dinner at Lost Dog Café, when he drank too much and left determined to win over Elaina. Mel had pumped Ben so full of bad advice and beer that he was bound to make a fool of himself. She'd convinced him to send several impassioned texts to his poet girlfriend about how beautiful she is before he showed up on her doorstep. Mel had hoped to learn the outcome of that, too, but they were barely speaking to each other, aside from the occasional text from him that she replied to cursorily.

Mel drives past a stand of bare bushes and brown ornamental grass in a landscaped bed on a corner lot. Emerging from the snow and sere foliage is what appears to be the hindquarters of either a large stuffed animal or a dead dog, whose beige fur closely matches the bleached stalks of grass. Her initial reaction is that she should stop, but a car tailgating her prevents it. Besides, how odd would she look getting out of her car to inspect a dead dog or a pile of garbage? It's also frigid out thanks to a spell of several below-zero nights in the area. What would she do with the body anyway? She's not in Chenango Forks, where she knows people and can ask them if their dog is missing or if they know whose it is. Though that's also a questionable prospect. Ever since the squirrel incident, her father's neighbors' once cautious politeness has now evolved into full-on stop-and-stare gossiping. At any moment, Mel imagines waking up to a scene straight out of the 1931 version of *Frankenstein* when the monster is caught at the windmill, but in her fantasy it's her father's neighbors massed in front of his house bearing torches and "For Sale by Owner" signs.

Driving past Pollon's house, she sees Ben entering with Elaina. Of course they're together because none of Mel's attempts at retribution have left a mark. Something protects Ben from being harmed. Or is it that her attempts are insufficient because she hasn't fully committed to revenge? Mel has heard nothing about him finding what she wrote under Sherry's lipstick print on his office hours sheet, which was replaced by a clean copy. The self-help book left propped against his door probably had no effect, like the bad GradeYourProfessor.com review she wrote, though she appreciated the few thumbs-up it garnered, which, if Ben saw them, would cause a twinge.

Scowling, Melody parks a few cars down and then tries to add to her masterpiece of a disgusted look by pursing her lips, which she imagines is how Marie Antoinette might respond if she was offered a boiled shoe for dinner. She flips down her shade with this expression frozen in place to tweak it to perfection in the mirror. Oscar walks past, offering her a tentative smile. Mel instantly puts her normal appearance back on and exits her car.

"Hey, Mel. You okay?"

"Fantastic. Never better."

With a theatrical flourish, she gestures for him to precede her up the narrow sidewalk. Inside Pollon's house, Oscar joins Cicely on the olive-green couch in the living room, while Mel collapses into an adjacent barrel chair. Her huddled posture, with coat bunched up around her ears, doesn't invite conversation. Oscar leaves them and returns, then wordlessly hands her a beer, for which she is tearfully grateful. Why can't more people be kind to each other, she wonders, taking a long sip from the bottle.

Mel surveys the guests—faculty and fellow grad students, many of whom she doesn't know now that she's finished her coursework. She wishes she were back at home, though it would mean spending more time with her father, who has been unnaturally quiet for the past few days. No, better if she could be at Drake's instead, where it's clean and odor free. Or a little place of her own, where no weird smells float up through the heating vents as though the house crouches on top of a landfill. The last time she saw Drake was when they met for an awkward lunch on campus. With her vow not to complain to him about anything going wrong in her life, Mel had much less to talk about with her former boyfriend/partner.

A loud voice attracts her attention. It's Annie from her C-Unit group, whose face looks especially tan. If she squints hard enough, Mel can morph Annie's head into an orange with a blond wig on it and a drawn-on mouth, eyes, and nose. She blinks hard several times to clear her vision, then drinks the rest of her beer in one long guzzle. Her gaze lands on Manfred and White-Leather Winston animatedly discussing something with another grad student. Most likely they're mocking the other guests for not understanding the differences between structuralism and poststructuralism. Mel imagines all three melding together to form a human Cerberus.

"By the way, Mel, I'm sorry about the fellowship," Oscar says, reaching out a comforting hand to pat her gray sweatpants-covered knee and interrupt her peculiar vision. She smiles at Oscar's consoling face. He's recently shaved off the lower half of his facial hair, leaving behind an unfortunate seventies-porn-star mustache.

She shrugs. "What is not meant to be, will not be," she says, in her best impression of Orson Welles.

A loud laugh prompts all three to turn around toward the adjacent dining room where Ben holds court. Tina rests a freckled hand possessively on his forearm and smiles up at him. The light from the chandelier above the table makes Ben's blond hair glow as if he's wearing a golden crown. His gaze lands on Mel and he gives her a tentative wave that she nods at. He puts his hand on Tina's fragile shoulder and squeezes gently. Elaina hands him a can of soda and clinks her wineglass to it. If only Imaginary Abe was here to see this.

"The patriarchy scores yet another victory," Cicely volunteers.

"With help from the matriarchy," Mel adds. "But what are you gonna do? Tina did encourage him to submit his novel." After their dinner at Lost Dog, Ben had forwarded Tina's email to Mel. In it she'd written that she "strongly recommended" he submit his novel to the fellowship selection committee (of which she was the chair) because of the quality of the work. Of course, this wasn't exactly how he'd put it when they met in person. He apologized again to Mel and swore he'd make it up to her by reading anything she gave him and putting in a good word on her behalf with Tina. As if she'd trust him to do the former or believed the latter would make a difference.

"So he's not as big a jerk as we think?" Oscar asks. Cicely looks as though she's giving this question some consideration but shakes her head and kicks the idea to the curb.

"Oh, no," Mel says, nodding confidently. "He's a dick of Empire State Building proportions."

They look at Mel with unblinking eyes.

"Right," Oscar says. "I'm hungry. Let's get something to eat." He rises from the couch.

Cicely scoots over to the space Oscar has vacated. Leaning toward Mel, a concerned look on her face, she says, "Are you okay? Because your last few blog posts have been . . . gloomy. I mean, they're enjoyable, and I love the new blog title, but they're not your usual amusing reflections."

Mel furrows her brow in thought, then furrows it some more. "My eyes have been opened and I'm telling it like it is for the females. I mean ladies. No, women."

Cicely nods. "And that's a good thing. But I'm worried about you." Mel shrugs to convey how blasé she is about everything. Cicely looks doubtful but rises to follow Oscar, while Mel remains seated, unwilling to face Ben up close. "Do you want anything?" Cicely asks.

To punch Ben in the face. To have Tina publicly denounce him as a liar and a fraud and give the fellowship to her, letting everyone know that she's the more worthy recipient. To have her father's dementia miraculously disappear. "No thanks. Have you seen Pollon?"

"Gertie's missing," Cicely tells her. She points her chin in the direction of a photo on a nearby bookcase.

The framed picture is of Pollon's Labradoodle and his ex-wife, who, rumor has it, left him decades earlier for the dean of one of VU's colleges. Mel rises to look more closely at the photo, taking in the dog's curly beige fur, noting the possessive hug Pollon's ex has Gertie wrapped up in. It's too much of a coincidence, Pollon's missing dog and the color of the dead dog in the bushes she'd driven past. Should she find him and tell him about it? Or if it is Gertie, would he forever associate her with the ill-tidings of his beloved pet's death?

When Ben and Elaina disappear down the hall into Pollon's home office, where empty liquor store boxes and stacks of books await the pillaging hands of greedy grad students, Mel visits the food on the dining table, the one positive of this party. She surveys the platters of cold cuts and cheeses, olives, pickles, pigs in blankets, and cocktail shrimp. There are also dishes brought by non-freeloading graduate students, vegan spreads of creamy hummus and carrots, some type of quinoa salad with red cranberries and broccoli giving it a Christmassy feel. Mel bypasses these healthier options to shove two pigs in blankets in her mouth at once, chewing them with blank-eyed apathy. She follows this with a hunk of some type of blue cheese, grimacing at the thick tang that runs down the back of her throat.

"What are your plans after graduation, Melanie?" Tina asks, surprising Mel as she chokes down a cracker to cleanse her palate of moldy cheese. Tina's glasses hang on for dear life on the end of her nose. Melody ignores the urge to push them back into place. The older woman's dark-pink lipstick looks as though she applied it while riding on the back of a four-wheeler traveling at high speed over a rutted trail.

Living with my demented father, acting as his housemaid, cook, chauffeur, and personal companion. Watching my writing ambitions die a slow, painful death. Being a composition adjunct for life. "No idea," Mel says.

"No luck at MLA?" Tina sips her wine. Pink lipstick smudges cover the rim of her glass, which she sets down on the table.

"Nope."

"Well, you know what they say. If at first you don't succeed..."

Fail, fail again. And apply for another seventy-five-plus jobs next year with degree in hand. "Yeah, I suppose."

"It'll happen, don't worry," she consoles Mel in her nasal Fran Drescher voice. "You're too strong a writer to give up."

"Thanks, Tina. That's so great of you to say," Mel tells her, noting how little it takes to make her feel grateful and willing to ignore that Tina got her name wrong. Perhaps glowing reviews of her writing ability had spread via faculty word of mouth. Surely Abe would have spoken about her before he left. And Tina was probably impressed by the novel she'd submitted for the fellowship, though it was in a drafty state. Now Mel pictures her hunched over a candlelit desk (why a candle, Mel doesn't know), both Ben's and her manuscripts in front of her, wringing her hands over which one to choose. "They're so close," Tina mutters, before resorting to "eeny, meeny, miny, moe," Of course, the good luck falls on Ben.

"Do you write fiction or poetry?" Tina asks.

Mel stares at her, allowing the reality to sink in that Tina has no idea who she is. She picks up the director's nearly full wineglass and drains it. But Tina continues smiling blandly.

"Fiction," Mel says. "I write fiction. Short stories. Novels. You know. Fiction. Prose. Not-poetry. Not nonfiction. And my name is not Melanie. It's Melody. Hollings." She stops herself from asking, Did you even read my book?

"Yes, fiction. That's right. I remember now." Tina's rhinoceros skin remains impervious to Mel's sarcasm. "Well, you keep persevering. It'll happen eventually."

"Thanks. That means ever so much to me." Mel assembles her mouth and teeth into a facsimile of a smile and walks away, still holding Tina's empty glass. In the kitchen, several liquor bottles lounge invitingly on a counter, offering Mel an opportunity to forget her troubles. Mel opens the first one—vodka—and fills the wineglass. She swallows several burning mouthfuls as a graduate student she hasn't met before watches. "What?" she asks him. He shakes his head and leaves the kitchen.

Mel heads back to the barrel chair in the living room with a beer from the fridge. Ben and Elaina emerge from the library. He motions for Elaina to hand over the box of books she's carrying, and she complies. Elaina kisses Ben quickly on the cheek, causing a glow of happiness to spread over his face.

Mel grimaces. Everything works out in Ben's favor while nothing does for her. How will justice be served if she doesn't up the ante with her revenge attempts? Stop being a coward, she tells herself, determinedly downing her beer and buttoning her coat, then striding unsteadily toward the front door. A plan of sorts, fueled by more alcohol than Mel is accustomed to, gels in her mind. There is something she can do to reduce Ben in front of his peers.

In the foyer, Pollon materializes in front of her. "Oh, hello," he says.

It's possible he emerged from the hall closet. This is her chance to tell him about his dog or beg him for a job. Mel weighs both options but anger at Ben wins.

"Forgot something in my car," she says, and a look of relief races across Pollon's face as she walks out of his house.

Mel heads toward the dog cadaver, zigzagging across the street and several yards. Her peripheral vision is compromised by her severe buzz. A few minutes later, she stoops behind the tall dead foliage to avoid being seen from the road, grateful she'd chosen to wear dark clothes she didn't care about, as if she'd been wearing anything else lately. Crouched in hiding, she's one of the soldiers on *Band of Brothers*, which she'd recently watched with her father. Prowling through enemy territory, she scans her surroundings to make sure there are no German soldiers training their sniper guns on her. She's the only woman to have been accepted in Easy Company, thanks to her stealth behind enemy lines. Sergeant Hollings prods the canine corpse with a gloved hand; it's as hard as a block of ice after days of frigid temperatures. Thank Athena. The tag on the dog's collar confirms it's Gertie. For a moment Mel feels a profound grief over the dog's passing. No creature should have to die in the cold, alone, at the side of a road.

Taking a deep breath to fuel her muscles and gird her determination, Mel lifts the dog's body, groaning at its weight as she straightens her legs, and nearly dropping it before regaining her balance. She shouldn't have drunk so much if she was going to do any heavy lifting.

When she stands upright, she realizes the full force of what she is going to do; she can never tell anyone about this. But it will be worth it if for once she can see Ben's perfect life take a hit. She staggers to a nearby evergreen bush, pausing behind it to catch her breath, refusing to look at the body and grateful for the gloves that prevent her from feeling Gertie's curly blond fur that's too similar to human hair. She continues her slog until she's hiding behind a car in a driveway across the street from Pollon's house. Ben's black Altima is parked on the other side of the road.

Mel puts the dog's body down and squats beside it as she considers her options. Make it look like Ben hit Gertie with his car? Place the body right in front of his new ride as though he didn't realize he'd run her over? What will damage Ben's reputation the most and topple him from his position on high? She looks at his brand-new car, shining in the light of the streetlamp, and it comes to her. She should place the corpse of Pollon's beloved Gertie in Ben's trunk. Most likely the car is unlocked since Ben doesn't have to worry about car theft in Binghamton. She can just open the front door and pull the trunk release. When the party winds down, Mel will leave with everyone. Ben will be the designated driver, given the soda he was drinking, and Mel can spread the word so that other guests ask him for rides and there won't be room for the boxes of books they've all acquired. The trunk will need to be opened.

"Jesus," someone will say.

"What the hell, Ben?" another will ask.

"I have no f-f-ucking idea," Ben will stutter.

"Isn't that Gertie?" someone will say, horrified.

"Holy fuck," Ben will say, and his ego, inflated throughout the party by all the congratulations he's received for winning the fellowship, finding an agent, and having his book accepted for publication by Graywolf, will sink like punched dough. He'll look around desperately, hoping for an explanation that makes sense and for allies among the witnesses.

Mel will feign a look of shock and bewilderment.

It's a beautiful scene to imagine. So damned perfect and sure to destroy Ben's carefully constructed persona. The problem is, what if no one believes Ben would do this? What if he somehow comes out of this as the victim of yet another practical joke and a determined effort is made to discover the culprit behind it? Knowing Ben's luck, this is exactly what would happen. And all of Mel's plotting would boomerang back to hit her.

"What are you doing out here?"

Mel lets out a small scream. Professor Pollon stands on the other side of his neighbor's car. "Jesus Christ Almighty Mother of God," Mel exclaims, falling back on her butt. She was so wrapped up in her fantasy of revenge that she didn't hear him approach. Her hand goes to her heart, like Fred Sanford calling to his wife, Elizabeth, and she imagines what it's like to be startled into a minor heart attack.

Pollon walks around the front of the vehicle but comes to a cartoonish abrupt stop when he sees the dog's body. "Is that . . . Gertie?"

Mel slowly rises from squatting by the car and puts a hand on the vehicle's rearview mirror to steady herself. She goads her buzzed brain into saying something reasonable. Mel bends down and places two fingers on Gertie's neck, searching for a pulse the way she's seen TV paramedics do. "I was checking to see if she was alive." Maybe she should attempt CPR. She measures Pollon's stunned expression. Adrenaline-fueled fear sobers her up enough to decide this is not a good option. Besides, it's evident from the stillness of the body that Gertie has gone on to the Great Beyond.

"Is that dog hair on your coat?" Pollon gestures toward Mel's torso.

Futilely, she tries to tamp down her panic while brushing the hair off. "Yeah. I saw her on the side of the road when I drove in." She gestures vaguely in the direction of where she first spotted Gertie's body.

"And you carried her here?"

"Um, I suppose it would have made more sense to have brought you to her. But I'm not gonna lie, I've had a couple drinks." Mel puts her hands out and sways as though she's on a ship during a storm.

"I guess I appreciate your bringing Gertie's demise to my attention."

"I'm really sorry. I know how much she meant to you." She takes in the dog cadaver, and hopes that Gertie's last moments weren't agonizing. Did she somehow escape the house and get run over? Mel thinks of the deer that ran into the highway in front of her mother's car but doesn't allow herself to contemplate her mother's last moments. Choking back an audible sob, she says, "Do you need help bringing her the rest of the way home?"

"No, that's okay. You go back to the party. I can take it from here."

Mel is profoundly grateful—both for being relieved of the burden and for not getting caught in carrying out her plan. Pollon is being so reasonable and kind in the face of such a bizarre sight. What has he experienced during his tenure as chair of the English department to make him so unmoved by this situation? He stares down at the dog with a strange expression. Mel heads back to the house, but after a moment, she turns to look one last time at the scene of her almost-crime. She freezes. Pollon is doing what appears to be an awkward rendition of a pop and lock dance next to the body. Confused, she whips back around to avoid witnessing this private moment.

Inside Pollon's house, she heads straight for the alcohol in the kitchen, where she finds Oscar.

"Hey," she says, taking off her gloves and shoving them into her coat pocket. Telltale curly blond hairs cling to them and her coat, which she quickly removes so Oscar won't see them. She washes her hands in the sink.

"What's up?" he says, before burying his head back in the fridge. "You want a beer?"

She stares at his back, working to compose herself and craft a response. What would a normal person who hasn't just done what she's done say to Oscar's question? "I could definitely be persuaded to take one off your hands, my good sir," she says, clutching the beer he passes to her. Mel realizes her hand is shaking. She tightens her grip around the bottle to hide it.

Oscar clinks his beer with hers and they both take a long drink. He clears his throat. "I read some of your stories, the ones online. And loved them. You're great, Mel. I wanted you to know that. Because you shouldn't feel bad about losing that fellowship. It was totally unfair for Ben to win."

"That is so nice of you," Mel says, tears springing to her eyes. "You don't know how much I needed to hear that right now." Oscar is the best. Such a nice man. Cicely is lucky.

He nods sympathetically. "And I'm sorry you and Drake didn't work out. Cicely said you two broke up."

"Yeah, romance is not in the cards for me at the moment." Mel pretends to fan out a deck of playing cards with one hand. She takes another deep drink from her beer, which is surprisingly almost empty. She looks sadly at the bottle. Beer can be quite tasty at times, especially after the first few, some wine, and a glass of vodka. She throws the empty bottle into a garbage can before grabbing another full one from the fridge. At this point, the only thing she can do is drown her embarrassment over Pollon finding her with his dead dog in a great deal of alcohol.

In the living room, Mel joins Oscar and Cicely next to a large bookcase. She gives the young man sitting in her barrel chair the evil eye, but he refuses to vacate his seat. For the next few hours, she keeps a calm, unexcited smile on her face, inserting herself into random conversations, steadily drinking beer. But thankfully, Pollon never reappears. She watches too many guests congratulate Ben as he inhales their good wishes like a supermodel absorbing compliments.

He's the guest of honor, and she imagines this won't be the last time he'll be in this position. It should have been her.

She has carefully navigated her way back to the food table when Ben approaches her, a sheepish look on his face. "Hey, Mel. How's it going?"

"Fine. How you?" She wobbles and places her hands on her hips, trying to stand straight in front of her nemesis. She would never have thought she'd have one of those, yet there he is. The damned good-looking bastard.

He seems concerned. "I'm okay. Listen . . ."

Mel puts a hand up to stop him, like Mussolini on his balcony, like Mindy during their C-Unit meeting. Then she extends it to him. "'Gratulations," she says, shaking his hand vigorously as if it's a defective voting lever. "The best man always wins, right?"

"I don't know about that. You're great yourself."

"I sure am," she says emphatically. As if she can believe anything he says about her writing. He probably thinks she sucks and was propping her up so he could knock her down. Like a scarecrow argument. No, that's not right. What's the word? Stupid logical fallacies. She'll be stuck teaching them in first-year writing classes forever.

Mel gives Ben a small bow that almost unbalances her before regaining her footing with help from his outstretched hand. Once she's fully upright, she brushes it aside and nods one last time before turning away. Her barrel chair is finally vacant so she flops into it. Cecily stops by and hands her a bottle of water. She pats Mel's shoulder and sits down on the sofa near her, silently keeping her company.

By midnight the party is beginning to break up. "Anyone want to give me a ride?" Annie shouts.

"I think Ben has room," Mel whispers to her. Since her nefarious plan has been thwarted, the least she can do is inconvenience him.

"Cool. Hey, Ben! You want to give me a ride?" she calls over to him, seductively waggling her eyebrows.

"Sure, no problem," he says, looking put on the spot. He was probably hoping it would be only him and Elaina in his car. The two have stayed together the entire night, their coupledom readily visible, the Helen and Paris of VU. Mel quietly sends several other people over to Ben for rides. No doubt he wonders why so many ask.

Guests file out of Pollon's house, most carrying boxes filled with books. Mel follows them out to watch Ben and his passengers while thinking about how her revenge might have played out. But he leads them across the street to a different black Altima two houses down from Pollon's. He pops open the trunk, which is of course empty.

Mel inhales sharply. Looks at the car she would have placed Gertie in and then at Ben's, relief washing over her that she didn't actually go through with putting a dead dog in the wrong person's car.

"You coming with us, Mel?" Oscar asks, standing beside Cicely's Honda. "We're going to the Belmar."

"No. I'm heading home. See you later," Mel says absently.

Oscar says something to Cicely, who gets out of her car to confront Mel. "You are not okay to drive," she says.

"Eh, I'm fine," she says, shooing them away. "I need to ask Professor Pollon something."

"We'll wait," Cicely says, staring at her resolutely before sitting back down in the driver's seat.

As several vehicles depart, Mel remains staring at the trunk of the black car in front of Pollon's house. She exhales into the cold air, her breath a dragon's vapor. Imagine being the innocent owner of this sedan and opening the trunk to put groceries in it. Or placing a child's hockey sticks inside before driving them to a game. Or needing to give someone a jump and retrieving the cables. A higher power, benign toward Ben and malevolent to her, must be preventing her vengeful actions from having any impact. Or maybe she's the one with the guardian angel, sending out Professor Pollon to stop her from doing something that would have hurt a stranger. Mel looks around for a sign of her own spiritual protector, but only winter-quiet houses encircle her.

"What are you doing out here, Melody?"

She jumps. "Son of a bitch," she mutters to herself. Pollon shoves a black garbage bag into one of the large plastic cans in front of his garage door. "Ah, Professor Pollon."

His stare is quizzical. "Do you have a ride home?"

"Yes." Mel gestures toward Cicely's car. She looks up at the dark sky. There are so many pinpricks of white staring down at her, their light impassive. Everything that has occurred this evening has been witnessed by an uncaring universe.

Pollon gestures at his house. "I'm heading back in. Is there anything you wanted to say?"

Mel considers telling him the truth about what she was about to do and why, even coming clean about the photocopy in Ben's syllabus. The urge to confess and be forgiven is strong. They stare at each other for several moments. Now is not the time to ask him to be on her committee. "Do you think you might avoid telling anyone about what happened earlier? I know it was weird."

"I wouldn't dream of discussing the events of this evening with anyone."

She nods gratefully and says good night to Pollon, then hops in the back of Cicely's car. On the ride home, Mel recalls how happy Ben looked when he left the party, holding a box of books for Elaina. She imagines them moving into a nice little place together, their joyful future assured. He will always be luckier than her. He has the right look, the right point of view in his writing, and the right genitalia.

Cicely and Oscar drop her off at her father's house, where she finds the TV blaring. He is sitting on the couch shoving his fingers into the back of his stuffed bear. His hair is buzzed off, his eyebrows almost nonexistent.

"What did you do to yourself?"

"Cut my hair with a shaver I found. Forgot I had it." He motions with his chin toward the kitchen counter, toward a stack of magazines and unopened mail. On top of these rests what looks like an Edwardian era vibrator.

Mel realizes her father is shoving his hair into the stuffed animal. She turns away, repulsed, and retreats to her bedroom.

The next morning she wakes up feeling only mildly hungover with a slight headache but no nausea. She is sleeping on what was briefly Drake's side of the bed. Mel moves her fingers and toes, then her legs and arms. She turns over onto her stomach, feeling gratefully healthy. Until she remembers the night before and Pollon's expression when he saw her next to Gertie's frozen body. A whimper emerges from her throat. She presses her face into the pillow, which bears a faint trace of Drake's smell, a combination of his shampoo and deodorant. But it offers no comfort. If she had drowned a sack of kittens, pushed an old woman into a busy street, or kicked a baby in the stomach, she couldn't feel worse. She is Pol Pot, Caligula, and Charles Manson, injected into the body of a largish woman. The best course of action is to pack up her belongings and head out of town, disappear into the wilderness for a few years until shame over her evil deeds abates.

Mel turns over and looks up at the ceiling. "Oh, god," she says, spasming in surprise.

Her gaze travels across the sad faces in the tongue-and-groove pine. But now the lion face has a Fu Manchu mustache, the owl a Salvador Dalí curlicue, the seal a soul patch, the howling Madonna a full-on Dutchman's beard, and the sad Labrador a set of seventies mutton chop sideburns. Perhaps her father is right: there is a ring of thieves breaking into his house, who've decided to graffiti her ceiling. Except she remembers waking up at some point in the middle of the night with the light still on in her bedroom and opening the drawer in her bedside table to rummage in there for a black Sharpie marker. Unsteadily, she'd stood on the mattress and reached up to the ceiling. With one hand braced on the wood above her, she'd drawn on the faces.

Mel's snort turns into a guffaw that evolves into a mad cackle. "What the fuck?" she asks herself through hysterical laughter.

29

A few nights later, Mel wakes up after 1:00 a.m. cocooned in her blankets yet freezing cold. She struggles to remember what day it is until realizing with relief that it's Sunday, near the end of March, and she has the week off for spring break. Shivering, she wonders if her father has opened all the windows in the house. Except her window is closed, so at least he hasn't snuck into her room while she was sleeping. Once she was roused by him tucking his teddy bear under the blankets in the spot beside her where Drake had slept.

With her quilt wrapped around her, Mel walks to her father's room, where the light is on. "Dad?" she whispers from the doorway. She hears no response and tiptoes into his bedroom. He's sleeping soundly, his mouth slightly open, a mountain of blankets covering him. Mel studies her father for several moments—the hair and eyebrows that are growing back since his self-administered barbering, the ruddy cheeks sprouting white whiskers because he no longer shaves as often as he used to. She tries to remember a younger version of him and the first memory that comes to mind is of him taking her to the used book store that used to be in the Northgate Plaza on Upper Front Street in Chenango Forks, handing her ten dollars and saying, "Go to town, kid." These trips happened regularly throughout her childhood. On their many antiquing and thrifting jaunts throughout the Southern Tier, her father was always willing to buy her whatever books she wanted or to stop at any bookstore.

Should she wake him so they can figure out why the house is so cold? He'd probably have no idea what to do, especially after being interrupted from a sound sleep. Mel walks back into her room to put on a sweatshirt over her pajamas and layer on another pair of thick socks. She holds her hand over the heating vent below her window but feels nothing.

Entering the kitchen, she braces herself and approaches the door to the staircase leading down to the basement, where the furnace is located. With a deep breath and a silent prayer to keep giant spiders at bay, she opens it. The stairwell light casts a murky glow. Mel cautiously makes her way down to the bottom step, where she takes in the pillars of boxes, old furniture, large plastic bins, and the hodge-podge of cast-off home goods that fill the space. The chemical stench she's grown familiar with accosts her. She imagines it wrapping itself around her like a boa constrictor and suffocating her. At the best of times, this basement is unpleasant—damp with a faint mildew smell, cobwebbed, and low-ceilinged. There are only four small casement windows around the perimeter that let in barely any natural light thanks to the dirt clouding them and to the assorted objects her father has leaning against the foundation wall. Over the past few years, whenever Mel has thought of this space, it was to dread the day her father passes and she'll have to clean it.

Her imagination hasn't done it justice. But despite the ceiling-high stacks, there is a narrow meandering path that leads from the last step of the stairs to the utility room where the furnace resides.

Before her is a large cardboard box with a water-stained bottom filled with wire hangers from a dry cleaner's. Is there some population of ancient TVs requiring antennas her father plans on fixing? Beyond the box and leaning against a support post are several old metal beer signs that are probably worth some actual money. Melody looks through them, pausing at the Guinness, Smithwick's, and Bass Ale signs. Drake would love these. But no, she won't offer them to him now that they're not together anymore. She'll have to help her father sell them on eBay.

A massive Curtis Mathes console TV from the late seventies hunches beside them. No one could possibly want this, nor could it still work after spending time in this dank dungeon. Mel has no recollection of this TV inhabiting their living room. Stacked on top of it and beside it are other pieces of furniture that as far as she can remember never belonged to them either: a desk, a fainting couch with fraying and faded floral upholstery, and several wooden chairs. It's possible these were all used in sets her father helped construct for the Chenango River Playhouse. She imagines the acting they witnessed: the wringing of hands, passionate soliloquies, and fists clenched in anger. But why not leave them at the theater instead of bringing them home?

Farther along the path is a section of sporting goods of varying ages and states of decay. Three golf bags. A badminton set. A stack of green plastic bins full of assorted balls for different sports, and a boomerang.

She shivers, hikes her quilt up off the floor, and moves on, but pauses beside a stack of her old board games. On top rest the most recently played (Monopoly, Life) with older ones from her early childhood (Operation, Candy Land, Chutes and Ladders) on the bottom. Mel runs her fingers down the boxes, and memories flood over her of playing these with her father and Oji at the kitchen table, the wagon-wheel ceiling light illuminating the board. Her father never let her win. If she did, and this happened more as she grew older, it was because she earned it.

Beside the games is another tall stack of dark-green bins. Inside are rows of VHS tapes of her favorite childhood movies that she watched repeatedly, sometimes with her father. By her third viewing he'd say, "Kiddo, you're on your own." She reads the titles on the spines: *Bambi*, *Snow White*, a plethora of other Disney movies, a boxed set of *Little House on the Prairie*, and collections of Warner Bros. cartoons, her favorites.

Mel rubs her eyes and travels deeper into the hoard, a suburban Marlow searching for Kurtz in the heart of Chenango Forks. She encounters an old bookcase with tilting shelves, filled with many of her favorite childhood books. They're now spotted with mildew. She squats down to read the titles, forgetting the quilt. The last time she saw these books was after she moved in with Drake. They'd been safely stowed in boxes, stacked on the floor of her old room, waiting for the day when she'd pass them on to her own children, if she ever decided to have any. How could her father have moved her most treasured belongings down here?

Rising, Mel surveys the basement. The urge to throw things out, to knock over bins, to smash anything in her vicinity is nearly overwhelming. Her earlier feelings, of nostalgia mixed with pity for her father's turning the basement into an Egyptian princess's underground burial tomb devoted to her, are transformed. How inconsiderate of him to let the basement get to such a point, knowing that the responsibility of having to sort through the rubble would fall on his only child. He had known of her plans for her books. Yet here they are, fit for nothing but a landfill.

But now she forces herself to focus on the reason she came down here. She heads straight for the heavy wooden door to the utility room, determined to figure out if the furnace's pilot light has gone out. Mel tries to imagine an HVAC repair technician maneuvering through the basement and groans. The embarrassment of having to reveal the state of her father's house to another stranger is as bad as the time Mel slipped in her middle school hallway and split her pants in front of the boys' soccer team. She turns the knob to the door and the toxic stench rushes out, a genie desperate to escape its captivity.

30

Once, during a teenage phase of blow-drying her hair straight before curling it with an iron, Mel accidentally left the heated cylinder touching a plastic cup from her bathroom vanity set. The smell of the furnace room reminds her of that but on an industrial chemical spill level. Near the furnace is a stack of quart- and gallon-sized containers with peeling or barely legible labels: paints, stains, and thinners. Several plastic jugs slump over, melted, most likely from their contact with other chemicals. Rust corrodes the bases of the metal cans, and a thick sludge spreads from the pile to the floor underneath the furnace. Mel imagines how flammable this goop is and thanks whatever guardian angel is watching over her that the house hasn't burned down. She holds up her sleeve to cover her face, futilely trying to keep the stench from invading her mouth, nostrils, and lungs.

The furnace itself resembles a steampunk contraption, something that could be attached to a hot-air balloon and used as a weapon against promenading Victorian crowds below. Appendages like the arms and legs of an ogre-sized Tin Man branch out from the top. Mel is sure that the fabric covering the ducts and pipes is asbestos, and she wonders how long it takes after being exposed to it to become sick with emphysema or lung cancer. She leans toward the monstrosity, an old-time doctor on a house call listening for a heartbeat from the chest of a dying patient. But Melody detects no sign of life. Using only the palm of her hand to rest on the sludge, she carefully kneels down to check the pilot light, but there is only darkness in the recessed area where the flame should be, for which she is grateful. There is no way she would relight the pilot now, even if she knew how.

Two old shower curtains hang from hooks screwed into the rafters. They bisect the furnace room into two equal halves. When Mel rises to clean her hand on one curtain, she trips over her quilt. Clenched in her fist, the curtain tears away from its hooks and Mel finds herself in the other half of the room. An old brown recliner, whose arms were shredded by Swift in his youth, is positioned in the center, so that it has a panoramic view of the three walls surrounding it.

Mel steps back to take in this triptych for several long moments as a choking sob emerges from her. With it comes a deep inhalation that refreshes the smell of the chemicals in her nostrils, making her eyes water.

The horror, the horror.

Her father has dissected their photo albums and scrapbooks to create a timeline detailing the years from when he first met her mother, their dating, marriage, and Mel's birth, to just beyond the car accident. Added to this is a collection of art along with collages and design boards of theater scenes her mother must have created, as well as letters and notes she'd written, like "Hope you like your lunch, punkin' bunny!" with a sketch of a rabbit nibbling on a carrot. Everything is neat and orderly. Each piece of history is regularly spaced and affixed to the wall with tape, the chair is free of all pet hair, the floor is spotless. Mel scans the wall, starting from the left and ending on the right, where the exhibit ends with two newspaper clippings.

She moves closer to read the articles describing her mother's car accident and the obituary notice from the *Press & Sun-Bulletin*.

Mel sits in the old recliner, where she realizes her father must also seat himself to worship at the shrine he's erected to his dead wife. Stunned at finding this memorial, she reclines the seat and settles back. When did he create the montage devoted to his wife? Across from Mel is a photo of her at approximately five years old with her arms thrown around her kneeling mother's neck. They are both grinning, and her father most likely took the photo. The front porch of the house, looking new and tidy, is the backdrop. Flowers fill the beds in front in a collage of pinks, yellows, reds, and purples with hanging baskets dripping the same colors at frequent intervals. Her mother had been a gardener, too, Mel recalls for the first time in years. She could stare at her round face and crooked smile for hours. How strange to realize that every time Mel looks in the mirror, she's seeing some of her mother.

She wonders what her mom would think of her now. She'd probably be proud of Mel for pursuing her calling to write and figuring out a way to make a living doing what she loves, which is what she herself had done by becoming an art teacher. But she wouldn't be proud of Mel's behavior toward Ben—neither her inept attempts at revenge nor her reliance on and caretaking of him before that. Shame percolates up through Mel. She draws a deep breath and feels how tired she is, from so many lost hours of sleep over the past few months. She'll close her eyes for just a few moments and then figure out what to do about the furnace.

"Baby, wake up. You have to wake up."

"Mommy?" Mel says.

"Rise and shine, punkin' bunny." Mel feels her mother's hands on her face. "It's all noise, baby. You have to remember, it's all noise."

"I don't understand."

"Get up. You have to get up now!" her mother shouts.

Mel sits up in her father's recliner and rubs her face to try to clear her head. Where is she? The basement. What was she doing? Checking the furnace. What did she find? Nothing good.

She stares over at the chemical sludge before looking again at her mother's photos, art, and words. As much as she wants to stay here among these memories, it can't be healthy living this way. Mel rises from the recliner with the quilt wadded up in her hands. Her father has been keeping himself rooted in the past. But hasn't she been doing the same thing by reliving the moment of being wronged over and over?

Mel leaves the furnace room and closes the door behind her. She reverses her course through her father's basement. He needs to be removed from the house immediately. She'll take him and Swift to a hotel to stay while she deals with the mess in the furnace room and brings heat back to the house. But what if some of his symptoms aren't dementia but constant exposure to toxic fumes? And what about her own behavior lately? Mel latches onto this idea like a shipwreck victim spotting a buoy. Maybe if the chemicals are removed, her father will go back to his pre-dementia state of being odd but not cognitively declining. And what about poor Swift, who's much lower to the ground and has been breathing in this air along with them?

"Dad, Dad. Wake up." She shakes his shoulder several times. "We have to leave the house."

He grimaces and stares at her blearily. "What happened? Is it a fire?"

"You have all those chemicals next to the furnace. I think that's what's been making me feel crappy the last few months. You've been breathing in the fumes too."

He remains supine, ready to ignore her. "Don't be ridiculous. There's nothing but some paint down there I took out of the garage."

"It's way worse than that and there's no heat in the house. Don't you see the mess down there? When you go down to . . . you know?" Mel doesn't know how to describe what her father was doing. She feels ashamed to label it, as though she found a collection of old *Playboy* magazines. "Seriously, we can't stay here without heat and with all those chemicals down there."

He swings his feet out from under the pile of blankets to reveal he is clothed in a uniform, possibly from World War II, with his work boots on.

"This is how you've been sleeping?"

He surveys his clothing, his expression turning to one of mild surprise before understanding replaces it. "'Course. This is how it's done in the army. This way I'm always ready to be on duty."

"You're not in the army."

He stands and salutes, clicking his heels twice. "Lieutenant Hollings at your service, ma'am."

Mel steps back. They had been watching *Sergeant York* the night before. "Okay, then. Well, lieutenant, we need to leave the barracks for an emergency."

"I'll have to find my wife and have her come with us."

"She's already left. I sent her with an escort to safety."

"Thank you, ma'am. That's much appreciated."

After procuring two rooms at the Fairfield Inn on Upper Front Street, one for her father and one for herself and Swift, who she leaves there with his cat litter and food and water, Mel stands in front of the reception desk in the emergency room at Lourdes Hospital. "I think my father and I may have been exposed to toxic fumes," she tells the young woman.

"Your Social Security number, please. For both of you."

Mel provides them and the other pieces of information requested, and the woman says, "Please have a seat. We'll be right with you."

She leads her father to the waiting area and slouches in one of the chairs, still in her pajamas and winter boots. Her father's eyes are closed. He's wearing his blue Carhartt coat unbuttoned over the military uniform. The receptionist had asked if he was a veteran. Mel's "no," which she provided after first wondering if a "yes" would speed up their being admitted, caused the woman's eyebrows to rise.

Images of what Mel found in the furnace room come back to her. She closes her eyes and wonders how she's going to deal with the enormous task before her of cleaning out her father's basement to have the furnace fixed. If that's even an option, given its age.

Mel starts when she hears the ER receptionist call out to them. She'd dozed off. "We're ready to see you two."

"C'mon, Dad." She pulls her father up and out of his seat.

After both of them are administered several routine tests—heart rate, temperature, and blood pressure—only her father is admitted to a room in the ER to undergo a more thorough examination while Mel is cleared to leave. Her father waves her off as a male nurse (Mel mentally corrects herself: Isn't he just a nurse?) offers to help him into a hospital gown. She heads back to the hotel room to make sure Swift is okay in unfamiliar surroundings.

Mel wakes up from a nap feeling more refreshed than she's felt in months. She calls Cicely and fills her in on all the details, including what she found in the furnace room.

"Wow, Mel! Why don't you come and stay with me? This way you don't have to pay for a hotel."

"I need to have the furnace replaced. Oh my god, the amount of cleaning that's going to take before anyone can work in that basement!"

"I'll help you, and Oscar will too. Maybe you should call Drake."

Mel strokes Swift's back where's he curled up in the center of the hotel bed as though he's lived there for years. "The ER doctor doubts Dad's behavior has to do with the chemicals, but how is that possible? We've literally been living on top of a toxic waste dump." She tries to recall when her father's behavior changed, hoping it started once he moved all the containers from the garage to the furnace room, but no, it was before that. Did her moving out trigger his dementia? She recalls Dr. Oberlin mentioning that changes in routine could have upset him. Great, she can add that to her list of misdeeds to feel guilty over.

Despite her better judgment, Mel does call Drake.

"You could move back in with me," he offers. "I miss you. It's not a home without you around, woman." Mel replaces the word "woman" with "kiddo" and hears her father saying the same thing. Over the past several months, the idea of a small place of her own has grown more appealing.

"I'll have to think about that."

"I took the job in Wisconsin."

"That's awesome. I'm so happy for you!"

"Thanks." There is a long pause. "You could come with me."

Mel rubs her thumb on the top of Swift's head. She could blame her father's health for not being able to move with Drake across the country, but that wouldn't be the whole truth. "I've never lived by myself. It's about time, don't you think?"

"I guess. You should at least stay with me until your father's furnace is fixed. You can't live without heat."

Mel surveys the hotel room with its neat if boring décor. There is something appealing about its monotony. Nothing of her past resides within the space to haunt her, it holds no reminders of everything that's wrong with her life, and it lacks overwhelming clutter. She could get a lot of writing done in a space with so few distractions, especially if her father remains in the hospital for any amount of time. But after that, he'll come back to the room she's procured for him and then what? Mel thinks about how much she needs to accomplish during the week she has off from teaching. Her father will have to stay in the hotel while all the work on the house is done.

"I appreciate the offer," she tells Drake. "But I think I'm good where I am."

31

The next morning, Mel returns to Lourdes to visit her father. He had been admitted to stay overnight for more tests to be run on him in the morning. She pauses in the doorway of his room taking in his uncomfortable posture in the bed, the back tilted at an upright angle. The TV is off, but the remote rests on the bedside table. His eyes are closed though it seems impossible he's sleeping, given the position of his bed. The clip on his right index finger measures the oxygen level in his blood as well as his pulse, which beats methodically on the digital pulse oximeter spiked on a post beside the bed. In his other hand, he holds what Mel first takes to be a business card.

"Hey, Dad. How's it going?" Mel whispers, hoping that if her father is asleep, she won't wake him. She can come back later.

He opens his eyes, a hesitant smile on his face. "Hey, kiddo."

Mel comes into the room and rests her hand on his arm. "How're you feeling?"

"Pretty good. Except I'm sick of them wheeling me off for more tests like I can't walk on my own. And constantly poking me with needles." He holds up his right arm, where the inner elbow is covered by a bandage. "Bunch of vampires. I got nothing left to me." Her father looks as if he's about to say more, but Mel doesn't wait for him to speak.

"We're going to have to clean the basement out before we can get the furnace fixed or replaced. I'm hiring some people to help and getting a dumpster delivered later."

"You need to wait for me to do that. What if they throw out things I want to keep?"

"I don't want to hear it," Mel says, adopting a voice as sharp as broken glass. Her father starts at her tone. "Be happy I'm willing to do this for you. For your health. Whatever you have in the basement that's worth something I'll sell at a yard sale or list on eBay or Craigslist. This is the last time I'm helping you do this. I can't spend my life cleaning up your mess."

Her father grimaces but nods. "Okay. Fine."

"Anyway, then I'll hire an HVAC company." Mel pauses before addressing the bigger issue. "I'm not exactly sure how we're going to clean up that Love Canal situation you have going on down there too."

"You can't let strangers into the furnace room!"

"Relax. I already took all of Mom's pictures and art down." That morning she had gone to Lowe's to buy a multipurpose respirator that allowed her to enter the furnace room and remove all the scrapbook photos and mementos from the walls. Mel watches her father's angry face relax into grudging acceptance. "Why didn't you say something about that? You could have told me how much you miss Mom."

Her father rubs at his pursed lips. "I didn't want you to miss her too."

Mel tries to compose a response out of the anger, sadness, and pity swirling within her. How old her father looks, how frail. "That wasn't your decision to make. And there's nothing you could do to prevent that."

"I thought if I didn't talk about her with you and took all her stuff out of the house, you'd forget you had a mother. You'd be all right just having me around."

"That's so messed up, I don't even know what to do with it. Jesus, Dad. Don't you think I'd want to know where half of me came from?"

Her father pulls the sheet over his head like a small child, and she hears him choke down a sob.

"Dad, stop," Mel says, pulling the sheet down.

"I didn't want you to be reminded that all you had was me. I know what a great mom you had, but I tried my best."

"I know you did. And I love you for it." She leans over and kisses him on the cheek.

"I don't know how someone like me was lucky enough to raise someone like you."

"Oh, yeah, you hit the Lotto with me," Mel says, as she thinks about her behavior over the past few months.

Her father looks out the window. "It wasn't always so bad, was it?"

Mel cocks her head. "You've had a problem with collecting forever. I tried to keep it in check when I lived with you. But, god, that was so tiring. All the fighting over stuff you wanted to bring into the house. It's part of why I moved out." Mel lets out a deep sigh. There's no point in rehashing the past. She is going to work out something to ensure her father is taken care of without making herself solely responsible for him, regardless of his reluctance to have a stranger in his home. "I talked to Dr. Oberlin and she said more than likely the chemicals we were breathing in didn't cause your issues, and her first diagnosis is what she's sticking with. But she did say it sounds a little like 'huffing paint,' if the concentrations of chemicals were high enough."

Mel recalls her own "research" into this phenomenon, which entailed googling it. Inhalant abuse could lead to oxidative stress to the brain, whatever that means, and to behavioral changes like the ones she and her father had both exhibited over the past few months. She terrified herself reading about central nervous system damage, neuropathies and toxic encephalopathies, memory loss, and impaired cognition resulting from prolonged and chronic exposure to chemical solvents like paint thinners. But the reality remains that her father's behavior began deteriorating long before his exposure to the chemicals.

He holds his hand up. "I don't want to know any more since there's nothing I can do about it."

"There is something you can do about it: keep the house clean and let other people help you, not just me." Mel knows that her father will have a difficult time doing either one of these on his own. "And never store chemicals inside. Where'd they all come from?"

"Here and there. They were in the garage for years. Till the roof started leaking in the back corner."

"There's a leak in the garage roof?"

"'Fraid so."

"And you left it?"

"'Course not. Tried to fix it myself. Put a bucket underneath it."

"C'mon, Dad!"

"I had a dream about your mother last night."

"Yeah. What happened in it?" Let it be an actual dream, and not a hallucination, Mel thinks.

"It was damn strange. Didn't make much sense. I don't remember it much now. But I know I felt stupid in it."

"Yeah, I've felt that way a lot lately too." She grimaces, thinking about Imaginary Abe visiting her in the middle of the night in a lucid dream, talking stuffed animals, a dog cadaver, her raving soliloquy as the moderator on the leadership panel. But she can't blame her behavior on the chemicals either since her desire for revenge on Ben started before she moved back in with her father.

"I've been doing some thinking while I've been stuck in here. About how I raised you." He reaches out and encloses her hand in his, the one with the IV tube inserted into the vein on top. "You've missed out on a lot because of me. Because I wanted to keep you close and safe."

"It's okay, Dad. I understand."

"But that's not enough, kiddo. You should get a chance to get out of here." He gestures toward the window. "See the world a little. Not stick around to take care of me. What's here for you besides me? A couple of friends? Places you know?"

Mel sinks into the chair beside her father's bed and realizes how tired she is. "One minute I can picture myself living somewhere else, and the next I'm scared of leaving you and being on my own."

"C'mon. If you can take care of someone like me and yourself, you can take care of just yourself somewhere else. How're you ever gonna know if you don't try?"

Mel nods. "I can always come back, right?"

Her father tilts his head from side to side. "Maybe." He grins. "I've been thinking about that lady you talked to a couple months back.

Maybe we hire her to stop by during the week." Mel squeezes his hand. "She didn't seem so bad."

"That's a great idea, Dad."

"And you should have this," he says with a sad smile, handing her the card he's been holding, which turns out to be his driver's license. "I don't need it anymore."

32

After spring break, when Mel returns to teaching at VU, the sun is shining and there's hope in the air. On her way to her morning composition class, she can't help but notice how the campus has transformed almost overnight. Tulips and daffodils push up through moist chocolate earth in all the flowerbeds. The tips of tree branches flaunt delicate chartreuse or red buds as shy as a turtle poking its head past its shell. Birds chirp in relief over the death of tyrannical cold. All the detritus of winter, the pods and leaves shed by trees and bushes, are decomposing into fertile material from which nature creates new growth.

Mel feels as purged as a Roman after vomiting up a gluttonous meal, though in her case, the feeling is mostly emotional. All her mother's art, photos, and notes that her father had arranged on the furnace room walls are safely ensconced in two new plastic bins in her bedroom, waiting for a moment when she has time to transfer them back into scrapbooks and photo albums and frames like the one she bought her father for Christmas. For three days she worked alongside a crew she hired to clean the basement, filling the dumpster in their driveway and making numerous trips to the Binghamton Salvation Army store with anything worth donating. Later in the week, an HVAC company arrived to update the entire heating system, installing an efficient natural gas furnace and new ductwork. A new pill was added to her father's routine, one that Dr. Oberlin prescribed once Mel conveyed the extent of his hoarding. "That behavior is often associated with either OCD or depression, though given your father's trauma over his wife's death and his loneliness, I believe it's depression," Dr. Oberlin said. By Saturday, Mel was able to retrieve Swift and her father from the hotel and put the latter to work cleaning his house.

In her classroom, Mel sits behind her desk and wishes she could open the windows to allow the cheerful noise of chirping juncos to fill the space. She surveys her class and wonders if she's provided them with stories to share with their friends and take into their later years whenever they recount the odd writing instructor they had during their first year of college.

"Hello, everyone." She clears her throat. "I hope you all had a restful spring break." Some students nod in the affirmative, while others tilt their heads from side to side in a physical manifestation of *comme ci, comme ça*. "I got to clean up my dad's house last week, which, given he's a hoarder, was not fun."

She considers telling them about the shrine to her dead mother, in case this increases their sympathy, thus reducing the chances they'll slam her in her end-of-semester evaluations or on GradeYourProfessor.com, but then decides the hoarding is more than enough of a reveal.

"He had this stockpile of old paint, strippers, thinners, you name it, all stored near his furnace." Mel envisions herself in a white lab coat wearing a pair of thick black glasses, standing in front of a chalkboard covered with various mathematical and chemical diagrams. She is pointing at some, giving a lesson in chemical bonds, atoms, electrons, and neutrons. "Every time the furnace kicked on, it circulated what smelled like cotton candy mixed with turpentine."

Sitting in the back, Jayson raises his hand with the conviction of a broken-down elevator. "Didn't it make you sick?" he asks.

"I did get lots of headaches. And some other stuff," Mel says vaguely.

Claire, who Mel has accidentally called Cher on several occasions because of her long black hair, raises her hand. "Is it true it makes you high?"

"Well, I wouldn't know from personal experience . . ." Mel overemphasizes the last two words, then theatrically clears her throat. The class rewards her performance with a laugh. "Most of the time, I felt sick—dizzy, headachy. I had a lot of weird dreams."

They smile at her in a way she hasn't seen before, and it occurs to Melody that this is the closest she has ever felt to a class.

"Okay, so let's get started and see where we are," she tells them, opening her binder. "Only a few more weeks until the semester's over, and I don't know about you, but I can't wait."

After class, as her students file out and the next ones arrive for the class taking place after Mel's, she gathers up her belongings. There's a knock on the door and she sees Professor Pollon staring at her through the small inset window. She's done her best to avoid him since his party, ducking down hallways, slipping into buildings. How ironic, after all her efforts to track him down. But in a few weeks, she'll be forced to see him at her defense since Dr. Gibson talked him into being the fourth faculty member.

Students continue to enter the room. "Hey, all," she says quietly, but with a welcoming smile. "Do you mind if I chat with you all for a bit and pretend I'm your professor?" The students look at each other and weigh this request. "Sure," one of them says as she wedges her long frame into the small rolling student desk.

An elderly man carrying a briefcase enters the room and stares pointedly at Mel, who stands behind the instructor's desk. She glances at the classroom windows. Even if they did open, she would never fit through them. Should she take a seat with the students and act like she's one of them? But Professor Pollon beckons to her from the open door and Mel accepts her fate.

"We need to talk," he says. He holds an envelope, which probably contains a photocopy of her bare behind along with a notification that she's fired or expelled from VU. "Come with me."

Mel follows him down the hall but considers making a run for it. The only thing that prevents her is that he's faster than her. She imagines Professor Pollon tackling her to the tile floor. Instead, he finds an empty classroom and holds the door open for her to precede him inside.

"Sit," he tells her, taking a seat at a student desk and rolling it to face hers. "How are you?"

"Good. Thanks." Despite her heart beating as though she just ran a 5K across campus, Mel keeps her face pleasantly blank.

Professor Pollon's expression is curious. "I've been wondering about you ever since the party."

Mel adopts a bashful expression and a southern accent. "Little ole me? Why on earth would you be doing such a thing?"

He scrutinizes her for several long seconds before saying slowly, "I think you already know the answer to that. There have been several mysterious goings-on in the department this semester centered on a particular graduate student. I thought you might know something about them."

"Like what?" Mel struggles to look blasé as a jolt of adrenaline floods her nervous system.

He tilts his head and squints at her. "Do I really have to tell you?"

Mel thinks, no, not particularly. "I have no idea what you're talking about."

"Hmm," Professor Pollon says skeptically. He holds her gaze until Mel buckles under the pressure.

"Okay, fine, I'll talk." In a rush, with frequent pauses for questions from him, Mel explains the last few months: what happened between her and Ben and his winning the fellowship, moving back in with her father, the lack of interviews at MLA or anywhere else, breaking up with Drake, the extra students she had to teach this semester, the inability to write except for *Mani/Femi* blog posts that were more venting than writing, her father's diagnosis and corresponding neediness, the toxic fumes circulating through his house, the car accident, the sheer accumulation of bad luck and circumstances that had plagued her since the previous September.

"It hasn't been a good year," she concludes.

"So the photocopy in Ben's syllabus. Can I assume that was you?"

"Absolutely not!" Mel lies with conviction. "I would never do such a thing. You know he has a lot of people on campus that don't like him. That man has a talent for making enemies." She taps the desk in a lawyerly fashion.

Professor Pollon rubs his chin and gazes out the window, then turns back to her with a look on his face she's never seen there before. Is it empathy? "When my wife left me, I tried to get back at her by keeping her damned dog. God how I hated that animal. She reeked no matter how often I took her to be groomed. She'd roll in garbage whenever she had the chance. And her hair. If you wore pants, you were covered in it. She used to purposely rub up against my legs." Pollon's near year-round shorts-wearing now makes sense. He thrusts out his hands, which are covered in old scars. "Bit me anytime I'd try to pet her. Or feed her. Or brush her. Or walk her. She used to urinate on my bed if I left the door open." Behind his large plastic-framed glasses, his eyes are wide with bewilderment "It's as if she knew the only reason I demanded her in the divorce settlement was out of spite."

"Did it work?"

He shrugs but looks sheepish. "Probably not. I'd make sure to walk past Eleanor's office in the history department whenever I brought Gertie to campus, but she never said a word about whether it bothered her. I suppose it must have, but she was so happy being married to someone else."

"Some people are immune to revenge. Like they're vaccinated against it." Mel crosses her ankles and leans back to ponder this. "She was frozen solid, you know. A dog popsicle."

"Good to know. Thankfully this didn't happen in the spring."

Mel nods with wide eyes, imagining that scenario. "Truth."

Professor Pollon sits back and ponders her, then nods as though making a decision. "I'm glad we talked. A lecturer's position has opened for next year. As long as your student evals are as solid this semester as they've always been—and there are no more strange goings-on—you can have it. It'll be some composition and literature survey classes since I have no control over the creative writing side of things. That's Tina's domain."

"Are you kidding me? That's fine. Lit and comp will be great."

"By the way, this is for you." He hands her the white envelope he'd been holding. Inside, Mel finds a letter and a check for $2,500, a bonus for teaching ten extra students in this semester's composition classes. Mindy, the director of the program, has come through.

33

Melody stands in front of the full-length mirror in her bedroom wearing only her underwear. It's several hours before her graduate reading. The partially open window behind her lets in fresh air while also revealing the state of her inner thighs, which look like skin-colored leg-shaped bags filled with cottage cheese. Mel realizes that in a decade or so, her knees will resemble the foreskin of an uncircumcised penis. How did she get so out of shape? Then again, when has she ever been fit? She pinches the fat at her upper hip and eyes the black dress hanging from a hook on the closet door. She'd planned on wearing it to her reading, but she's going to need some help reining her body in.

At T. J. Maxx on Vestal Parkway, she heads toward the underwear section, where she finds a shaping garment that spans from below her breasts to above her knees. A vague recollection of her mother pulling on a girdle comes to mind as she races back to the cashier, hoping to avoid running into anyone she knows. Mel stands in line, clutching the thing to her stomach to hide it from the young man in front of her. He turns around and it's Joshie Grubber.

"Hey, Mrs. Hollings. How's it going?"

"Good, good," Mel says, wadding the girdle into a ball and hoping Joshie has no idea what it is.

"Funny I should meet up with you here. I was wondering if I could get a recommendation letter from you. I'm applying for an internship and you said students could ask you for one if they worked hard in the class, even if they didn't get an A."

Mel recalls the report, not argument, he wrote on poor people needing to do better with their finances, one that quoted several conservative commentators instead of the scholarly sources required for the assignment. It was also short by two pages. She'd given it a C to match his overall grade for the course due to his absences, lack of participation, and frequent napping.

"Look, Jeremy," she says, "I don't think I'm the best person to ask."

"My name's not Jeremy."

"And mine's not Mrs. Hollings. That was my mom's name and she's dead." Mel now has her PhD after successfully defending her dissertation a few weeks earlier. Her correct title is Dr. Hollings.

They stare at each other for several moments before a female computer voice intones, "Cashier Number Two is open." Mel gestures for Joshie to proceed and he turns around without another word.

A few moments later, another register opens. The cashier, a young woman, holds Mel's garment out in front of her, stretching it like it's a slingshot she's thinking of shooting at someone. "What is this?" she asks loudly.

"It holds fat in under dresses," Melody says. "You know, to smooth things out."

The cashier looks skeptical, as though Melody is lying and plans to use the girdle for some nefarious purpose she should report to the authorities. "Oh, I've never needed one."

"And I've never worked in retail," Mel says, smiling. "But sometimes life makes you do things you never thought you would."

Later that afternoon she arrives on campus, tightly swaddled. This summer she will exercise and rebuild muscle lost from being held captive in front of her computer for all these years. Who cares what she weighs or what size she is as long as she has energy and is healthy. She needs to learn to accept her body as it is.

Mel cuts through the English department hallway but makes a detour to collect her mail. Ads for textbooks flow from her hands to the recycling bin beside the mail cabinet. But she pauses at the sight of an envelope in her mailbox that's addressed to Ben in cursive. A heart drawn on the seal makes up Mel's mind. Looking around to be sure no one is present, she opens the envelope and reads the letter inside. Jesus.

The door is opened by an undergrad, and Mel shoves the letter into her messenger bag. She heads to the engineering building, where she spots Drake waiting outside.

"Are you nervous?" he asks her as they head into the building.

"Most certainly. But I want to get it over with."

"You're going to do great. Your novel is hilarious." She recalls what Professors Gibson, Russell, Zeigler, and Pollon had said about it during her defense when she'd read from portions of the book, how they also thought it was funny, with pathos and insights into the struggles the female characters underwent. Every approving nod and snort of laughter from her committee and the attendees was a balm on the wounds created by Ben's notes. But even better, her committee had given her so many ideas on how to improve the book.

Mel and Drake find seats near the doorway. When Ben enters the auditorium with Elaina, people turn to watch them because they're so good-looking. Ben glances at Mel and nods. He hadn't attended her defense, though he'd texted her to see if he could. She'd rejected his offer. "It would be weird," she wrote back.

Elaina, who is this semester's director of the graduate reading series, leaves Ben to take her place on the stage and introduce each graduating MA or PhD student. Mel and Drake listen to the two writers who read before her. When it's Mel's turn, Elaina introduces her as a "talented writer with multiple publications," and Mel goes to stand behind the podium. She carefully positions a copy of a short chapter from her novel in front of her, then smiles at the audience, giving Cicely and Oscar a wave. Then she reads. Mel looks up as she progresses through the chapter, making frequent eye contact with her audience. She catches Ben chuckling at all the right spots and is disgusted by what a fraud he is. He shouldn't need an audience to help frame his response to her humor.

When she finishes, the boisterous round of applause fills her with gratitude and pleasure. Drake shoots her a proud thumbs-up from his seat and then gestures toward the door. He rises and leaves the room to teach.

Mel finds a seat next to Cicely and Oscar. "That was great!" Cicely says.

Sitting several rows down from them, Ben waits for his turn to read. Melody stares at the spot of thinning hair at the crown of his head, something she'd never noticed before. May that spot grow and grow, she prays, until it engulfs his whole head. She pictures herself dressed like a New Orleans Voodoo priestess, sticking pins into a Ben doll and plucking strands of hair from the top of its burlap head.

But she stops herself. What if she instead wished him well, wished him to grow into a less self-centered human being?

She's not quite there yet. Especially given the letter she found in her mailbox.

The second-to-last student to read is the poet Valerie Amilio. Her work includes an extended metaphor of a bride being a wedding cake devoured by guests, the image of a collapsed rural home abandoned to its memories, and gorgeous lines like one describing a field covered in snow like ash from a volcano.

When Valerie finishes, Elaina returns to the podium to introduce the final reader. "I'd like to welcome our last reader, an esteemed peer, with too many stories to mention out there in the literary world. His brilliant novel *The Stinkfist Chronicle* will be published next year by Graywolf Press. Ben will be staying on after he graduates this year, having won the Alumni Emerging Writer Fellowship. He's also a good friend, who's as generous with his time as he is with his feedback. In fact, my poems wouldn't be half what they are without him. Ladies and gentlemen, Dr. Ben Howe."

Mel struggles to prevent her eyes from rolling back into their sockets and her face from turning into a rictus of revulsion.

"He doesn't seem to have much support," Cicely says quietly, gesturing with her chin behind them toward a small clump of people sitting in the center of the auditorium wearing the facial equivalent of beige linen. "I guess some people don't think it's fair that a professionally edited book won the fellowship."

Ben stands at the podium, his expression modest. Over his normal uniform of ironed shirt and dark jeans, he's wearing a navy suit jacket. If Mel was better looking, would he have been so begrudging of his time to help her with her novel? What kind of advice does he give Elaina about her poetry? Does his attraction to her make him praise her work more than it deserves? Is that what Mel would have wanted from him? Definitely not.

"What a nice introduction, Elaina. Thank you." He shakes his head and turns to face the audience. "I'm lucky to work with so many talented writers in VU's creative writing program." Ben gestures vaguely at the audience, and Mel acknowledges this with a queenly nod. "I thought I'd read something I wrote awhile ago. I've revised it a lot since then. It's called 'My Daughter's Toy.' Hope you all like it."

Melody recalls the story, a first-person narrative from a father's perspective. She'd read it when she first met Ben. He launches into the reading in his low voice, with appropriate self-deprecating pauses when he looks at the crowd and semi-rolls his eyes at something absurd, spinning his image as the humble writer acting as the conduit for his muse. Mel thinks of all the doors that will open for him. Meanwhile, she hasn't written anything since the race-through revision of her dissertation, only picking away here and there at the constructive feedback her committee gave her. Nothing comes to her, and anytime she starts something new, she thinks it's corny, hokey, flat, all words Ben used to describe parts of her manuscript.

Mel reaches into her bag to touch the letter for Ben she'd found in her mailbox. It's from Sherry. A residual desire for revenge makes her want to place it on Kelly's desk or chair when she finds her office empty. Kelly would see the heart on the outside and examine the open envelope. Nosy as she is, she wouldn't be able to resist reading the letter. Her eyes would grow wide as she took in the two-page rambling attempt at nonchalance, felt the young woman's confusion over why Ben stopped seeing her, and scoured lines such as "Didn't we have fun together?" Kelly would immediately bring this letter to Professor Pollon, possibly causing Ben to lose the fellowship for next year. Mel imagines this happening with pleasure. But what will it gain *her* to continue feeding this hunger for revenge?

Maybe nothing, but given his behavior, Ben shouldn't be teaching at VU—or anywhere—if he has taken advantage of an undergraduate.

Ben's reading comes to an end and the audience claps, though not as much as they did for Mel. He waves it off as though it's undeserved. Melody rises to leave, but spots Sherry walking down the aisle heading toward the stage. Her former student holds a sheaf of papers and looks determined. Before Mel knows what she's doing, she rises to intercept Sherry. As she does this, Mel realizes that she's doing it not for Ben's sake but for Sherry's. She glances behind her where Ben and Elaina stand next to each other at the podium.

"Hey, Sherry. Whatcha got there?" she asks gently.

"I have something I want to read. A love story that's real and true," the younger woman says, her blue eyes bright with tears.

Mel feels her own eyes water on Sherry's behalf. "I'm sure it's a great story. But why don't you read it to me and let me help you with it?"

Sherry stares beyond Melody, who follows her glance to see Ben hurriedly leading Elaina off the stage toward the exit.

Mel turns back to the younger woman and offers her a sympathetic smile.

"He doesn't care at all, does he?" Sherry asks.

"Nope, I'm afraid not. But it's okay that you did." Melody guides Sherry to an empty row of seats and gestures for the young woman to sit down. She will definitely give Kelly the letter. She has to. It's the one last bit of revenge she'll take.

Epilogue

Over a year later, Melody sits in a café on Second Avenue in Manhattan, around the corner from KGB Bar, nursing a coffee. The trees lining the sidewalk in their concrete playpens are in full leaf. An early June blue sky creates a stark contrast to the tan-and-orange-brick buildings below it. It's late in the afternoon and Second Avenue is busy, but not as much as it will be in an hour or so. Mel has her laptop open and is scrolling through Facebook. She quickly types a post reminding friends about her reading at KGB tonight, a place where Ben had been a frequent reader at its fiction nights during his New York University MFA years.

It's close to 7:00 p.m. when she stands beneath the Soviet flag pinpointing the bar's location. Mel climbs the stairs and slips into the red-walled room, which reminds her of a womb. Wooden tables and chairs take up most of the space. Above the liquor bottles arrayed on the bar are internally lit stained-glass cabinets. Stools are occupied by an assortment of East Village types: there are a lot of plaid shirts, beards, and bold eyeglass frames. The room is crowded, and Mel alerts the Frank Zappa lookalike running the reading that she's arrived. She stands by the bar waiting her turn to read. Zappa introduces her and she heads for the mic in the far-left corner of the room, where a tiny arc of a stage in front of a deep-red curtain awaits her. Smiling at the audience, Mel thanks them for coming and launches into her reading.

After last year's spring semester ended, Ben left her several friendly messages, but she didn't return his calls. There were a few texts, too, which she also ignored. Helping her father sell the unique vintage items she'd found in his hoard, graduating and grading final portfolios, finding and moving into her own place, and establishing Diana Lane as her father's housecleaner and caretaker while also easing back into writing took up all of her time that summer. It turned out her father was right. The multiple listings she created on eBay and Craigslist earned him a sizable chunk of money which he insisted on giving to Mel.

She'd saved it in case she didn't find anything permanent when her year-long lectureship at VU ended. But it hadn't been necessary, because Mel landed a tenure-track assistant professor position at a small private liberal arts college in Pennsylvania, teaching comp, literature, and creative writing. She's already built her syllabi, and there are no old white men on any of the reading lists. The school has also asked her to run the Visiting Writers Series, and Mel already has a wish list of female, POC, and LGBT writers she will invite. She'll also be close enough to see her father every weekend, though thanks to Diana, who stays with him several days a week, and her father's restored friendship with Oji, courtesy of the right meds, he no longer needs her quite as much. Who would have thought he and Diana would hit it off as well as they have? How quickly his dementia progresses will determine how long this arrangement will continue, a thought Mel finds painful to contemplate though she knows she'll have to one day.

She had reached out to Abe in the fall for a recommendation letter, which solved the mystery of why he left VU. According to his side of things, Tina had pressured him into early retirement because of his attempts to implement recommendations made by outside evaluators who had audited the creative writing program. Abe was happy enough to move to Montana, where he had a summer home. Now he was thrilled to be retired and have time to travel and write as he pleased. Tina is still the director of the creative writing program at VU.

After her graduate reading, Mel had walked Sherry over to the university's counseling center. Sherry refused to speak with Professor Pollon or the dean of students because she didn't want to hurt Ben. But Mel did pass her letter along to Kelly, who told her that Professor Pollon tried to get Tina to rescind the alumni fellowship, though she refused.

Instead, Ben's book contract enabled him to land a tenure-track assistant professor position at Hunter College after graduation. But this also meant he and Mel didn't have to run into each other at VU, for which she was grateful. Elaina left the program to follow him.

When Mel finishes reading, she heads for the bar, smiling at customers who tell her how much they enjoyed her story. She's waiting for her beer when Ben appears beside her.

"Oh, hello," Mel says.

"Look at you, getting a reading at KGB," he says. "You were great."

"Thanks. I won this mini–writing residency with a lit journal. And doing a reading here was part of it."

"Very cool. How are things with your dad?"

"Good." Dr. Oberlin had definitively diagnosed her father as being in the mild cognitive impairment phase, which could last for several years. The meds she prescribed seemed to help, as did the routine established through Diana's, Mel's, and Oji's visits. There are a lot of good days when her father is himself, which Mel tries to memorize for when he isn't.

"Are you still at VU?"

Melody shakes her head. "Not anymore." She doesn't offer any other information because she doesn't want to. She will only share with Ben what she'd tell a stranger. There's no desire to relate to him how excited and nervous she is to start this next phase of her life, which includes the new job and a second novel project she looks forward to sitting down with every day. Or how anxious she is about leaving her father.

"You have a job, then, for next year?"

"Yep."

"I like what you read. Is it new?"

"Yeah," Mel says. "Trying something different."

He gives her a sideways look as though expecting her to say more, maybe ask how his writing is going. For the first time Melody realizes that in many ways the collapse of their friendship was a much greater loss for him than for her.

He gestures with his thumb toward the bar's entrance to guide Mel's gaze. She spots Elaina, who looks very pregnant. The younger woman watches them with a solemn expression. She waves at Mel, gestures to her belly with two hands, an expression of good-humored disbelief animating her features. Mel smiles and calls out, "Congratulations!"

"Well," Mel says. "I would never have expected that."

Ben nods. "Maybe it'll stop me from being a selfish asshole."

"Can anything do that?" Mel asks half-jokingly, and he laughs. She wonders if he ever read her blog posts from the year before. Did he ever connect her to the comment on his office hours sheets, the defacement of his syllabus, the copy of the self-help book by his office door or the *Hamlet* text by his classroom?

"I recommended you as my replacement for the fellowship when I got hired at Hunter," he says.

"Did you? That was nice." Mel considers reminding him that he'd received the award unfairly to begin with, but why bother? She also wonders if he knows how close he came to having it rescinded.

"What do I have to do for us to be friends again?" He sounds more sincere than she's ever heard him and his expression matches his tone.

But Mel wonders if it's possible to go back to a place that never existed. "We're good," she says. "I'm good."

Acknowledgments

This book exists in printed form thanks to the tireless advocacy and revision ideas of editor extraordinaire Jennifer Savran Kelly. I am so fortunate to have had an editor who understood my vision for this book. Further appreciation goes to the readers at Cornell University Press's Three Hills imprint who participated in the process of this novel being accepted for publication.

Much thanks to the first readers of *Unlucky Mel*—Olivia Chadha, Kathy Henion, and Barrett Bowlin, who provided helpful feedback on early drafts. During my graduate studies at Binghamton University, I had so many wonderful writing and literature professors, but Jaimee Wriston Colbert and Jack Vernon were instrumental in helping me improve my work and see myself as a writer.

To my husband, Jeff, the builder of my dream life: There will be a comprehensive exam on the novel one week after you've read it. Take good notes.

Finally, there's Mooch, who Swift is based on. He was the most loving, outgoing, and grateful of creatures, an exemplar for us all.